SNOW GLOBE

Jeanne Skartsiaris

ACKNOWLEDGMENTS

Snow Globe was inspired by a friend's godchild, Paizley Sloan. Paizley has an intuitive gift and some of the stories in the book are based on true events. Another person who inspired me is my aunt, Anne Emerman (in the book she's the inspiration for Aja's mom). My aunt has rallied for causes, especially for the disabled, her whole life. In the late 80s she was the Director of The Mayor's Office For People with Disabilities in New York. She's been paralyzed and wheelchair bound since she was seven after being stricken with polio.

I'm indebted to all who read and helped critique Snow Globe: My wonderful writer's group, Mary Turner, Ian Pierce, Kathy Yank, Lou Tasciotti and Jean Reynolds Page (author of six amazing novels). Jacquelyn Smith, author of "Cemetery Tours" and "Between Worlds" and who has helped me branch out with marketing. My fabulous sister-in-law Angela Sheets who initially edited my hot mess of a book. When my editor, Alicia Street, received it, she was impressed with how "clean" the writing was. My dear friend Cheryl Duncan who reads all my stuff and gives me the confidence to keep going. Sally Harvey my bookie-buddy offered kind comments and good advice. My sweet granddaughter, Emma Robinson who, at eleven, is an avid reader. My friend, Donna Holmes, who got so mad while she was reading threw the book across the room because of all the bad stuff that was happening to Aja. I attended a Donald Maas seminar (a literary agent) after that and he said, "If you can get someone to throw your book across the room because of the conflict, then you have a good book." I must mention my cover artist Erin Dameron-Hill who designs such excellent book covers that people actually gasp when they see them. Formatting expert, Amy Atwell makes the books "real."

And last, but certainly not least, my daughter Alexandra who puts the spark in my soul and is always in my heart. And my husband, Terry, who has always encouraged me to write and never gets upset when I disappear for hours with my computer.

Thank you all.

SNOW GLOBE

For Alexandra

Live your dreams.

CHAPTER 1

"Face it. She's not worth our time."

The halls outside the principal's office echoed with the last few after-school stragglers. Aja could hear the muffled conversation of her teachers, principal, and counselor through the closed door.

"I disagree. Aja's IQ is higher than most of the students here," Mrs. Burnett, her counselor, said. She seemed the only one willing to bat for Aja.

"Damn lot of good it's done her." Principal Carlisle's voice boomed through the thin door.

They know I'm sitting here, Aja thought, fiddling with the clasp of her worn patchwork book bag. *Is he being loud to make sure I hear him? Just to piss me off?*

"She's had more absences than any other student this year and she is certainly the most disrespectful kid on campus—when she bothers to show up," Carlisle went on. "And look at this school history. She's changed schools almost every year. I vote for suspension, let her get her GED. She's obviously a troublemaker."

"Mike, where is your sense of compassion?" Mrs. Burnett asked. "She's had a...well, an interesting home life. Give her a chance. School's almost out. Let her graduate with her class."

"She's lacking credits and her absentee rate is off the charts. And she has a record; look at this charge. She's a juvenile delinquent," Carlisle snapped.

"I'll work with her," Mrs. Burnett pleaded. "She's taken more AP and college courses than most of the students here. The only credits she lacks are from missing assignments."

1

"Barbara, we can't save everybody. She's had too many chances."

Aja recognized the voice of her English teacher, Mrs. Dempsey. A hag of a woman who wouldn't let the kids read any books with the "F" word in them or the Harry Potter series because of the evils of witchcraft. It just wasn't Christian.

These people are so clueless. They have no idea about the real world. She wanted to smash into the office and tell them all to "F" off. It would be so worth it to see Dumpster Dempsey fall out of her chair and onto her fat ass.

"But it *is* our job to save everybody. We're teachers, *guidance* counselors. Hello!" Mrs. Burnett pleaded. "This poor child needs us. We have the power to help."

Aja felt bad that Mrs. Burnett was pitching so hard for her, especially since Aja had dissed her too. But that woman was so nosy, asking a million questions about her home life, her future life, her *weird* life.

It was the same wherever she went. She squeezed her eyes shut, fighting tears. All she wanted was to fly under the radar and be normal.

Just let me live the way I want to, Aja thought, glaring at the closed door, willing them to get her telepathic message. *You guys have no idea what I need.* Aja looked around the office and considered getting up and walking out. If only she wasn't on a first name relationship with the school's truant officer, Rocky. No doubt because she was the new kid. Quiet, easy to blame.

"Well, if she's so damned smart, then why is she failing?" Mr. Carlisle asked.

"She's misguided; she needs direction. Those marks are assignments not turned in yet," Mrs. Burnett said. "Aja is a free spirit and doesn't like to be told what to do."

"*Aja.* What kind of name is that? Why would anyone name their child after a continent, then misspell it? She's a misfit," Dumpster Dempsey said. "I have my hands full enough with students who are willing to help themselves. Why spend energy on someone who couldn't care less?"

Aja gritted her teeth. She was used to people messing up her name—A-jay, A-Ja. Very few knew it was pronounced *Asia*. Now she was a misfit too?

"The child understands the work," Mrs. Burnett said. "She's probably bored. We have two months until graduation; I'm sure I can talk her into buckling down."

Carlisle barked out a laugh. "It says here her mother is a palm reader! Is she that psycho lady who has a waving palm reading sign in her front yard? I wonder what else she sells out of her home," he said sarcastically. "If she's psychic, why don't we just ask her about her daughter's future? No wonder the kid's a nutcase."

Aja cringed. She hated when people found out about her mother. And now it was in her school record. Her mom called it "her gift" and, although Aja also possessed the same intuitive power, she fought it down hard. It scared her. It was another mark against her being normal.

"Shhh..." Mrs. Burnett hushed him. "You know she's sitting in the office."

"Not for long, suckers," Aja whispered. She waited a beat, then stood to leave. As she tiptoed out, she noticed a purse under a desk, opened wide. Two twenty-dollar bills stuck out over the top. She'd never stolen anything before, but the bills were beckoning to her. *You're a bad kid, Aja,* echoed in her head. Isn't that what all the teachers thought? What they always thought? She looked at the bills and justified her decision by proving them right. If they thought she was a hopeless case, then, yeah, maybe she was. Maybe being bad would feel better, Aja reasoned as she quickly stuffed the bills in her bag. You guys are so stupid, she thought as she escaped out of the office.

CHAPTER 2

Aja ran to her car, ducking so the teachers wouldn't see her. Forty bucks wasn't going to pay for much, but she'd add it to her California money. As soon as she could ditch Dallas, a hot airbag of a city, she'd be on her way to sun and surf. She'd been working at Abercrombie in the mall for two months, but too much of her paycheck went to the merchandise instead of adding to her sun-fund. Aja knew better than to spend her money on cute outfits, but she hated all the thrift store clothes her mom found for her. Aja wanted to look normal, cool, like the other kids, even if the rest of the world thought she was nuts.

Her 1981 Tercel's engine bucked and choked out a wad of smoke when she started it. She gave a finger flip at the school as she drove by, hoping the group of teachers would see her from Principal Carlisle's office window.

When she got home, a bunch of cars were parked in front of her house. Now what? Aja thought. Her mom's palm reading sign, which looked too much like the Hamburger Helper hand, practically drooped from the heat. When the wind kicked up, it waved back and forth, reminiscent of a bobble-head toy. Aja was embarrassed whenever anyone figured out that her mom was the town psychic—even though a lot of those same people came for readings. In all the places Aja had lived, and there were many, people swore her mom was the "real deal," generating spirits of loved ones and reading past and future events in her customer's lives.

Aja loved her mom but wished there was a little more normal and less freak. Her mom also painted and sold art, and sang in a folk band, like the true hippie she was. She fought for every cause

4

possible: peace, equal-rights, save the wildlife, LGBT support, help the disabled, fight for the underdog, climate change. She and Aja got along well, but Aja longed for things she'd never had, like a stable home life. And a bedroom she didn't have to pack up and move every year. The free spirit, live-off-the-land attitude stunk and it was one of the main reasons Aja tried to fight down her own psychic abilities. Another reason was that sometimes the visions scared her.

She pulled into the driveway next to her mom's dusty Nissan pickup. Her car hissed and coughed after she turned it off, then let out a final sigh of exhaust. There was never enough money to fix it right.

Aja went around back and let herself in through the kitchen screen door of their run-down small frame home. The door, like the rest of the house, was in bad need of paint and repair. The rental agent who showed them the house said it had good bones, but to Aja it sagged and bore the scars of life. Often, in some of the homes they'd moved to, Aja could feel the spirits of previous tenants. Not this place though. It was just old and smelled funny when it rained. She tried to keep the squeak of the old rusty door quiet as she slipped inside.

Peeling her shoes off and leaving them on the worn linoleum, Aja started to call out to her mom but stopped in case those cars out front belonged to people here for readings. Her mom begged her to be quiet whenever she had a customer in the tiny bedroom at the front of the house. The room was dark with a card table in the middle draped with a shroud of purple silk. The table sat under a vaulted pyramid of gold-painted PVC pipe. Crystals of all sizes were placed on tables in the small space. Instead of a crystal ball in the center of the table, her mom had a snow globe that rained sparkly glitter on a tiny angel inside. Her mom had a thing for angels and gave small guardian angel coins to her friends. She insisted Aja carry hers with her always.

Considering all the cars out front, Aja expected to see a waiting room full of people in her living room. Instead when she peeked, she was shocked to see a stark-naked man standing on a sheet-draped pedestal. He looked close to Aja's age, about eighteen or nineteen, which surprised her. Four or five people sat with sketchpads in their laps or on easels, drawing.

"Oh, hi, honey." Her mom looked up from her charcoal drawing. "Mrs. Wells brought her delicious coffee cake. It's on the counter. Help yourself."

"Um, Mom?" Aja nodded at the naked man, who turned his head and smiled. Not bad looking, Aja thought, then blushed. *He* managed to blush crimson all the way to his butt cheeks.

"It was my turn to host the art class." Her mom looked over her reading glasses at Aja. "Care to join us, or are you working tonight?"

"I'm working." Aja shook her head, smiling as she turned to go to her room. "Can't you guys draw fruit bowls or something?"

"The human body is a beautiful thing," her mom called out. "Think of Michelangelo's David."

"Oh, the agony and ecstasy," Aja muttered. "Think of still life with flowers," she yelled back. Didn't most mothers have cookies and milk when their kids came home?

"Make sure you eat something before you go to work. There's a nice tuna salad in the fridge," her mom said. "I made it with dill and capers, your favorite." Her mom scrimped on everything but food. They only ate wholesome, nutritious, organic fare, but if Aja wanted to burn a wad on cool jeans, her mom wouldn't offer a nickel.

"And take an extra big piece of my coffee cake," Mrs. Wells called to her.

Aja turned back to the fridge and slapped together a tuna sandwich before she went to her room to change for work. Clara Wells's sour cream and buttery coffee cake was legendary. Aja was tempted to eat that first.

She'd just opened her closet when she heard a car door slam out front. Chewing her tuna sandwich, she debated on the red tank top with her orange bra or denim mini skirt and blue embroidered shirt. It had to be from Abercrombie when she was working. She grabbed the strappy gold sandals her mom hated so much. She encouraged Aja to wear Birkenstocks, "not those cheap shoes that will ruin your feet."

Aja heard heavy footsteps on the walk, and she peeked out her front window. Rocky, the school's truant officer, and another uniformed policeman approached her porch. The police officer was a lanky creepy guy with evil eyes. He gave her the willies. Kind of like Freddy Kruger with a badge.

"Oh, crap," she whispered, as she backed away from the window, remembering the money she'd taken.

There was a hard knock on the door and loud voices when the door opened. Aja heard a lot of shocked exclamations about a nude man in the living room.

"Hey, what's going on here?" Aja recognized Rocky's voice. "Is this some kind of sex ring?"

"I thought you read palms." The other officer sneered. "This is a family neighborhood."

Clara Wells spoke up. "It's an art class."

"Can I help you, officers?" her mother asked.

That was about all Aja heard before she dashed to her mother's room in the back of the house and snuck out the window, almost yanking off her mom's crystal light catcher hanging from the window frame. Barefoot, holding her sandals, she ran down the alley, careful to stay out of sight, and wondered how she would be able to go back to her car to get to work on time.

"Damn. I can't lose another job," Aja murmured as she hid behind her neighbor's big oak tree and slipped her shoes on. She looked at her phone clock, realizing she had just a little more than thirty minutes to get to the mall. An easy ten-minute drive, but an impossible walk. Then, she never got a piece of Mrs. Wells's coffee cake. Almost worth getting busted for.

She heard her mother call her. "Aja?"

Aja peeked from behind the tree and saw her mom stick her head out the screen door. "Aja?"

Aja caught her mom's eye, then hid behind the tree again, trying to make herself as small as possible.

"I'm sorry, I don't know where she went." The creaky screen door bounced shut. Aja knew her mom wouldn't give her up.

Rocky opened the door and stepped into the backyard. Aja held her breath, praying he didn't see her.

"She couldn't have gone far," Rocky's big voice boomed. "Her car's still hissing."

"I'm sure she got a ride or something," Aja's mom said. "Let's check out front."

"Is that naked man still there?" Rocky bellowed. "Mrs. Harmon..."

"That's Ms. I'm not married."

Aja snuck a quick glance from behind the tree and saw her mom hold the screen door open for Rocky.

"And you allow your teenage child to view nude men standing in your living room? What kind of home is this?" Rocky said.

Aja heard the creepy officer say, "We need to report a 311 indecent exposure here."

"I'm hosting an art class," her mom said. Before the door shut, Aja's mom glanced at her. "Call me," she mouthed as she surreptitiously signaled, miming a phone to her ear.

Aja had no choice but to walk to work. She could already feel the fake leather of the uncomfortable sandals rubbing her heels as she set off down the alley. She was wearing shorts she'd bought at Target, a big no-no at Abercrombie. But there'd been no time to change. Stealing a glance between the houses, Aja saw Rocky sitting in his car, waiting.

"Damn," Aja said to herself. "All for forty stupid dollars." She hoisted her purse on her shoulder and ducked through the neighborhood to the main street.

A few scorching blocks later, she turned to face oncoming traffic and was considering sticking her thumb out when an old sky-blue Buick pulled to the side of the road.

"Need a ride?" a male voice asked.

Aja backed away. This was a guy, alone, and she didn't want to do something else stupid like get abducted while she was trying to ditch the police. She felt in her purse for her trusty needle-nose pliers her mom made her keep for protection—or in case a rivet needed tightening.

"I'll be happy to give a fugitive a ride, unless I'm putting myself in danger."

Aja peeked in the window and noticed the male model from her mom's art class behind the wheel, now dressed in jeans and a T-shirt. Foil packages were wrapped on the seat beside him. No doubt leftovers, including her piece of Mrs. Wells's coffee cake.

"I'm not a fugitive..." She saw Rocky's car pull into the street to turn from her subdivision. Quickly she jumped in beside the model and closed the door.

"Hi, I'm Walker. Your mom sent me to check on you."

"I'm Aja." She cut a glance behind her as Rocky turned into traffic. She slunk down in her seat.

"Asia? As in the continent?" Walker asked.

"No, Aja, as in Steely Dan."

"Who? Aren't they like an old rock band?"

"Yeah, sort of. My mom likes them. I know it's a weird name, but it fits. Can I use your phone to text my mom? I left mine at home."

Walker smiled and handed Aja his phone. "So you're not a fugitive, but you're afraid of the police?"

"It's a long story," Aja said, typing. "Any chance you could drop me at the mall?"

"My pleasure," Walker said, and flashed a wide grin as Rocky's car passed by. "What's a nice girl like you doing on the lam?" he asked as he pulled into traffic.

Aja stayed low in her seat and tossed his phone on the seat. "I'm sort of a problem kid at school, and I proved it to them again today. Officer Rocky and I are old friends, and I can't be late for work again. That's why I didn't want to hang around while he was there." Aja sat up a little higher. "So what's your story? A male stripper wannabe?"

"Very funny. I'm a student making some extra money posing for a nice group of artists. One of the art teachers posted the ad at school. I'm, um, trying new things." He blushed a little. "I didn't expect anyone else except some older ladies. Did you see anything?"

"You were on a pedestal." Aja settled in her seat and smiled. "Hard to miss."

Walker laughed. "Then I hope I made a good first impression." He glanced at her. "So where do you work?"

"Abercrombie. And they'll be mad if I'm late again." She looked at her outfit. "Plus, I didn't have time to change into their clothes, so I'll probably have to fold all night."

"What time do you get off tonight? Will you need a ride home?" Walker looked at her. "Maybe we could hang out."

Aja hesitated. He was cute, but she wasn't sure she could get interested in a guy that stripped for money. Although he had an aura of goodness around him that pulled her in more than she wanted. "Thanks, I'll call my mom," Aja said, shaking the lure of this guy's magnetic energy. "Where do you go to school?"

"At the community college. I just started this fall."

"Where did you go to high school?"

"Chicago area," Walker said. "Just graduated high school last year."

"And you came all the way to Dallas for a community college education?"

"Yeah, sort of." He turned into the mall parking lot. "My grandfather has Alzheimer's and is in an assisted living home. My grandmother decided to move with him but couldn't bear to sell their house." Walker stopped at the entrance. "They said they'd pay for me to go to school if I'd stay in their house and keep it up." He shook his head. "It's really sad to see him go in and out of his life."

"That's rough. Sorry," Aja said. "It's nice of you to be here for them."

"Yeah, and I get to shake life up a little by moving to Texas." Walker turned to her and smiled. "I'm heading to the home now to have dinner with them." He laughed. "I used to sleep till noon, eat lunch at five o'clock. When I have dinner with them the food's so bland it's like eating air and we're done by six."

Aja eyed his foil-wrapped packages. "And I suppose you're going to eat my piece of Mrs. Wells's coffee cake later tonight."

Walker grinned and raised an eyebrow. "It was worth getting naked for." He reached for a pen and paper. "Here's my number in case your mom can't pick you up. I'd be happy to."

Aja took his number and put it in her purse. "Thanks."

Walker looked at her. "It must be pretty cool to have a mom like yours, being a psychic and all. I hear she also sings with a band."

Aja shrugged. "She's cool most of the time, but mostly I feel like we're the town idiots."

"Does she ever do readings for you?"

"Hardly ever. She says it's hard for her to see my aura, and she gets really weird afterward. Usually a psychic can't read people that are close to them."

"Really?"

Aja shifted the focus from her mom's intuitive gift. Aja hated her own abilities to "see dead people" or see inside a person's heart. She'd discovered her talent when she was four or five but didn't realize it until years later. She could see colors in her mom's angel snow globe, especially after she shook it. Somehow she knew they were from people, but she was never afraid of them. About the same age, when Aja watched TV, she was often joined by a young boy who wore a baseball cap and would sit on the floor next to the couch, never letting Aja see his face. He said he was in a fire and looked weird. Her mom had at first thought he was an imaginary friend Aja had invented, but then sensed Aja was seeing a spirit. As soon as her mom tried to seek his aura, he never came back.

Aja glanced at Walker. "Apparently, according to my psychic Mom, I'm either an old soul or have a bunch of old souls around me." Aja closed her floppy denim purse.

"Maybe you need to come to dinner with me and my grandparents tonight. Make your mom's 'old soul' vision come true." Walker raised his eyebrows playfully.

Aja shook her head. "No thanks; old people annoy me. They drool, shuffle, and...I don't know—it all kind of weirds me out." Aja opened the car door. "Thanks again for the ride. I've got to run. I'm already late."

"Maybe another time?" Walker looked hopeful.

"Sure. I've got your number," Aja said, as she got out. She stood on the sidewalk and watched him drive away. He was pretty cute, seemed nice enough, but the last thing Aja needed was an anchor to hold her to Dallas even though she was hypnotically drawn to his radiant personality.

CHAPTER 3

Aja punched in ten minutes late while her manager stood and watched, arms crossed. He made a point to look at his watch.

"Sorry, I had to get a ride."

"Again? You need to get rid of the rust bucket you drive. How many times have you used that excuse?" He looked her up and down. "And why aren't you wearing our line? You've been warned about that, too." He raised an eyebrow and pointed at her butt. "Please don't tell me those shorts say Massimo on them. Target?"

I'm surprised the alarms didn't go off when I came in, Aja thought, and smiled uncomfortably. "I was in a huge hurry and didn't have time to change."

"Go buy something you can wear, then fold and stock these." He pushed forward a messy rack stuffed with clothes that customers had tried on. "This should keep you busy."

Aja didn't argue but went to the clearance rack and picked a madras skirt marked fifty percent off. She'd been waiting for it to go to seventy percent, but, oh, well. Aja went to the counter to pay. The perky cashier, Taylor, rang her up at the register. "Got stuck with the rack again tonight?" She tossed her blonde curly hair. "Good, because after the register I get to model the new line." Abercrombie employees had to be beautiful or they didn't get hired. The privileged got to stand around and look good for the customers. "Guess you won't have to worry about that tonight, wearing a clearance skirt."

"Guess not." Aja glowered as she grabbed the skirt and stomped off to the dressing rooms.

About an hour into her shift, she'd gotten most of the clothes put away, Aja went to the dressing rooms to clean up the new piles of clothes customers dropped on the floor.

"Slobs," she muttered, clipping shorts onto a hanger. A kid, wailing and crying, was dragged into the dressing room by her young mother.

"I want to go!" the little girl cried, trying to pull away from her mother's tight grip around her arm.

Aja hated screaming kids but was appalled by the tight hold the mother had on the child. She could see red marks on her little arm from the woman's fingers.

"We'll go when I say." The mother shook the child. "Do you understand?"

"I'm hungry." The girl couldn't have been more than five or six. Her big brown eyes were filled with tears, and her face was swollen and red.

"Shut-up!" The mom gave the child another shake, almost pushing the kid to the floor. "I don't want to hear another word."

Aja stared hard at the woman hoping to embarrass her enough to stop. Aja saw the woman's aura as angry red. She forced herself to stop the psychic vision. The girl rubbed her arm and hiccupped sobs.

"I'm...hungry," the little girl whispered.

The mother slapped the girl across the face. "Didn't I tell you to shut up?"

The sound was like a shot. Aja dropped the handful of clothes and ran to the mother. "Stop! Are you nuts?"

The child's mouth was open in a silent cry, and she held her face where red marks and tears glistened on her cheek.

"Don't tell me what to do with my kid." The young mother faced Aja. "Unless you want a piece of me."

"You do that to me, and I'll have your ass thrown in jail." Aja got in the woman's face, her fists clenched. "I'm calling the police."

"Aja, what's going on?" Her manager ran into the dressing room.

"That woman just slapped the crap out of her kid."

"I'm going to file a complaint with this store." The woman crossed her arms, baring a large tattoo of a cross on her upper arm. "I don't need this stupid-assed clerk telling me what to do."

"I'm sorry, ma'am. I'll talk to her," her manager said.

"Damn right you will."

"Wait, this woman just hit her kid and I'm the one being talked to?" Aja shook her head. "We need to call CPS or the police." Aja bit her tongue on the word police. The way things were going, she'd get tossed in jail.

"Aja, back off." Her manager got between them.

The little girl, still crying silently but watching the grown-ups intently, moved closer to her mother.

"Don't take that, kid," Aja said to the child. "Dial 911." Aja glared at the mother. "If you didn't want kids, you shouldn't have had them. They're not punching bags."

"Aja," her manager warned.

"People like that shouldn't be allowed to have kids." Aja threw her hands up.

"I want her ass fired," the mother said. "I'm never shopping here again. Come on." She grabbed the child's arm and dragged her behind her. The poor kid had to run to keep up, but she stared at Aja as she was pulled along.

The manager followed her out. "I'm terribly sorry ma'am, let me give you a shopping pass for your next visit."

The woman kept walking. "Yeah, you better."

"Why is she getting freebies after beating her kid?" Aja yelled after them. A small group of people had gathered but no one said anything.

Aja angrily picked up the clothes she'd dropped. Her manager stormed into the dressing room.

"That's the last straw, Aja. I'm going to have to let you go."

"What? Why?"

"You can't talk to a customer like that."

"She was beating her kid."

"That wasn't your business."

"Then whose business is it? If she's smacking her kid in public, what do you think she does at home? We should report her." Aja held the clothes to her chest.

"It's not just that. You're always late, and you don't come to work dressed properly." He put his hands on his hips. "You're a liability. What if that woman sues?"

"For what? Beating her kid?'

"Aja, I'm sorry, you're fired."

Aja tossed her armload of clothes to the floor and made sure to step on them as she stormed off.

Chapter 4

Aja wandered around the mall. She needed to call her mom. She hated that she left her cell phone in her race to escape. She would not go back to Abercrombie to use their phone. Pay phones were scarce so she looked around for a friendly face, someone who might be willing to let her make a call. She found an empty table at the food court and sat sulking about being fired. She scanned the crowd, hoping to find that mother so she could give her a real piece of her mind.

"Hey, Aja. Are you on break?"

Aja looked up to see Javier, one of the workers at Sonic in the food court and a student at her school. He was also Taylor's boyfriend.

"No, I just got fired."

"Bummer. What happened?"

Aja filled him in on what happened. "Plus my car is so unreliable that I'm always late anyway."

"Good luck finding another job." Javier sipped on a drink. "Most of my friends can't find any work, and if they do, they're only given about eight hours a week. Not enough to even put gas in your car." He offered her a French fry. "Cool skirt, you just get that?"

"Yeah, how did you know?"

"The price tag is still hanging off it. Not that I'm checking you out or anything."

"I should smear French fry grease on it and take it back," Aja smiled.

"Hey, you did the right thing."

"Thanks." Aja took a fry and ate it. "Can I borrow your phone? I need to call my mom for a ride."

"Sure." Javier fished his cell phone from his pocket. "I'd offer to take you home when I get off, but Taylor would probably freak out."

"Yeah, she's modeling the clothes tonight at Abercrombie."

Javier nodded. "Good. She was thinking you were going to get to do it."

"Me?" Aja dialed the phone and waited for her mom to pick up.

"You give her a run, since you're pretty hot." He held the French fry bag out.

"Thanks," Aja said, grabbing another greasy fry. People often told her she was "so pretty," but she never made any popular lists. Aja tried her mom's cell; it went right to voice mail. Some nights her mom sang with a folk group. Aja couldn't remember if her mom said she had a gig tonight or was she at one of her human right's protest? Aja didn't want to walk home in the dark and in uncomfortable shoes. She opened her purse and took Walker's phone number from her purse and debated calling him.

"Hey, don't use all my minutes," Javier scolded. "My parents are already on me for using it too much."

"I'll be quick," Aja said, and dialed Walker's number.

He picked up on the first ring.

"Walker, hey, this is Aja."

"I was hoping you'd call."

"I hate to ask you this, but is your offer still good for a ride home?"

"You're already off work?"

"It's a long story, but yeah."

"You seem to have a lot of long stories. I can be there in fifteen minutes. Same place I dropped you off?"

"Sure, thanks."

Aja handed the phone to Javier. "I owe you, thanks."

"No problemo. I'm gonna run to see if Taylor is modeling." He looked at the clock on his phone. "My break's almost over, and I may have to crack a few heads if I find any guys going gaga over her." He tossed his almost-full order of fries in the trash as he stood.

Aja licked her lips. Dang, she was starving and seriously

considered Dumpster diving for the trashed food. She stood to leave and saw a uniformed police officer ascending the escalator. She froze. He looked very much like the Freddy Krueger cop. She couldn't imagine them trying to track her at the mall. It was only forty stupid dollars, now less the fifteen bucks she had to spend on the skirt.

The officer turned toward her. It wasn't him, but Aja still felt like a wanted criminal. *Am I going to have to duck and run every time I see a uniform?* She sorely wished she hadn't taken the money. She did not want to go to jail—again.

She took a deep breath and headed to the mall exit to wait for Walker, a guy she'd only met today, didn't know his last name, and had already seen naked.

My life is too weird.

CHAPTER 5

Aja hid in the shadows near the entrance of the mall until she saw Walker's sky blue Buick pull to the curb.

"Thanks for coming to get me," Aja said, as she slid into the car.

"Dinner was over and I really didn't want to stay for dessert bingo anyway," Walker said, flashing a big grin.

"I don't know how you deal with all those old people. Don't they creep you out?"

"No. I really get into talking to them. They're interesting. I mean, it's like having a personal history book." Walker went on. "And I can't help feeling sorry for some. Their families hardly ever visit."

"So you really are a nice guy," Aja said, leaning back in the car seat to look at him.

Walker nodded, laughing. "Yeah, but don't tell too many people. It'll ruin my incredibly cool image. Like driving my grandparent's Buick. Way cool." He stopped at a light. "What happened at work? You weren't there more than two hours."

"I got fired." Aja tugged at her skirt.

"Long story?"

Aja sighed. "It's pretty stupid, really. Some lady was smacking her kid around and I yelled at her." Aja told Walker the ugly details. "My manager was looking for an excuse to get rid of me anyway."

Walker watched Aja as she told her story. A car horn beeped behind them. The light had turned green.

"That's a great reason to get fired," Walker said, driving through the intersection. He gave a friendly wave to the driver behind him. "You totally did the right thing."

"Tell that to my bank account."

"So let me get this straight. You're a wanted criminal, a fugitive from the law. You're a hothead employee who can't hold down a job. And you have a bunch of long stories to tell." Walker smiled and kept looking ahead at the road. "Do you want to go get some coffee or something?"

"Sure," Aja said, warming up to him. "Did you happen to eat all of my coffee cake?"

"If I'm going to have to share the cake with you, then maybe I should just take you home." Walker grinned.

"I'll bet if you pose naked again Mrs. Wells will make you another one."

They decided on a Starbucks and took the foil package of cake in with them.

Sitting at a table sipping tea, Aja asked, "What are you studying?"

Walker leaned back and sighed. "Good question. So far I'm just getting my basics done, but I'm pretty interested in history and art. And I love writing. Let's just say I have no idea." He pinched off a buttery chunk of cake and took a bite. "What about you?" he asked with a full mouth.

Aja shrugged. "If I can get out of high school, then I'm thinking about heading to the West Coast."

"To go to school?"

"Eventually."

Walker's phone rang. He looked at caller ID and frowned. He hit the cancel button and put the phone in his pocket.

"Screening your calls?" Aja asked.

"Yeah, sort of." Walker changed the subject. "What do you mean *if* you get out of high school?"

Aja told Walker about the meeting at school she overheard. "I probably won't get my diploma, thanks to that jerk of a principal."

"So you're living on the edge, huh?" He sipped his coffee. "Most principals are jerks anyway. Part of the job description."

"I don't mean to be a problem, but trouble seems to follow me." Aja looked out the window. "I just want to get the hell out of Dodge, but I don't have enough money to cross state lines." Aja stirred her tea. "And now I'm unemployed."

"You could be a nude model." Walker smiled.

Aja giggled. "Yeah, in front of my mother and her friends. That's about the creepiest idea ever."

He shook his head. "If my mother ever found out..." He let the comment hang.

"Yeah, I doubt most moms would approve of nude modeling."

He scrunched his face. "She's too proper and uptight."

Aja thought of her own mother. Hiring teenage nude models. Didn't people get arrested for that? "No, she's probably just normal." Aja sighed and looked away. Wondered how she'd have turned out if she grew up in a real home with a real family.

Walker changed the subject. "You should apply at the nursing home where my grandparents are. They really need help there. Plus, you'd really love all the residents."

"I don't think so. I can't relate to kids or old people."

"Sure you can. Didn't you just rescue a kid today?"

"Not the same thing. I didn't have to wipe drool and snot off her face." Aja shook her head. "I don't have what it takes to change diapers—old or young." She grimaced. "Yuck."

"Two waitresses quit, so I know you'd get hired for that. No diapers. Maybe a little drool though. Especially when they put their dentures on the table on soup night."

"Ugh, no thanks."

"Think about it. You'd be perfect. The residents would love you." Walker's phone rang again. He punched the button without even looking at the caller ID.

"Important call?" Aja asked.

Walker got serious and looked at Aja. He sighed and said, "Long story."

Aja noticed his mood shifted down-gear after the call. "Thanks again for driving me home. I owe you."

"Hey, my pleasure. It was fun." Walker stood and threw their cups away. "Maybe we could do it again sometime."

Aja nodded, hesitant. She was reluctant to get involved with someone who could waylay her plans.

"And I hope you really consider a job at the retirement center. You'd enjoy it."

"No way." Aja shook her head emphatically. "Not in a million years."

CHAPTER 6

Two days later, after school, Aja sat in the HR office of the Golden Leaves Retirement Community. The director of the home was reviewing her job application. Frustrated, Aja had not been able to find another job at the mall. Her car was chugging and coughing more than ever. She needed money to get the car fixed, or better yet, buy a newer one. And she had to pay back the stolen money.

Plus, every time she was in the mall applying for jobs, she saw a uniformed officer that she feared was keeping an eye on her.

Principal Carlisle had called her mom, telling her that if Aja didn't finish her assignments she wouldn't graduate. They were still considering holding her diploma because of her attendance record and would review her file with the school board. He also said Mrs. Dempsey wanted to press charges but hadn't yet because the counselor, Mrs. Burnett, had given Dumpster Dempsey the money out of her own pocket. Aja needed to pay her back soon, or *he'd* bring charges against Aja.

Her mom had hung up on Carlisle when he called Aja a bad seed.

Aja could handle the lecture from her mom: "*Stealing is never okay and you reap what you sow. You'll only create bad karma for yourself.*" Yada, yada. And it was up to Aja to make it right. Her mother insisted Aja take care of it herself. To get out of karma jail.

So, right now she was hoping to get this stupid job with drooly old people. She'd pay back the money, get a car that worked, and be a beach bum. Who needs college anyway?

"And why did you leave your last job?" Edna Jones, the director of the retirement center asked. She was a roly-poly apple of a woman and Aja saw the colors of her aura as a mix of butterscotch yellow and orange. Aja could often see objects in auras if she stared hard enough and if she focused on one object she'd learn what it meant to that person. It was distracting and got her into trouble a lot with teachers thinking she was spacing out in a daydream. Aja shut down the image immediately before any objects came in to focus. "You were only there two months."

Aja looked away. "Personal differences." She watched Edna make some notes.

"Can I call them for a reference?"

Aja shrugged and shook her head. "Probably not."

"I see," Edna said, scoring the page with another black mark.

Aja could see her career sliding to continued unemployment forever.

"Aja! I'm glad you decided to apply here." Walker appeared at the door, his cute face bore a smile that lit the room.

"Walker, sweetie," Edna blushed a Gala apple red. "Do you know"—Edna looked at the application—"Aja?"

"Yeah, I thought she'd be perfect to work here." Walker strode into the room and took a seat next to Aja. "Did she tell you why she got fired from Abercrombie?"

Edna's blush cooled. "Fired?"

Walker nodded. "Yeah, she's a real hero. Some lady was smacking her kid around, and Aja told her to stop."

Edna looked over her reading glasses at Aja. "Now why would you get fired for that?"

Aja glanced at Walker. His energy radiated throughout the room. "I guess because I yelled at her."

"Did you hit her?"

"No! Of course not."

"Good." Edna made a few notes. "We can't have anyone here with a short temper."

Walker laughed. "She fights for the underdog. She'll be perfect here." He squeezed Aja's arm.

"Do you have any experience working with the elderly?"

"No, ma'am."

"One must have a great deal of patience," Edna said. "Our residents need someone to keep up with their pace. Usually slower than what you may be used to."

"You'll get to know everybody here. They'll love you," Walker said, standing to leave. "Call me when you're done. I'll show you around." He turned to Edna. "I'll introduce her to everybody. You're a doll for hiring her."

Edna blushed again. "I still need to do a background check. But if you recommend her, she must be special." Edna giggled.

"I highly recommend her." Walker put his right hand over his heart.

Aja smiled nervously at the mention of a background check and glanced at Walker. He had only met her a few days ago, picked her up as she was running from the law and gave her a ride after she'd been fired from a job. Maybe he wasn't such a good judge of character. But at least he was cute.

She considered asking Edna if she was interested in taking a drawing class. That poor woman would have died and gone to heaven had she been in her mom's studio.

"It's not that hard," Janie, the woman training Aja in the kitchen said. Janie was probably in her early thirties, had short thick hair, and a warm energy that Aja could practically feel. Her aura was green-hued, nurturing and comforting; filled with hugs. "You ask if they want soup or salad, what kind of dressing, and what they want to eat. Two dinner choices: beef, chicken, or occasionally fish. Sometimes we'll have pork chops, but when we do most of the residents need them blended to mush. Then you take it to their table."

Aja tied the apron over her white shirt and black pants she had to use the rest of the stolen money on. The ugly orthopedic-looking shoes she'd found at Payless for under ten bucks were already hurting her feet. She'd better start making some money soon, or she was afraid she'd be looking at the world from behind bars. Her mother would not help pay back the loot. "Karma," she'd said. "*You* need to make it right."

"Drinks are easy," Janie went on. "Water, juice, coffee, tea. Have you ever been a server?"

"No, this is my first time. I was a hostess at a steak restaurant once."

"Just don't drop anything, especially on one of the residents."

"Okay."

"This place is like a soap opera. It's hilarious to see who's eating with who. It's worse than high school—they have the popular table and the nerd table." Janie hoisted a tray of water pitchers. "And everybody gets dressed up for dinner." She shook her head. "I can barely get dressed up for a date. Come, follow and learn."

"What did you mean when you said you blend stuff to mush?" Aja asked, trying to keep up with Janie, who was a head shorter than Aja but moved with quick efficiency.

"A lot of the people here can't chew their food, so Gabe, the cook, blends it down. Tastes the same, but looks gross." Janie handed a water pitcher to Aja. "Go fill the water glasses on the tables. Hurry, the line is starting." Janie nodded to the entrance, where a few people hovered over walkers or on motorized scooters.

Aja took the pitcher and started filling. The dining area was big; tables had linen tablecloths and napkins and were adorned with flower centerpieces. It looked like a nice restaurant. Aja could also sense ghosts of others here but focused on her work to keep her intuitive powers quiet. Her brain could barely deal with her own problems, she didn't need others in there too.

"Who's the new girl?" a woman with steel blue hair coifed to a hardened football helmet asked Janie. She wore a red silk dress with lipstick to match. The coral color feathered into the lines around her lips.

"This is Aja. Aja, say hi to Mrs. Poston."

Aja stood behind Janie and waved. "Hi."

"I hope you're better than that last waitress. She was a lazy bore. You'll have to hop to keep up with this crowd." Mrs. Poston stood ramrod straight. "And no back talking either. Young people are so impertinent these days." She looked at Janie. "I'll have cranberry juice tonight." She walked to a table in the middle of the room and took her seat.

"I'll bring it right out, ma'am," Janie said. She turned to Aja and raised an eyebrow. "Queen Bee. Don't piss her off. She'll have the whole place turned against you."

As soon as Mrs. Poston took her seat, the rest of the crowd shuffled or drove in.

"Janie, have the new girl bring me my drink," Mrs. Poston called across the room.

Janie poured a wine glass full of juice and handed it to Aja. "Don't spill a drop. I don't want to deal with her complaining tonight."

Aja took the glass in two hands and walked to Mrs. Poston's table as if she held combustible liquid. Her hands shook as she carefully placed it in front of Mrs. Poston. Not a drop was spilled.

"My right. Put it on the right side of my setting. Don't you young people have any idea about how to set a proper table?"

Aja leaned over, picked up the glass, and set it next to the water glass. A drop, a mere smidge, plopped onto the white tablecloth. Red seeped into the fibers looking like a crime scene.

Mrs. Poston looked on with a horrified expression as if Aja had just committed a bloody murder on the linen.

"Get me a napkin. Now!" Mrs. Poston pushed back from the table.

"Oh, get over yourself, Bea. You're going to scare this pretty girl off before she even gets started." A tall gentleman in beige slacks and a maroon sweater walked to her. He took a cloth napkin from another table and handed it to Mrs. Poston. "Don't sweat the small stuff, Bea."

"Hello, Miss, I'm Dr. Brad Landers." He held a hand out to Aja. "Welcome. I'm sure you'll do just fine here."

"Thank you," she said, shaking his hand. "I'm Aja."

"Asia?" What kind of name is that?" Mrs. Poston grumped. "You don't even look Oriental."

"It's spelled A-j-a."

"Oh, like the Steely Dan album?" Dr. Landers asked.

"Yes, sir."

"You're named after a record album? That's dumb." Mrs. Poston waved spidery fingers in the air.

Dr. Landers winked at Aja, "I'm learning iTunes and will be happy to burn you a CD of some of my favorite music. Steely Dan is high on that list."

"Evening, Doc, what can I get you to drink tonight?" Janie came up behind Aja.

"Since we're having chicken, I'll do white tonight, Janie. Thank you." He tilted his head and winked.

"Apple juice it is, sir," Janie said and pulled Aja along with her. "We'll have it right out."

Janie took Aja's arm and dragged her along to the kitchen. "Take Dr. Landers his juice and start asking the others what they want to drink." She pointed to a tray of pre-made salads. "Find out who wants soup or salad."

"What if I spill again? This is a tough crowd."

"You'll be fine. Before you know it, you'll know what everybody eats and drinks. They'll love you." Janie pushed her to the dining room, which was almost full.

Once Aja got in the rhythm of it, she served the drinks without too many mistakes. Janie had Aja dole out the salads while Janie served hot soup, in case Aja dumped a bowl on someone.

After everyone had been served dinner, Aja and Janie went to the kitchen to cut cakes and pies for dessert. "How did you find out about this job?" Janie asked.

"I met this guy, Walker, who told me about this place needing help."

"Walker? What a dreamboat." Janie tasted a finger full of chocolate frosting. "Just don't get near his girlfriend, Kendall. She's a piece of work."

"Oh, he never mentioned her," Aja said, more disappointed than she would have expected.

Janie paused and wiped chocolate from her face. "I don't know the whole story with them, but she's always coming to visit him. I think she lives in the Chicago area." She stacked the dessert plates on a big tray. "Just be careful with her. She's the type that would cut you with her claws." Janie meowed, and scratched the air at Aja. "Come on, let's get these desserts out before our guests start falling asleep in their plates."

Aja took a smaller tray of sugar-free apple pie while Janie hefted the platter of chocolate cake. They'd just gotten out the door of the kitchen, and Aja noticed a frail gentleman standing alone near the door.

"Hey, Mr. Jenson. How's your wife?" Janie set the tray down and said to Aja, "She just had surgery."

"She came home today," Mr. Jensen said. His voice was soft

and trembled a little. "I was hoping to take some dinner to her." He held his shaky hands up. "I just can't cook like she does, and she's too weak to come to the dining room."

"Have you eaten today?" Janie asked, concerned.

"No, no. But I'm okay. I'm just worried about my Buttercup." He smiled wistfully and said to Aja, "That's what I've always called her. She's my special flower."

"Let me get some dinner for you both. And I'll cut an extra big piece of chocolate cake for her. I know it's her favorite," Janie said.

"Thank you, love." Mr. Jensen wearily sat in a chair near the kitchen door.

"China, or whatever your name is," Mrs. Poston called across the room. "I'm ready for my coffee."

Janie told Aja to grab the pots of coffee and start pouring. "We'll get the desserts in a minute. I want to make sure the Jensens have a good dinner. He won't eat without her, and look how thin he is." She shook her head. "I hope Mrs. Jensen makes it. She's been real sick for a long time, and this surgery may be the final straw. If anything happens to her it would crush him."

Aja took the coffee, being extra careful with the hot liquid, and went to each table, pouring more decaf than regular.

"You're the new girl?"

"So pretty."

"You'll love it here."

"Oh, you know Walker?"

Everybody had something nice to say to Aja as she went to each table. Except Mrs. Poston. "My coffee's cold. Get me a fresh cup."

As Aja poured a fresh cup for Mrs. Poston, Janie came up, holding two covered dishes. "Can you walk Mr. Jensen to his room with these?"

"Sure," Aja said.

"Why does he get his food to go?" Mrs. Poston griped. "Next thing, we'll have a drive-through window." She turned toward Mr. Jenson and yelled, "Steve, you need to get Leigh up walking. That's the best way to get her back in shape."

Mr. Jensen slowly walked toward Aja and Mrs. Poston. "She's just too tired, Bea. We're going to rest tonight, but thanks for the advice."

"You shouldn't mollycoddle her," Mrs. Poston said. "I've had hip surgery, and now both are titanium and stronger than when I was a teenager."

Janie rolled her eyes and handed the dishes to Aja.

Aja followed Mr. Jensen out of the dining room. For every one of her steps he'd take three. His body was so thin his pants, belt buckle just below his nipples, still looked like they'd fall off him. The trek was painfully slow, and the hot dishes burned her hands.

Probably sensing her impatience, Mr. Jensen said, "If I had young legs, I'd sprint back to my Buttercup." He smiled sadly. "How old are you, young lady?"

"Eighteen."

"Ah, that's how old my wife was when we met. I took one look at her and was smitten for life." His shuffle slowed even more. "She's been my sweetheart ever since."

Aja couldn't imagine being with someone for as long as they'd been together. He looked like a thousand years old. "Do you have children?" Aja asked.

"Yes, two daughters and five grandchildren. We've been blessed."

The walk had taken so long the plates had cooled in Aja's hands; either that or she'd lost feeling in them. The residence complex reminded Aja of a hotel. All the doors opened to an interior hall. Most of the entries had small tables decorated with flowers or photos. Again Aja felt spirits of others, strong, along the decorated corridors but she didn't want to open her mind to them. Finally, they reached a door adorned with a wood sign that said "Welcome All" on it.

"Here we are," Mr. Jensen said as he tried to fit the key into the hole, his hand shaking so much he couldn't hit the target.

The heavy dishes strained Aja's arms. *Anytime, dude.*

After a few tries, Mr. Jensen got the key in the tumbler, opened the door, and they went in. "Buttercup, I'm home," he called out.

Aja followed him in and was shocked to see a wisp of a woman reclining, eyes closed, in a lounge chair. Aja feared they were too late and she was already dead. The small apartment smelled of old people and medicine.

Mr. Jensen went to her and said, "Janie got you an extra big piece of chocolate cake." The woman didn't move. "Let me get you upright, Buttercup." He struggled with the recliner. Aja stood, holding the dishes, not sure what to do. She was tempted to call 911.

He couldn't work the chair lever, so Aja set the dishes down on a table and went to help. "Is she okay?" Aja hesitated when she got closer.

The woman's eyes fluttered open. "Lauren, is that you?"

"No, Buttercup." Mr. Jensen looked at Aja. "Lauren's our daughter." He turned back to his wife. "This is the new girl who works in the dining room." He brushed a thin wisp of hair off his wife's wrinkled face. "She looks just like Princess Buttercup, too." He glanced at Aja. "*The Princess Bride* is one of our favorite movies. But I was calling *my* princess Buttercup long before the movie came out. It's as if they made the movie about us." He turned to his wife and whispered affectionately, "As you wish."

Realizing the woman was alive, Aja moved next to Mr. Jensen and adjusted the chair to a sitting position. Mrs. Jensen almost fell completely forward with the movement. "Oh, no," Aja said, and grabbed the old woman's shoulder to steady her. Aja could feel every bone and almost jumped back in horror.

Mr. Jensen helped her sit upright and opened a tray of the food, almost spilling it over with his trembling hand. He then filled a spoon. His hands shook so much he dropped the mushed spoonful on the chair before it reached Mrs. Jensen's mouth.

Aja wanted to run back to the dining room, the scene so pathetic it scared her. Mrs. Jensen's cheeks were sunken in, she could barely open her eyes, IVs hung on a pole next to the chair. Aja drew a deep breath and took the spoon from Mr. Jensen and brought it to his wife's lips. Like an infant, the old woman ate a small amount and dribbled out the rest.

I'm going to throw up, Aja thought.

"Isn't she beautiful?" Mr. Jensen asked.

Are we watching the same movie? She looks like a wrinkled prune with eyes.

Aja hesitated, took a napkin and wiped the food away and offered another spoonful, fighting a gag reflex.

"You are an angel, young lady," Mr. Jensen whispered as he took a seat next to his wife and held her paper-thin hand.

CHAPTER 7

Sitting in Dumpster Dempsey's class the next day, Aja thought about the Jensens. She was touched by his affection for his wife but couldn't imagine being that old and not seeing the flaws in each other. Weren't they grossed out when they kissed? Aja looked at the taut skin on her arm and considered how it would look wrinkled and bony.

She'd almost gotten fired last night because she'd been at the Jensens too long. Poor Janie handled the desserts and coffee refills by herself. Mrs. Poston was armed with fresh criticism as soon as Aja returned to the dining hall.

"Breaks aren't allowed during the dinner rush," Mrs. Poston said. "You young people have no respect."

Janie, frazzled by serving alone, was still glad that Aja had helped the Jensen's. "I was going up after dinner to check on them," Janie said. "They're both so frail. I hope Mr. Jensen ate something."

"Are you planning on joining us this morning?" Mrs. Dempsey asked, jolting Aja back to reality. She stood over Aja and said, "You look like you're in another world."

Aja cast a sideways glance at her teacher but didn't respond.

"Maybe she's using her psychic powers to find out the answers on the test," one of the kids yelled. "Oh, wait, that's your mom who's the psycho."

Mrs. Dempsey chuckled and didn't admonish the boy. "Aja, do you want to take this test today?" She leaned closer and stage whispered, "You're already so far behind in your work I'm not sure you're ready." She stood taller. "Did you read the material?"

Aja, slumped in her chair, felt defiant. She wanted desperately to kick Dumpster in the knees and watch her fall like a turtle on its back. "Let me take a look at it and I'll see if I feel like taking it." Aja held her hand out for the paper.

"You can leave your attitude at the door or in Mr. Carlisle's office," Mrs. Dempsey said.

And you can shove your attitude up your fat butt. Aja bit her tongue. The thought of having to go to summer school if she didn't graduate made her keep her mouth shut. "I was planning on taking it today." Glaring at Dempsey, Aja continued to hold her hand out for the test.

"Well, good luck with it," Mrs. Dempsey said as she put the test on Aja's desk face down.

Aja turned the pages over, looked at the test. "Romeo and Juliet." She'd studied Shakespeare in ninth grade while living in Boston. Her English class in Ohio, in tenth grade, started to touch on the Bard when they moved to Georgia. The school system there was years behind what she'd already done. By the time they got to Texas, the work was so different she'd gotten tired of trying to keep up with the curriculum. Her elementary years were the same, moving almost every year to another state, thanks to her mother's free spirit and a determination to try everything and live everywhere. Luckily, the planned moved to Antarctica to save the seals was scrapped because of the lack of a school system.

Aja yearned for northern California. She had vague but happy memories from when she lived there.

"Are you going to stare at the test or take it?" Mrs. Dempsey still hovered over Aja.

"It's hard to concentrate with you standing over my shoulder," Aja shot back.

"Would you rather take it in Mr. Carlisle's office?" Dempsey snorted.

"No, I doubt he knows the answers," Aja said. A few of the kids snickered.

"Quiet!" Mrs. Dempsey shouted and began to hand out the rest of the tests.

Aja took a pencil and started working. Unrequited love. She

thought of the Jensens again. Would Romeo and Juliet have stayed in love, or would they have divorced and fought over who got custody of the brats? She sighed. No, they would have been in love forever, just like Mr. and Mrs. Jensen.

CHAPTER 8

Later at work, Aja piled iceberg lettuce on plates, making sure each had a wedge of tomato and a sprinkle of carrots. She stacked the plates on a large tray and headed to the dining room to serve them. Mrs. Poston's drink order had gone much better today, and the woman had been less critical.

"Great job, thanks," Janie said, as she started brewing coffee. "I'll take care of the soup."

"Have you seen the Jensens today?" Aja asked, wondering if Mrs. Jensen was better.

Janie shook her head. "I doubt they'll make it down tonight."

Romeo and Juliet, Princess Buttercup and true love, Aja thought. "I hope Mrs. Jensen's still alive. She looked real scary."

"I'll check on them later," Janie said.

Aja shifted the heavy tray and pushed through the doors to the dining room. She stopped short when she saw Walker at a table with his grandparents. A beautiful girl sat next to him.

He looked as if he'd been caught doing something wrong.

"Aja, hi." He couldn't look her in the eye. "These are my grandparents, and this is Kendall. "

"It's nice to meet you," Aja said, the tray weighing heavy on her shoulder. She tried not to look at the beautiful girl next to Walker.

"Oh, you must be the new girl. We're glad to have you," Walker's grandmother said. "You're busy, but please come by and say hello when you can."

Walker's grandfather smiled but didn't say anything. His gaze went from one face to another, as if trying to take in the mood of each person.

JEANNE SKARTSIARIS

Aja set the tray down on a serving buffet and began to hand out the salads.

When Aja set the plate of salad next to Walker's grandfather, she asked him what kind of dressing he wanted. He looked helplessly at his wife. His lips moved, but Aja didn't hear him speak.

"How about Italian tonight, Charles?" Walker's grandmother said to Aja as she patted her husband's arm.

Aja began to see different pictures of Walker's grandfather in her own head. First young and vibrant, then words, incoherent, jumbled her brain. She worked to shut off the vision, afraid to let it play out.

Aja turned to Walker and asked what kind of dressing he wanted. He looked at his anemic salad and answered, "Ranch."

"I'll have oil and vinegar on the side," the beautiful girl said, but she pushed her plate away from her. "Is this lettuce brown?" She picked up a wilted leaf with her long, elegant and perfectly manicured fingers.

"Then don't eat it," Walker snapped.

"China girl, my table needs some decaf." Mrs. Poston waved her hand at Aja. She sat at a round table with a few other women and seemed to hold court over them.

The dinner rush kept Aja so busy she didn't have a chance to speak to Walker. Before they served dessert, Janie said, "Did you see Walker's girlfriend? I'm surprised she's eating here. Usually she sticks her nose up at anything we serve."

"Does she come here often?" Aja was disappointed in herself that she'd not sensed Walker had a girlfriend.

Janie shrugged. "I don't see her much, but when she's here, she's usually rude to everybody." Janie looked thoughtfully at Aja. "I don't know Walker's story, so I'm not sure how serious they are."

"I didn't ask," Aja said, putting plates on a tray.

"You didn't have to." Janie smiled.

Everybody's a psychic, Aja thought cynically.

After work, Aja headed to her car in the dark parking lot. She saw Walker and Kendall under the portico. She couldn't hear what they were saying, but she could tell that they were arguing about something.

34

It's for the best, Aja thought. Glad she hadn't invested her heart in Walker. Besides, Aja felt like she couldn't hold a candle to the sleek young woman. They were a beautiful couple. Aja sighed.

She got in her car and started it. The exhaust popped like a gunshot. She wanted to sink into the cracked, vinyl upholstery but couldn't help smiling when she saw Kendall jump like a scared rabbit at the noise.

She headed out of the parking lot, chugging and clunking. A car in the lot turned its headlights on as she drove by. She got a sick feeing when she realized it was the Freddy Kruger cop watching her as she pulled out.

CHAPTER 9

"Aja, if you miss any more school, you'll have to go to summer school," her mother said as she stood over Aja's bed the next morning. "I'll leave it up to you if you want to sleep in. I know you're tired from work." Her mom's usual attitude: do what feels right, let the universe guide you—which was why Aja's absentee rate was so high.

"I'm getting up." Aja rolled over and stretched. The last place she wanted to go was school. She spent a few minutes trying to rouse her brain; she remembered Walker's stunning girlfriend, and Freddy Kruger following her home. He'd kept on driving when she turned into her driveway, but Aja felt violated anyway.

The news was on their tiny analog TV in the kitchen. Her mom buttered a piece of sprouted whole grain toast for Aja. "Here, you need to eat something." She put a plate in front of Aja. "Have you paid your counselor back the money yet?"

"No, I will when I get my check."

"Please get it done soon. I don't want a black cloud of bad energy around you because of it. You're too smart for that." She sat across from Aja and sipped on coffee. "That awful police officer came by while you were at work. I told him that no charges had been filed, so back off. I also let him know I'll file a complaint against him if he keeps harassing us." She shuddered. "He gives me the willies."

Aja started to say that he'd followed her home, but stopped. Knowing her mom, she'd be at the police station raising a ruckus, filing orders against him and probably picketing outside the station citing police abuse. Her mom fought for any cause and looked for any excuse for a protest. She lived for righteous causes. Aja didn't need the aggravation or embarrassment. "I gotta run," Aja said, standing. "I'm working tonight, too, so I won't be home after school."

"Okay, honey. Go out and change the world." Her mom smiled. It was her favorite catch phrase. "I think working at the assisted living center is great for you. Take time to talk to the people there."

"Yeah, I know. So far, they're all hard of hearing, rude, or pass gas all the time." Aja opened the screen door and thought of the Jensens.

"Everybody has a light in them. Try to find it." Her mom gave her a hug. "I have some clients later this afternoon, so be quiet if you do come home."

Aja fought to stay awake in English. Working late at such a physical job was wearing her down. Her arms ached from lifting the trays, and her feet throbbed from the cheap shoes.

Mrs. Dempsey squeezed through the desks, handing out the Romeo and Juliet tests, offering comments to each student. "Good job. Needs a little work." When she got to Aja's desk, she slapped the paper facedown, saying nothing.

Aja peeked at her score and smiled when she saw her grade: ninety-seven. She could see the only points off were on the essay section, where Mrs. Dempsey was able to offer her own opinion, and where Aja could read between the comments that she didn't deserve this grade.

"So did you cheat, or what?" Aja heard a voice behind her. Her face burned, but she didn't turn around. Instead, she flipped the test over with the grade on top and stared at the front of the classroom.

In between classes, Aja felt her phone vibrate in her pocket. It was a text from Walker. *Can I see you later?* She stopped in the hallway, forcing other kids to go around her, and texted back. *No, I'm working.* She snapped her phone closed and went to her next class. The phone buzzed again as she took a seat, but she ignored it.

Later, at work, Aja ducked into a bathroom and changed clothes. She only had the one outfit, and her shirt was getting gamey. She'd not had time to do laundry. As she laced her cheap shoes, Aja thought she felt another blister pop. She stopped by the mirror to put her hair up. She was so tired it showed in her whole body. Her long blonde hair was greasy, and her shirt had a chocolate stain from the cake she'd brought to the Jensen's apartment the other night. She thought of Walker and his perfect, shiny girlfriend complaining about the brown salad leaves. Please, would Kendall's hair even get dirty? She and Walker looked like they were meant to be together. The perfect couple. Aja stuffed her school clothes in her backpack and ran out of the bathroom.

"China girl, help me out here." Mrs. Poston stood in the lobby of the residence home, holding a small box and a stack of mail. "Carry this to my room." She handed the box to Aja.

"I'd love to help Mrs. Poston, but Janie's expecting me." Aja glanced at her watch. "Ten minutes ago."

"Then she can wait a few more minutes." Mrs. Poston walked ahead, flipping through the stack of mail. "You need to be more dependable."

Aja sighed and dutifully followed the old lady, surprised at the spring in the woman's step. Mrs. Poston's hair was a helmet seared with a single flip of a curl in the front. Aja thought if she touched it, the hair would break into pieces. She wondered how she slept at night without messing it up—if she slept at all since she was always cranky.

"Bills, junk and catalogs," Mrs. Poston said waving the mail. "You young people don't write letters anymore. Everything is science fiction now. Phones that take pictures and computers that do your work. Lazy, lazy."

It took a few minutes before they reached Mrs. Poston's apartment, and Aja knew Janie was cursing her by now. "Here you go, Mrs. Poston. I really need to run."

"You will excuse yourself properly *after* you put the box inside," Mrs. Poston said with a raised eyebrow. The alcove to her door had a small table decorated with an eyelet doily and a fake potted geranium on top. She lifted the plant and took a hidden key from under it and opened the door. "Set it on the dining room table." Mrs. Poston waved her inside and put the key back under the pot.

Aja ran in and placed the box on a table in a small kitchen. Mrs. Poston's apartment was neat and clean, not a speck of dust anywhere, and it felt like the thermostat was set to a searing ninety degrees. "Okay, I'll see you at dinner." Aja dashed to the door.

"What are we having tonight?" Mrs. Poston asked.

"I don't know yet." Aja fidgeted, ready to sprint. "But I'm sure Janie needs my help. Bye." She ran out before Mrs. Poston could say anything else.

Janie was busy filling water glasses when Aja ran into the kitchen. She looked at the clock, then at Aja.

"I'm sorry, Janie. Mrs. Poston held me hostage, and I couldn't break away." Aja grabbed an apron and took a bucket of lettuce from the fridge.

Janie sighed. "I'd hoped to bring the Jensens something before the dinner rush started. Mrs. Jensen's not doing well and really should be in the hospital."

"Then why doesn't she go?" Aja asked.

"Mr. Jensen says he can take better care of her here, but he's about to run himself into the ground."

"His hands shake so bad he couldn't even hold a spoonful of food steady when he tried to feed her the other night," Aja said. She looked around the kitchen. "You go. I'll take care of the soup and salad."

"No, there's too much," Janie said.

"I'll be fine. You'll be back before the main course." Aja grabbed a tray and a stack of salad plates. "What could go wrong?"

CHAPTER 10

After Janie left to go to the Jensen's with dishes of food, Aja and Gabe, the cook, slapped lettuce on each plate and garnished each with tomatoes and carrots. She could already hear voices out in the dining hall. She grabbed a pad to write the orders down so she wouldn't forget, heaven forbid, Mrs. Poston's order. She grabbed two pitchers of water and headed into the dining room, where most of the tables were already occupied.

"We thought you'd deserted us," Mrs. Poston yelled across the room. "What's taking so long?"

"Coming," Aja said, hastily filling water glasses. She got to Mrs. Poston's table and filled her glass. A few drops splattered on the tablecloth. "Sorry," Aja said.

"I want apple juice and decaf coffee," Mrs. Poston demanded, blotting the water with her napkin. "And bring me a fresh napkin."

Aja set one of the pitchers on the table to write the order. Mrs. Poston gasped so loud Aja thought the woman had breathed her last breath. "Are you okay?"

Mrs. Poston pointed to the sweaty pitcher. "Get that off my table. Where did you learn your manners? *Bad* manners, I might add." The two women sitting with her squirmed in their seats. "Where's Janie?"

"She'll be right back." Aja grabbed the pitcher. "I'll get your drinks in a sec." She ran to fill up the rest of the diners' glasses.

"No, not in a 'sec.' Now." Mrs. Poston glared at Aja.

"Here, let me help." Aja felt someone take the water from her hand.

"Walker, this is not your job," Mrs. Poston said.

"But it would be my pleasure to serve such a beautiful group of women." Walker bowed. The two women giggled while Mrs. Poston continued to glare at Aja.

"Walker, don't be gross." Kendall came up behind him. "Don't bring yourself down to this level. You're not a server."

The way she said 'server' made Aja's skin crawl.

"I think I can handle pouring a few glasses of water." Walker stepped away from Kendall and nodded at Aja.

"Thank you," Aja whispered.

Walker winked at her and poured out water and charm at each table.

Aja got the rest of the drinks and began with the food orders. She stopped short when she noticed Freddy Kruger, in full uniform, his big gun holstered at his hip, take a seat with one of the residents. He smiled, an eerily sinister smile at Aja, and waved her over.

"Aja Harmon, right?" he asked.

"Yeah." She felt defensive and scared at the same time. "Are you eating here tonight?"

"Yes, with my favorite uncle." He waved toward an elderly man sitting next to him who didn't respond much except to nod. The poor guy's wrinkled, grimy button-down made Aja's shirt look sparkly clean.

"What can I get you to drink?" Aja asked, trying to keep her voice steady.

"There's not much here that I'd want." Freddy Kruger sneered. "How about you and me go get something later?"

Desperately wishing she'd been serving steaming hot coffee so she could pour it on his lap, Aja ignored his remark. "How about you, sir?" she asked his uncle.

"What?" he yelled, cupping his ear.

Aja heard a high-pitched whistle coming from his ear and noticed a hearing aid. "What do you want to drink?" she asked loudly.

"Milk," he wheezed. "Helps my peptic ulcer." He patted his belly.

Aja took their food order and went to get the rest of the drinks. She'd have to hustle to get the salads and soup out. Where was Janie?

Walker stepped in beside her. "What else can I help with?"

"Really?" Aja turned. "Janie should've have been back by now. Can you help serve the salads?"

"Sure, show me what to do."

Kendall appeared in the kitchen and grabbed Walker's arm. "This is not funny. Don't you think you should eat with your family?" She looked with disdain at Aja. "I mean, it's not like you need to train for future life skills here. There's no waiting tables in law school." She flipped her silky, shiny hair as if to make a point. Aja got a glimpse of her psychic aura as a colorless blob.

Aja could practically feel the grease congeal in her own hair and noticed Kendall had on one of the new spring skirts from Abercrombie.

"China girl, pack my dinner to go. I don't have time to sit here all night," Mrs. Poston shouted. "I don't pay for my meals to be self-serve. Hurry!"

Aja ran to the kitchen, where the cook had started serving the plates of food by looking at her order slips. "Thanks, Gabe. Janie's still not back, and Mrs. Poston wants her food to go."

He gruffly waved her off. "I'll take care of her. Get these orders out."

Aja grabbed a tray of food and ran out the door, crashing into Walker as he was coming into the kitchen. Food went everywhere, plates shattered to the floor.

"Oh, I'm so sorry!" Aja cried, grabbed a napkin and wiped blended roast beef off Walker's shirt.

Gabe took a broom and swept the mess into one big pile. "Go get the next tray and serve. We'll finish cleaning up later." He set the broom to the side and took another stack of plates, dealing them on a tray like a deck of cards. "I'll re-do this order. Go on."

Aja didn't have time to check on Walker as she took the food tray and began serving. After the third tray, she saw Gabe walk a box of food to Mrs. Poston.

"This is unconscionable. I pay too much money to live here to be treated like trailer trash," Mrs. Poston said. "You can be sure I will file a complaint."

"Sorry for your troubles," Gabe said, as he placed the box on the table in front of Mrs. Poston.

Aja served the two women who were sitting with Mrs. Poston. "I'm sorry for the delay."

"That's fine, honey. They need to hire a few more girls, though," one of the women said.

Aja smiled at her gratefully, then ran to serve Walker's table. Walker was in good humor with a bib tucked into his stained shirt. Kendall, fuming, glared at Aja.

"Miss Stafford." Mrs. Poston was suddenly next to Walker's table, addressing Kendall. "Do you mind helping me carry my food and drink to my apartment? I need someone who can show some responsibility to help me." Her eyes bore into Aja.

Kendall grimaced, obviously not willing to help.

"I'll help you." Walker stood.

"No, I'll do it," Kendall huffed, and threw her napkin on the table. "You've done more than enough for this place," she hissed, angrily scooting her chair away from the table.

"Thank you, dear." Mrs. Poston handed the box to Kendall. "You know, you remind me of myself when I was your age."

"Don't flatter yourself," Kendall whispered to herself, but Aja heard. She wasn't sure that Walker heard and was certain that the elders didn't because no one reacted.

What an awful person, Aja thought as she left them and headed toward the kitchen. She felt a hand on her arm and turned smiling, expecting to see Walker. It was Freddy Kruger.

"My uncle wants more milk and his dinner."

"Sure, let me get it." Aja tried to wiggle from his grip, but he only held her tighter. "Let me go, so I can get your food."

He took her by both arms and faced her and pressed his body into her. "You look like you need some help."

"I can't do anything if you don't let go." Aja did not want another scene, so she didn't kick him in the balls like she wanted to.

"Do you do any nude modeling?" he said contemptuously. "I want to take pictures of you."

"Well, look at that," Aja heard Mrs. Poston say. "China girl, I don't think you should be flirting with the guests, especially considering the disaster you served tonight."

"I'm not." She wrestled from Kruger's grip, darted to the kitchen and tried not to cry.

An hour later, everyone had been served, and Aja was so exhausted and sore she could barely move. The kitchen still needed to be cleaned, and she felt obligated to help Gabe since he'd been so good to her during dinner. She still had hours of homework to do and would be up till 2:00 a.m. doing that and laundry.

Janie walked into the kitchen and took in the mess. "What happened?"

"Don't ask. Where were you?" Aja asked, angrily rubbing her blistered feet.

Janie shook her head. "We had to call an ambulance to take Mrs. Jensen to the hospital. She didn't look like she'd make it through the night. Mr. Jensen is beside himself, cried like a baby when they took her. I had to drive him to the hospital." She grabbed a broom and began sweeping. "I'm sorry. I should've come by here first."

"That's okay." Aja sighed. "You did the right thing." She wearily leaned against a counter. "But I'm probably going to be fired after this."

"Let me talk to them. It's my fault."

"Well, don't get yourself fired. This place would fall apart without you."

"I've worked here so long." Janie shook her head. "I can't help but get attached to the residents. It never gets easy when we lose somebody." She swept the pile of broken plates and food together.

"How is Mrs. Jensen?" Aja asked.

"Not good. I hope she rallies, but I could see that her pee bag was empty. I'm sure her kidneys are shutting down. And then her breathing was ragged." She bent and scooped the mess onto a duster. "The Jensens are people you want to see go together. He'll be lost without her."

Then Aja felt it. Sorrow. Deep endless pain. "She's not going to make it," Aja whispered.

"Don't be so negative." Janie looked at her strangely.

"I...when I saw her the other night, she looked so sick." Aja grabbed a mop and began cleaning the food spills. She'd always kept her mouth shut about her psychic abilities, hating to be thought of as a freak. The feelings she got didn't happen all the time and they didn't always come true. But sometimes she just knew things were going to happen before they did or she could envision scenes from a person's past. Like a puzzle, but she never knew how to put it together.

Aja heard voices in the dining room.

"Don't go in there. Are you training to be a bus boy?"

"Kendall, stop. It wouldn't kill you to help out a little."

"Eww, like I'd actually work in a kitchen?"

The door opened and Walker came in, Kendall trailing him. He'd changed into a fresh shirt. "I thought you could use a hand here."

Janie, carrying a stack of dirty plates, laughed. "Walker, I wish everybody in the world was like you. But we're good. Thanks, anyway." She turned her smile to Aja. "Since you busted your butt tonight, why don't you take off. I can get this place cleaned up in no time."

Gabe, standing by the sink, wiped his hands on his stained apron. "So I can leave too?"

Janie's smile faded. "Well..."

Gabe waved his hand at Janie and kept rinsing the dishes.

"Good." Kendall pulled Walker's arm. "Let's get out of here. Now." She looked with contempt at Aja, scrutinizing every stain and glob of food stuck to her. "How can you stand yourself?"

"Kendall!" Walker said. "That was rude."

"Oh, it's fine," Aja said lightly, while seething inside. "Here, give me a big hug; we should all learn to get along." Sarcasm laced her voice. She walked toward Kendall, arms outstretched.

"Gross," Kendall shrieked, and backed away out of the kitchen.

"I'm sorry," Walker said. "Now you know the reason I left Chicago."

Aja looked at Walker, all polished and handsome. She'd never felt so dirty or grimy in her life, especially with the stain of Freddy Kruger's touch on her.

In the parking lot, Aja saw Freddy's car. Should she just confront the jerk? *No, he's a police officer.* It'd be her word against his, plus he had a gun. The chill she felt when she looked at his silhouette in the car was profound. He was not one to mess with.

It took a few tries, but her car finally started. As she pulled out, she noticed Freddy Kruger's headlights come on and he followed behind her. She fought down nausea and a deep paralyzing fear. What if her car broke down? She chugged out of the lot and onto the main road, watching him in her rearview mirror. She nervously felt for the guardian angel coin in her pocket. Silly, she knew, but sometimes rubbing the etching gave her a minute to think.

On impulse, as she drove by the hospital, she turned in quickly. Too quick for him to follow. She drove to the emergency entrance and parked. Aja saw him turn around and drive into the lot. Maybe she should sic her mother on him. He wouldn't know how to handle her and her sit-in protests.

Unless he retaliated.

That sent another wave of fear over her, and she jumped out of her car and ran inside.

"Can I help you?" an attendant sitting at a desk asked.

Aja looked back at the parking lot and noticed Freddy parking near her car. "Umm, yes. I was checking on Mrs. Jensen." Aja realized she didn't know the woman's first name.

"Are you family?"

"No, a friend."

"Visiting hours are over." The attendant looked at a clock on the wall. It was after ten o'clock.

"I know. I work at the assisted living home were she lives, and I just wanted to check on her."

The attendant took in Aja's stained clothes and greasy hair, then typed into a computer. "She's on the third floor, but they may chase you out of there."

"Thanks." Aja ran to the elevators.

The third floor was quiet. It smelled of stale mold, disinfectant, and urine. She didn't want to ask a nurse which room and risk getting shooed out, so she walked the hall looking at the names posted on the doors. She should have brought some food or something but she hadn't planned on coming here.

Outside one of the rooms, she saw Mr. Jensen arguing with a doctor. "No, you need to make her better," she heard him cry.

"I'm sorry, sir. We can send her home with hospice care."

Mr. Jensen looked up and saw Aja. "Princess Bride," he addressed Aja. "My Buttercup needs to get better. She's real sick." His eyes begged Aja for help.

Aja sensed the loss again. Mrs. Jensen would not survive.

"Spend some time with her," the doctor said to Mr. Jensen.

"Give her another IV," Mr. Jensen pleaded as he turned back to the doctor. "She just needs to get healthy."

"Her kidneys can't take any fluid, sir. We've done all we can."

Aja felt Mr. Jensen's sadness. He looked so frail and small and completely helpless. "Come on, Mr. Jensen, let's go and talk to your wife, your Buttercup." Aja took the man's withered hand and led him into the room. "Can I call your daughters?"

He seemed shell-shocked but let Aja take him into the hospital room. Aja almost recoiled at the sight of Mrs. Jensen. The poor woman was even thinner than the other night, but her abdomen was bloated like a beach ball. Her eyes sunk into the sockets of her skull, and her cheekbones protruded like a Halloween skeleton. Aja didn't want to look but couldn't take her eyes off of her. Like when people hang around gawking at a car accident.

"Isn't she beautiful?" Mr. Jensen asked, as he took his trembling hand to try and move some disheveled hair from her face. Aja noticed a night kit with a brush in it on the bedside table. She took it and began gently brushing Mrs. Jensen's hair.

CHAPTER 11

A loud pop started Aja out of a dream.

Mrs. Dempsey stood over her, a book in her hand. She must have slammed the book closed, waking Aja up.

"I'm sorry to have disturbed your sleep," Mrs. Dempsey snapped.

Aja swiped at a thin line of drool that ran from her mouth to her desk like a spider web. She sat for a second trying to regain composure.

"I guess you partied too much last night?" Mrs. Dempsey scoffed.

"Yeah, that's it." Aja glared at her fat English teacher. Aja had only slept two hours. She'd stayed at the hospital until 1:00 a.m., consoling Mr. Jensen while she used his old duct-taped cell phone to call his daughters. She waited until one of them arrived before she left.

Aja asked for a security escort to her car and was relieved to see Freddy Kruger was no longer waiting for her. At home, she had to wait for the laundry cycle to run so she could get her clothes in the dryer. They were still damp and drying in the back of her car for her shift tonight.

"So, what was the answer to my question, Sleeping Beauty?" Mrs. Dempsey sneered.

"I'm sorry, could you repeat the question?" Aja asked, still shaking sleep off.

"No, I will not. If you can't stay awake for my class, then maybe you should spend some time in the principal's office."

"Maybe if your class was interesting I'd be wide-eyed and

bushy tailed." Aja crossed her arms defiantly and stared at the teacher.

The other kids snickered and whispered.

"I'll let Mr. Carlisle know you're coming." Mrs. Dempsey snapped her fingers and pointed to the door. "Go on." She clucked and shook her head. "Such a waste of a life. You only have yourself to blame for your troubles."

Aja wasn't going to beg for mercy. She stood up, grabbed her books and bag and stormed out of the classroom.

Aja flopped into a chair outside the principal's office. The same chair she'd been in when she'd overheard them talking about her. The door opened and Principal Carlisle walked out with another student. Aja recognized him as the quarterback of the football team.

"Get your grades up, son." Principal Carlisle patted the boy on his back. "We need you on the team. You might have to miss a few of the pre-season games next fall because of the DUI, but we'll help get you back on track."

"Yes, sir," the kid said as he left.

Aja shook her head. This kid had been caught drinking during the season. Now the principal was going to help him so he could continue to play football? What a whiff.

"You again? You want an indefinite suspension? It'd sure be easier on all of us."

"Would I get my high school diploma with it?" Aja shot back.

"No, of course not. But if you're as smart as Mrs. Burnett says, then maybe you'll ace your GED."

"Too bad I don't play football. Sounds like I'd get some extra help if I did."

"Don't smart talk me, young lady. "

"Aja, how about we take a few minutes to talk." Mrs. Burnett appeared from her office. "Mr. Carlisle, I need to meet with Aja anyway. Let me visit with her."

"Send her back to me when you're done." Principal Carlisle waved her on. "Did you pay the stolen money back yet?"

"Not yet. I will as soon as I get paid," Aja said quietly.

"She's working on it," Mrs. Burnett said.

"Another good reason to suspend you," Carlisle threatened.

Aja and Mrs. Burnett went into the counselor's office and sat.

Mrs. Burnett clicked on her computer and opened Aja's school record.

"Aja, I know you can do the schoolwork." She looked directly at her. "You're smarter than most of the students here. Your scores are way above average as are all your aptitude tests. I don't want to see someone as talented as you fall through the cracks. What can I do to help you?"

Aja just sat and shrugged.

"Mrs. Dempsey emailed us that you'd fallen asleep in her class and you talk back to her all the time. What's going on?" Mrs. Burnett sounded sincere. "Are you working or just out late?"

"Working," Aja mumbled.

"What job keeps you out so late?" Mrs. Burnett put her elbows on the desk and tried to make eye contact with Aja.

"Pole dancer."

Mrs. Burnett jerked backward. "Oh, Aja, I hope not. Why, you're not old enough to get into those places. What about your mother..."

Aja remembered Mrs. Burnett going to bat for her with Dempsey and Carlisle, not to mention bailing her out with the forty dollars she'd stolen. "I'm not working as a stripper." Aja slouched lower in her chair. "Just as a waitress."

"*Just* a waitress? That's a tough job. I'd be sawing logs at my desk, too."

Aja smiled a little.

"Are you planning on going to college?"

"Yeah, I think. I want to get out of high school first."

"Good point." Mrs. Burnett began typing on her computer again. "You need to get through these next two months without missing any more school or assignments, and you'll have to learn to deal with Mrs. Dempsey. I'll help you any way I can."

"You already have, Mrs. Burnett," Aja said. "I'll get you the money back as soon as I can."

"I know you will." Mrs. Burnett leaned over her desk. "Look, maybe I can work something out with Mr. Carlisle where you can 'assist' me in the office. I'd like to help you apply to some colleges."

"I'm planning on moving to California."

"To study?"

Aja shook her head. "I don't know. I just want to leave this place."

Mrs. Burnett sighed. "California schools are tough to get into, plus they're expensive. You're smart, but"—Mrs. Burnett pointed to Aja's page on the computer—"your student record is spotty with the different schools, even if your grades are good. I could probably pull some strings here, but I don't know anybody in California."

"I just want to get out of Texas."

"Are you running from something?"

Aja felt her defenses rising. "No."

"Based on your school records, you've moved around a lot. That's great if you're looking for adventure, but it's also okay to put some roots down, too. Don't be afraid to leave your mark."

"The only mark I'd want to leave in this town would stink."

"Aja, why so angry?"

Aja smiled. "I guess I have a problem with authority."

Mrs. Burnett laughed deeply. "*That's* an understatement. Here, let me check to see if you can meet with an Army recruiter."

Aja stared at her and hugged her book bag tight.

"I'm joking," Mrs. Burnett said, still smiling. "I don't want to see you waste an opportunity to spread your wings. You can fly or you can fall flat. Your choice." She rummaged in her desk and handed Aja some college brochures. "Look these over; get some ideas, even if you start by taking a few classes at the community college. I'll check with Mrs. Dempsey to see if you can make up today's work. I'll recommend she add an extra assignment or something to appease her ego." Mrs. Burnett leaned closer and whispered, "She likes to be the boss. Let her feel like it's her decision." She held up two fingers. "Two months, Aja. Then you're out of here. You can do it."

"Thanks," Aja said, she stood to leave.

"Wait." Mrs. Burnett waved her back to her seat and looked out the door. "Mr. Carlisle is leaving. Give him a few minutes to get out the door and forget that he was supposed to meet with you. Then you can run to your next class."

Aja smiled and tucked the brochures in her bag.

CHAPTER 12

In the bathroom at work, Aja buttoned her black pants, still damp from the late night laundry. Trying to dry them in the car didn't quite work for the areas of her clothes that had been in the shade. Thankfully they were clean even if they were wrinkled. She was about to fall flat on her face from exhaustion, but at least she didn't smell like blended roast beef and apple juice.

After dressing, she glanced out the door of the bathroom, making sure Mrs. Poston was nowhere in sight. Aja wanted to make a mad dash to the kitchen and to check on Mrs. Jensen. She came home today with hospice care.

Aja pulled her long hair up in a ponytail and stuffed her clothes in her bag, then double-checked the hallway. Good, the coast was clear.

She'd just made it past the office when she heard her name. Damn.

"Aja, do you have a minute?"

Aja turned and saw Edna Jones, the woman she'd interviewed with. "Yeah, sure, but Janie is expecting me."

"I'll let her know you'll be late."

The way Edna said "late" made Aja wonder if it would be a permanent situation.

Aja dutifully followed Edna into her office, where she closed the door. "Please, have a seat." Edna scooted in behind her desk and sat. The air escaping from the cushion made Aja wonder if the woman had just passed gas.

"Aja, it's come to my attention that you've been arrested before." Edna opened a file that had been sitting on her desk.

Aja sunk lower in her chair. "Yes, but I was never charged with anything." She wondered how much information was in the record that Edna was perusing. As a juvenile, her records were supposed to be sealed. "Is that from the background check you did on me?"

"Yes, that as well as Officer Clay's research on you." Edna looked at Aja, raising her heavily penciled eyebrows. "I believe you know Officer Clay Richards. According to Mrs. Poston, you were rather, umm, close to him during the dinner disaster last night. Which is another issue we need to talk about."

"That weirdo was hitting on me. The guy creeps me out." Aja chilled, remembering Freddy Kruger's headlights in her rearview mirror.

Edna sat silent, continued to read the file. "Both the charges here are for disorderly conduct and one for resisting arrest. And then there was a complaint listed from Georgia."

"Georgia? How did you find out about that? I wasn't arrested for anything." Aja sighed. She hadn't even gotten one paycheck yet, and she was already going to be unemployed again.

"Officer Clay did some research," Edna said. "Aja, I can't see us employing someone with a record. I'm sorry." She closed the file. "I have to think of the residents first."

"Yeah, whatever. I get it." Aja stood to leave.

"As far as the dinner service last night, I've already spoken to Janie, and she's on notice for that. But you should have been able to handle it better than you did."

"Don't fire her; she was helping the Jensens."

"Don't worry about Janie." Edna got out of her chair. "If this address is good, I'll send your check there." She walked to the door to let Aja out.

"Okay." Aja was so dejected she didn't even have a snappy rude comeback. She was tired, depressed and still felt a responsibility to poor Janie, who would be busting her ass alone tonight.

"Aja, our angel." Lauren Jensen caught up to them in the hallway outside Edna's door. She gave Aja a big hug. "Dad keeps talking about how much help you were last night. Thank you so much for being with him." She turned to Edna. "Did Aja tell you she stayed with Dad until one o'clock in the morning? She wouldn't leave until I got there."

"No, she didn't." Edna glanced at Aja.

"He calls her Princess Bride." Lauren looked at Aja. "I can see why. You do look a lot like her."

"How's your mom?" Aja asked.

Tears filled Lauren's eyes. "She's resting, but..." She wiped away the tears that fell on her cheeks. "I still can't thank you enough for calling all of us. Dad wouldn't have been able to." She sniffled and took a Kleenex and blew her nose. "You are an angel."

Edna turned to Aja. "You didn't mention this."

"What was there to say? She was really sick the other night. I don't know. Mr. Jensen was so worried about her. Is it okay if I go and visit her?" Aja asked Edna. "I mean, since I'm not working here anymore."

"You quit?" Lauren asked. "I hate to see you go." She turned to Edna. "Why can't you keep the good ones here?" She looked at Aja. "Of course, you are welcome to visit anytime."

Aja took off her apron and handed it to Edna.

Edna waved at the apron. "Aja, why don't you go see how Janie is doing in the kitchen first? She's probably looking for you. Please do a good job. We need good employees."

"Really? Thanks," Aja said, then turned to Lauren. "I'll come by after serving dinner if that's okay."

Lauren hugged her. "Anytime, Aja."

Over Lauren's shoulder, Aja saw Kendall standing near the front desk, staring hard at her. Aja wondered why she was always there if she hated the place so much. Walker had tried calling a few times, but Aja ignored his calls. She didn't want to play second fiddle to Kendall.

In the kitchen, Aja told Janie and Gabe that she'd almost been fired. She left out the part about her criminal record.

"Was it because of last night?" Janie asked. "I'm so sorry."

Aja shrugged. "Long story. Let me start the salads tonight."

CHAPTER 13

Later that night at home, Aja's head bobbed sleepily over her homework. Her mom had left a note saying she'd gone to the Hill Country near Austin to sing with a folk band and that there was a vegan casserole in the fridge.

Math was stupid easy. Geography was interesting, but Aja didn't have time to spend savoring her book because she had to finish reading for English, including the extra assignment Dempsey gave her. Her eyes would not stay open as she tried to track the pages. Instead, she decided to read in bed after showering.

She'd only spent an hour at the Jensens' after work. Mrs. Jensen slept the whole time Aja was there. Her family sat around her, seeming afraid to miss a second with their mother. Mr. Jensen nervously worked to keep up with the activity and spend time holding his wife's hand. The commotion seemed to make him more anxious, and Aja only felt like she was in the way. She didn't leave until she made sure he'd eaten a cup of soup, though.

Aja glanced at the clock. It was almost midnight. The lack of sleep the night before was wearing on her every nerve. She was a little apprehensive about staying alone but was so tired she figured the house could implode and she'd probably sleep through it. She got up from her studies to take her dirty dishes to the kitchen. As she rinsed her dishes, she looked out the window over the sink and froze when she saw a figure under the oak tree near the alley. A familiar shadow. The police officer, Clay Richards, the one she called Freddy Kruger.

She jumped so hard she dropped her plate in the sink, cracking it in two. Aja ignored the broken dish and ran from the kitchen, turning out the light behind her. Her heart fluttered like a scared animal ready to take flight. She was trapped. This guy wasn't like other adults that Aja easily flipped off. His presence was so evil she shook to her core. And, worse, he wouldn't leave her alone.

She crouched in the darkened hallway, chewing her nails, wondering where she could go and *if* she could get out. She was trapped like a caged bird. Her cell phone was in her room so she crawled toward her open door. The light in her room was on, leaving no place to hide. As she shuffled by her mom's room, she glanced out the window to the backyard. He stood under the tree, but had moved closer. This was worse than a horror movie. At least in the theater, she could close her eyes and make the scary parts go away.

She wanted to run to her car and drive away, but he'd no doubt pull her over for some reason and then she'd be at his mercy. She wished that she'd grabbed a big butcher knife before she ran from the kitchen.

She made it to her bedroom and turned off the light. As she reached for her cell phone, she heard the squeak of the screen door. In her purse were the needle-nose pliers, a gift from her mom who swore every girl should have this multi-use tool. Her mom used one when she was hitchhiking years ago. Pressed them against the neck of a driver who decided he wanted payment for the ride he'd given her. Since then, she was never without hers and made sure Aja had a pair too. Aja used it mostly on their garage-sale crockpot whose knob had broken off leaving no grip.

The screen door squeaked again, and this time Aja heard the doorknob jiggle. Luckily, she'd locked all the doors when she got home. She never liked to stay alone, but she usually did okay—until tonight. The veil of fear shocked her so much she could barely breathe, much less think of what to do.

Aja knew the door would be nothing to break through. She took her phone off the desk and tried to dial. Her hand shook so hard and she couldn't remember what numbers to dial.

911, 911. She finally hit the buttons.

The door opened.

"911 operator," a voice came on the line.

"I'm at 324 Willow and a man is breaking in. He's coming in the house!" Aja whispered loudly. "Hurry."

"What's your zip code? You're calling from a cell phone."

Aja couldn't remember. Her mind was blank with fear. "Hurry!"

"Give me a cross street," the operator stayed calm.

"He's in the house," Aja cried. She heard boots on the kitchen floor. "Oh, God, hurry."

"Okay, stay on the line with me; I'm sending someone out." There was a pause and click, then the operator somehow zeroed on her address. "Is this where you are?"

"Yes," Aja whispered. Another scuff sound closer to her room. Aja dropped the phone, took her pliers, and crawled to the window. She unlocked it and pulled it open. The screen was already ripped, and Aja tore through the screen with the pliers and rolled outside. She landed hard in some scraggly bushes but barely registered the sharp twigs jabbing into her back. She stood, tool in hand, and looked into her darkened window. Freddy was in her bedroom doorway looking at her. She saw the light of her cell phone on the floor. He crunched the phone under his boot. Aja turned and ran.

She sprinted in a panic through the neighborhood, dogs barking at almost every house. He'd find her just by the noise. Aja dashed between two houses and tried to gulp some air and think. The more air she got in, the more her cuts hurt. Her head ached from being so keenly aware of fight-or-flight fear, layered with exhaustion.

Before long, she saw red-and-blue flashing lights ricochet through the houses. She debated about going home. What if he was still there? He was, after all, a police officer. She looked down the dark alley where she hid. But what if he's here? She blanched at the tomblike darkness and headed toward her house, pliers at the ready.

By now a few of the neighbors had come out of their houses to check out the police visit.

"Aja?" Fiona, one of her neighbors caught up to her. "What's going on at your house?"

"Someone tried to break in." The relief of being safe brought on uncontrolled sobs. She put her tool into the back pocket of her jeans.

"This neighborhood is getting so bad." Fiona shook her head.

"It's getting that a lady can't live alone here anymore. "Fiona was a middle-aged divorced woman, who'd raised three kids in her small home until they'd all moved out. "You okay? Where's your mom?" Fiona put a comforting arm around Aja. "Why, you're all cut up. What the hell happened?"

Aja continued to cry. "I-I jumped out the window. I guess I landed in the bushes."

"You're alone? Come on." Fiona walked Aja toward her house.

Aja headed to a cluster of police officers, who turned to her and Fiona. She saw Clay Richards among the group, and she froze in her spot.

"Are you the young lady that called about a break-in?" one of the officers turned and asked her.

Aja pointed to Richards. "It was him. He's been following me and I saw him in my backyard."

Richards leered at her and laughed. "I was the first to the scene. I'd been patrolling and heard the call."

"Did you see anybody?" a female officer asked Richards.

"No, and I drove around to make sure."

Aja shook her head. "No, he *is* the guy."

Fiona patted Aja's sore back. "Honey, he's a police officer. Are you sure?" She pulled out a pack of cigarettes from her tattered robe's pocket and lit one.

Richards took a few steps towards Aja. "You're alone here tonight?"

It was a question, but Aja was certain he knew she was.

Aja backed away and tried to hide behind Fiona's smokescreen. She began shaking. "I want a restraining order against this guy. I don't care if he is a police officer, he's been following me for days."

Richards laughed heartily, seeming so good-ol-boy. "I'm sure you're exaggerating because I saw you at the old folks home the other night. You're just looking to start trouble."

The female officer stepped up and told one of the other officers, "Doug go check the back door for signs of a break in. Clay, thanks for everything, but I think we've got it under control here."

"Look, why don't I take over this call, babe," Richards said to her condescendingly.

"Babe?" She rolled her eyes. "Aren't you supposed to be off duty?"

"Yeah, go," Aja cried. "And I'm filing a restraining order against you." Her boldness wasn't as firm as she'd wanted. She turned to the female officer. "I am allowed to file a restraining order even if he is a police officer?"

"We'll talk," the woman said.

"He's one of the more decorated officers we have here," the police officer named Doug said. "He's here to help you, little-bit."

"Doug, go check the back," the female officer ordered.

"Did he just call me little-bit?" Aja asked. She was so tired and wide awake at the same time.

"I'm Officer Smith," the woman said, introducing herself. "Are your parents home?"

"No, my mom is out of town. I'm here alone."

"How old are you?"

"Eighteen."

"Is your father home?"

"No," Aja said. She didn't want to have to answer questions about not ever having a father. In first grade, a teacher who'd planned a "breakfast with daddy day" had the children tell what their fathers did. Hands went up, and kids gave answers like accountant, fireman, doctor. Aja, waving her hand enthusiastically, yelled out, "sperm donor," which stopped the teacher in her tracks. To this day, Aja still didn't know if the teacher was laughing or crying as she escorted Aja to the principal's office.

Fiona stepped into the conversation, stubbing her cigarette out on the street. "Aja and her momma are friends of mine. Why don't you stay with me until she gets home?"

Smith ignored Fiona. "How often are you here alone?"

"Not much. She had a job out of town tonight. I need to call her but 'Mr. Decorated Hero,' officer Clay Richards, crunched my phone under his boot."

"Why would he do that?" Smith was taking notes.

"Ask him. He's been following me around for days now."

"Did you provoke him?"

"Are you kidding me?"

"Don't use a tone with me."

Aja backed down. She'd dealt with police before; they always stuck together.

By the time the police left, they'd determined that someone had forced the back door open, and they found Aja's phone in pieces on her bedroom floor. Aja had seen enough *CSI* episodes to know they did nothing to investigate who might have done it.

It was two o'clock, and Aja was weak with exhaustion. She'd had less sleep all week than she needed in one night. Fiona let her come in and clean up, catch a few hours' sleep and change at her house. By then, it was time to leave for school.

CHAPTER 14

Aja plopped into a desk in Dempsey's class. Just get through this day, Aja thought. She was off work tonight and her mother was coming home. She'd be able to sleep all afternoon and night.

She wanted to talk to Walker but thought of Kendall. And, since her phone was smashed, she couldn't call anybody. Since she'd been ignoring Walker's texts and phone calls for the past few days he'd probably moved on anyway. Right into Kendall's arms.

Dempsey called on her a few times in class, and Aja managed to answer the questions. She could tell Dempsey was pissed and got some satisfaction from that. The rest of the day, Aja managed with energy drinks and pinching herself.

When the final bell rang, Aja headed to her car. Relieved. She was going straight home to sleep. She prayed her mom had made it home.

Standing next to her car was Walker.

"Hey." He jogged up to take her book bag. "I've been calling and texting you."

Aja let him take her books. "My phone's broken. And I'm sure Kendall's not interested in a threesome."

"That's what I want to talk to you about. I broke up with her a few months ago and moved to Texas to get away from her. She just won't take no for an answer." He opened her car door for her. "That's why Kendall is always here. She refuses to believe it."

"I thought you came to help your grandparents."

"That, too. Kendall and I were in school at Northwestern together. We've dated since high school. I've tried to end our relationship for a while now, and I thought moving here would help me make a clean break." He ran a hand through his thick, dark hair. "I told you that I'm working to be a different person, trying new things, but sometimes it's hard to break from my past. My family is so traditional that any change really shakes them up."

"Look, it's fine. I mean, we're not an item or anything. Plus, I've been really busy." Aja wished she wasn't drawn to him, his eyes, his smile that goodness he seemed to glow with.

"Can we go somewhere and talk?"

"Walker, I've had maybe two hours of sleep all week. I just want to go home and take a nap. Then I need to catch up on homework." She summarized the last few nights with the Jensens and the break-in. "I know that creep is following me. I'm so tired I don't even know what to do."

"Let me take you home and watch you snooze." He smiled.

Aja had a flash of him standing naked on the pedestal, and she blushed. It was sort of tempting, but all she wanted to do was sleep.

"I'll even get dinner and help you study."

"I don't know, Walker, since I don't have a phone I don't know if my mom made it home yet."

He took his phone from his pocket. "Here, call her. Tell your mom I'll bring dinner for all of us. You nap, I'll cook."

"You drive a hard bargain."

He followed her home, where her mom waited anxiously for her. She gave Aja a big hug when she got out of her car.

"Are you okay?" Her mom released Aja. "I've already tried to file a complaint against the jerk, but they need your statement. We can go there right now. Then I can call my friends, and we'll have a picket set up outside the police station in no time." She opened the door for Aja and Walker. "Hey, Walker, good to see you again."

"Mrs. Harmon." Walker smiled. "It sounds like Aja is real tired."

"Yeah, Mom. I haven't slept in forever. Can I take a nap first?"

"Sure, but I don't want this guy to be out on the streets. The public needs to know about him."

Aja's emotions were in turmoil about what to do. Her mom fought causes. She never just filed a complaint and let the proper channels take over. No, she marched with signs and handed out flyers. Aja never liked to go but was always dragged along. All of

Aja's incarcerations were because her mom had taken her along on various protests. Each of Aja's jail sentences was celebrated by her mom and friends because Aja had taken a stand for something important. One time, when she was fourteen, Aja had her favorite shirt on. A cool, stylish and expensive piece she'd saved and saved for. Her mom forced her to stick a huge "Peace is the Answer" button through it. The big pin left a noticeable hole in it.

Walker put Aja's book bag on the couch. "I promised to make dinner for you two. I'll run to the store and get food while Aja takes a nap. I'll make my specialty—spaghetti and meat sauce. With bottled sauce, of course."

Aja's mom said, "That sounds perfect, but we only eat grass-fed beef from humanely killed animals." She went to the kitchen and opened the freezer. "I have a little bit here, we'll mix it with this ground soy. If you want to pick up some bread and sauce, I'll start the meat."

Aja flopped on the couch not sure if she should be embarrassed by or proud of her mom.

"Soy meat?" Walker looked skeptical.

"You really can't tell the difference, especially if it's mixed with the real stuff," Aja said. "I'm going to take a shower and a nap. You two can wake me up when dinner is ready." She stood and considered calling Janie first, just to make sure she wasn't understaffed and to check on the Jensens. No, I need sleep, she convinced herself, and went into her room.

The pieces of her phone were piled in a shoe box. She heard Walker leave and her mom came into her room.

"I am so pissed that this guy thinks he can get away with something like this." Aja's mom nodded to the broken phone. "We might have to reactivate one of our old phones, since our contract isn't up yet."

"I thought you donated them to some women's shelter." Aja dropped the shoe box on her desk. It would be so cool to get a smart phone like everybody else in the world.

"I think I still have one around here somewhere." Aja's mom sat on the bed. "He had to have been watching you. How else would he have known I was gone? We may have to move again."

"No, not again. Not yet." Aja wanted to cry. "I'm so tired of moving all the time. Let me finish high school; then maybe we can go to California."

"We can't afford California."

"We can't afford anyplace. I'm going to San Francisco even if I have to be a beach bum." Aja grabbed some clothes from her dresser. "I'm going to take a shower."

"I'm sorry, Aja." Her mom stood and hugged her. Aja felt the sting of the scratches she'd gotten last night. "I thought a life of adventure would be the best for you. You know, living in different places, seeing the world. But we always seem to wind up on the same side of town."

"It's okay, Mom. It has been fun...most of the time." Aja stepped out of the hug. "How many kids can say they lived in an ice cream truck?" When Aja was seven, they'd lived in North Carolina for a summer. They never found a real home to settle in so the two of them stayed with friends of friends until their welcome wore out. Her mom thought she could make enough to support them by driving the truck and doing her readings.

"It was only for a few weeks." Aja's mom sat back on the bed. "Until the thing broke down."

"That was a day to remember." Aja sat next to her. "We had to eat all the ice cream before it melted. It was a dream come true."

"You're a great kid. We've had some times."

"Yeah, how many kids can say they shared a jail cell with their mom? Hey, how was the trip?"

"Good." Aja's mom got that wistful look. "Austin, now that would be a cool place to live."

CHAPTER 15

True to his word, Walker was a great cook. The kitchen smelled of fresh butter-sautéed garlic. The three sat in Aja's kitchen sopping their soy meat sauce with heavily buttered garlic bread.

"Now I'm really tired," Aja said as she took a mouthful of food. She'd had almost two hours of sleep while Walker and her mom made dinner.

"Go back to bed. You need your rest more than you need to do homework," her mom said, standing and picking up the plates.

Aja thought of seeing Freddy-Kruger-Clay-Richards under the tree. She shivered. "If I don't get this work done I won't graduate. I'm sick of that stupid school, and I want to get out no matter what."

"You will, honey," her mom said as she went to the sink. "Walker, tell me about your schooling. What are you studying?"

Walker smiled, melting the butter even more. "Good question. Basics mostly, but I'm interested in history, writing, everything. I was thinking of law school, but now I'm not so sure."

"With Kendall?" Aja asked. "Or is she studying how to be the perfect beautiful housewife?"

"Who's Kendall?" Aja's mom asked.

"Kendall Stafford, Walker's girlfriend," Aja answered.

"My ex-girlfriend." Walker pushed back from the table. "We are no longer an item."

"Except she's not aware of that." Aja crossed her arms.

Aja's mom watched with amusement, her hands coated with

soapsuds. "If it's meant to be, then let it happen." She smiled at Aja, then asked Walker, "Aren't you in an art class, too? How did you find out about the modeling position?"

This time, Walker's blush blossomed so much Aja thought the room would glow red if she turned the lights off.

"I, uh, saw the flyer at school," he stammered, playing with the breadbasket on the table. "Did you ever watch that show *Fear Factor*?"

"Yeah, a few times," Aja said.

"It used to be my favorite show, and I swore I could have done all the challenges. I'm trying to step out of my comfort zone. You know, like bungee jumping or diving with sharks. My life has always been so predictable and stable, and I thought if I moved to Texas I would try new things." He smiled again. "It was a sort of leap of faith. I wanted to do something unstable for a change."

"What's wrong with being stable?" Aja asked. "We've moved all over the place, and I sure don't feel grounded." She looked at her mother. "Not that it's all bad, but sometimes I've wished for a real old-fashioned home." She regretted saying it when she saw the sadness on her mom's face.

"I'm sorry, honey. I thought it would be good for you." Her mom was convinced the only way to really know a city was to live in it.

Walker grabbed the rest of the dishes from the table. "I guess nobody's ever happy with their life."

Walker's phone rang, and he glanced at caller ID before he answered. He got a funny look on his face and glanced at Aja. "Yeah, she's here. Her phone's broken." He handed his phone to Aja. "It's Janie."

Aja groaned. "I knew I should've called her." She took the phone. "Hey, were you working by yourself tonight?"

"Yeah, but it's restaurant night. Once a week there's a bus that takes whoever wants to go out to eat, so we were slow." Janie paused. "Mrs. Jensen passed away earlier this evening. I thought you'd want to know."

The ache Aja felt surprised her. She didn't really know the family, had never even spoken to Mrs. Jensen. But after being in her apartment, looking at all the framed pictures of a vibrant young woman, mother and wife, the news of her death pierced

Aja's soul. And Mr. Jensen, how was he? How would his life be after losing his Princess Buttercup?

Aja glanced at the clock. It was only eight. She'd have time to visit the family and still be able to study.

"I'll be right there."

CHAPTER 16

Aja had to tiptoe past Mrs. Poston's apartment to get to the Jensens. She did not want the old woman to see her in case she asked her to fold laundry or do some other menial chore. She noticed Mrs. Poston's door opened and raced past.

"China girl, is that you?"

Aja groaned and took a few steps back. "Yes, Mrs. Poston. I'm going to visit the Jensens."

"Why? You're not family."

Aja stood in the doorway. "I know, but I feel bad for Mr. Jensen."

"He has his daughters there. You'll just get in the way. Come here and help me with something."

Aja sighed and stepped into the apartment. The thermostat was still set to ninety and she could almost feel her skin blister. "Yes, Mrs. Poston."

"I have some old photo albums up on that shelf." She waved to a large bookcase against the wall. "I can't reach the top, and I'm too unsteady to stand on a chair."

Aja pulled a ladder-back chair from a dining room set and went to the case.

"Don't use one of my good chairs," Mrs. Poston huffed. "Get one of the kitchen chairs and take your grimy shoes off."

Aja was tempted to knock the chair over and leave, but she felt a little bit sorry for the mean woman. As she walked to the kitchen, she saw some photographs on a credenza. It made her think of the many pictures in the Jensen's apartment. There were only a few here. A wedding picture of Mrs. Poston, her hair still helmet sprayed in the same style. The only difference was that it was blonde. "Is this you?" Aja asked. She noticed Mrs. Poston towered over the groom, who wasn't smiling, but then neither was the bride. She touched the frame and saw a vision of a young girl's wrists being smacked with a riding crop. The image was so strong she actually felt the snap of pain. What she wasn't sure was whether the girl was a young Mrs. Poston or her daughter.

She was jolted out of the vision by Mrs. Poston's screechy voice.

"Are you being a nosy busy body?"

"Sorry, whatever." Aja sighed. "I was just asking." She set the picture down and rubbed her wrists of the phantom pain and dutifully followed Mrs. Poston into the living room.

"Get me the photo albums. I want to show Kendall some pictures."

Aja bristled at Kendall's name. "I'm sure you two have a lot in common."

"Yes, we do." Mrs. Poston seemed to have missed the sarcasm in Aja's voice.

Aja put the chair under the case and took her shoes off before she stood on it and retrieved two albums. She stepped off, grabbed her shoes and the chair, and hustled into the kitchen to put it away. She'd put her shoes on out in the hallway. "See you tomorrow."

Mrs. Poston waved her off without even a thank you.

Aja scrambled into her shoes and took off to the Jensen's. She realized she hadn't brought flowers or a card. Was she supposed to? Aja didn't know. She'd never lost anyone before.

The door to the Jensens' was opened, and the small apartment was filled with people. Janie was there sitting on the sofa with Mr. Jensen. His daughters sat in chairs across from them, and a few other people, probably husbands and friends, milled around the living room. Two young children played on the floor in front of the TV. Mrs. Jensen's hospital bed was still in the room, the sheets wadded and crumpled as if she'd just gotten out of bed. The IV stand still had a bag of medicine hanging from it, its tube dangled and twisted.

Poor Mr. Jensen looked dazed, but his eyes lit up a little when he saw Aja. "Princess Bride." Then his countenance grew painfully sad again. "We lost her," he whispered.

"I'm sorry, Mr. Jensen."

He sat comatose, unmoving. Janie spoke up. "Hey, Aja. It's nice of you to come. There's a bunch of food in the kitchen. Help yourself."

Lauren Jensen stood and hugged Aja. "Thanks for being here. You've been such a help." Lauren's face was puffy and blotched from crying. "We're going to miss her so much."

"She was our anchor," the woman next to Lauren said as she stood. "I'm Katie, Lauren's sister. I've heard all about you from Dad. Thank you for helping him at the hospital."

"He really loved your mom," Aja said. "I wish I could have done more."

Aja took a seat next to Janie on the couch. She sat with the family and listened to them tell stories of happier times. Vacations they'd taken, holidays they'd celebrated. Every now and then, Mr. Jensen would smile, remembering, but Aja could practically feel his suffering pain.

"What am I going to do without her?" Mr. Jensen asked his daughters.

By now, the young kids were getting restless, so Aja took them into the kitchen and gave them some treats. Janie was right: the kitchen was filled with food. Covered casseroles, cakes, cookies, there was enough to feed everybody in the retirement home for weeks.

Aja put as much food away as would fit into the fridge. She went into the living room to say goodbye. It was after ten o'clock, and she still had homework to do.

"I'm going to head out," Aja said. "I'll come visit tomorrow after work."

Janie stood. "Yeah, I'm going to go, too. Try to get some sleep, Mr. Jensen."

He nodded but didn't move. Lauren and Katie stood to see them out.

"Thanks, you two. We'll have to make funeral arrangements tomorrow. I just can't stand to think of dad here alone. They were inseparable."

Aja turned to go, saddened by the loss of this family. A family she really didn't know but felt an odd compassionate connection to.

CHAPTER 17

For the next few days, Aja barely kept up with school and work. Her mom wanted her to file a restraining order and complaint against the creepy police officer right away. She was thankful she'd not seen him around.

Mrs. Jensen's funeral was the next day, on Friday. Aja wanted to go, but couldn't miss any more school. She went to see Mrs. Burnett to ask if she could miss her last two classes so she could attend.

"How well do you know the Jensens?" Mrs. Burnett asked as she ushered Aja into her office.

"That's what's so weird; I don't really know them at all. I just met them at the retirement home. I really feel sorry for Mr. Jensen."

"Did you know Leigh Jensen taught English here? Her daughter Lauren and I were classmates," Mrs. Burnett said, smiling. "I was one of Leigh's favorite students."

"You were?"

"Steven Jensen taught physics. I never had his class, but all his students loved him. His experiments were legendary."

"Wow, that's pretty cool. To look at the pictures of them when they were younger is strange, like they're completely different people. I've only seen them as old people; it's hard to think of them as being anything else." Aja leaned back in her chair. "I've never lost anyone close to me. He seemed so sad and, I don't know, helpless."

"So you're not all tough-as-nails as you want us to think," Mrs. Burnett said. "I always knew there was more to you."

Aja became defensive. "Don't get your hopes up. I'm still the same rude girl you've always known."

"I won't tell anyone you harbor a nice side. Your secret is safe with me."

"Yeah, whatever." Aja stood to leave. "I don't need to go to the funeral. I just sort of wanted to."

"Let me check with your teachers. You're really on a thin thread, and to miss any school would be tough. If it were a family member, there would be no problem." Mrs. Burnett stood and opened the door. "Get your assignments today, and I'll try to sweet-talk the staff."

"Thanks, but on second thought, maybe I shouldn't go. You're right; I don't know anything about the family. It's probably a little creepy that I even wanted to." Aja turned and ran out before Mrs. Burnett could say anything else.

Later, at work, Aja scooped salad on cold plates and worked math problems at the same time. She was just about caught up on her assignments, but she had overextended her absences. She was disappointed, but okay with not going to the funeral.

Janie rushed into the kitchen still tying her apron. "Hey, kiddo, Edna Jones wants to see you. Is everything okay here?"

"Yeah, I think so. Why does she want to see me?" Aja closed her book and pushed it aside.

"I don't know. She seemed pretty hot under the collar though." Janie stacked the salads on trays.

"Should I wait until after the dinner rush?" Aja asked.

"No, Gabe and I can handle it. She said for you to get over there pronto."

Now what, Aja thought. She felt like she'd been called into the principal's office in front of a classroom of students. Not uncommon for her, but always embarrassing.

She took her apron off as she walked and haphazardly folded it. Edna was standing outside her office door with Mrs. Poston and a security guard.

Mrs. Poston waved a crooked finger at her. "Take her in now."

Edna moved in front of Mrs. Poston. "I'll handle this, Bea." She walked right up to Aja and handed her a document. "You have been terminated from Golden Leaves assisted living home and are never welcome back here again. Here's your first and last check. This security officer will escort you out."

"Wh-what? Why?" Aja stammered. "What did I do?"

"You stole my jewelry, you little thief." Mrs. Poston's finger continued to wag in the air. "You knew where my key was, even came into my apartment, and you were skulking around here the other night." Mrs. Poston took a step toward Aja. "I'm pressing charges against you, you tramp."

"I didn't take your jewelry. What are you talking about?"

"You were looking at my things, I'll bet scouting for loot."

Edna pointed to the front door. "There is an officer waiting to take you to the station where you'll be questioned."

"Can I use the handcuffs, Miss Edna?" the security officer asked, hopefully.

"No, I'm sure Officer Richards can take care of that." Edna looked toward the door.

Aja felt a cold fear run down her spine. Freddy Kruger was standing next to his car, a scary smile on his thin lips. Aja remembered reading once about a dog trainer and how he chose dogs by the way they tracked the target with their keen eyes, never letting the mark out of their site. How they honed in for the kill. Aja thought the same about the officer.

"I won't go with him. I'm filing a restraining order against that guy." She turned to Mrs. Poston. "I don't know what you have against me, old lady, but I didn't steal anything from you. You asked me, no, demanded that I come in and help you. My life would be better if you..." Aja stopped before she said, "drop dead." Lauren Jensen stood near the mailboxes across the lobby, watching. "I didn't do it," Aja cried.

"You have a criminal record," Edna said.

Aja saw Freddy Kruger step toward the front door.

"I'm not going with him. He's been following and harassing me."

"That's the man you were smooching all over in the dining hall," Mrs. Poston retorted. "Stop lying. You're only digging yourself in deeper."

Aja looked at her, helpless. No matter where she went, she was the kid that the finger pointed to. New kid, juvenile delinquent, freak. Never normal. She panicked as Freddy walked into the lobby. Like a hunted animal, Aja turned and took flight, nearly running through Kendall and Walker.

"Aja! What's going on?" Walker yelled after her.

She bolted down a long hallway, bracing herself for the bark of a gunshot and a bullet piercing her back. She heard jingling behind her, probably Freddy running after her. She didn't know, wouldn't turn around, and she ran as fast as she could through an emergency exit door. A loud buzz sounded as she ran to the back parking lot. There was an empty loading dock and a few cars parked in the small lot. Her car was on the other side of the building closer to the dining room where she'd left her purse and books.

Behind the parking lot was a creek. She ran toward the trees and took cover just as she heard the door slam open.

CHAPTER 18

It was getting dark and Aja continued along the creek bed heading, she hoped, toward home. She needed to call her mom and warn her about what had happened, she was sure the police were there waiting and telling her mom about Aja being a thief.

It took more than an hour to get close to her subdivision. She was starving, sweating and exhausted. At her house, she saw a police car parked in front. Too tired to face them, she decided to backtrack and go into a grocery store nearby and see if she could borrow someone's cell phone to call her mom.

Walking into the store, Aja looked around for a friendly face. A security guard took note of her and began to follow.

Damn, damn. Do I look like a criminal? Aja wondered. Then realized she was dirty and smeared with mud from her creek trek. She dug in her pockets for money and only came up with three dollars and some change. Aja headed to the deli counter, suddenly craving a turkey and cheese sandwich on a crusty French roll. She ordered just enough meat and cheese to make a sandwich but stay under the three bucks. After she paid, she went to the little café there and made a sandwich. Her mouth watered as she globbed mayo on the bread. She piled on the meat and cheese and wrapped it in a napkin. She couldn't wait to take a crunchy bite but when she noticed the security officer still eyeing her, she decided to eat outside.

She threw her shoulders back and walked right past him. He didn't say anything but followed a few paces behind. He left her after she exited the store.

By now the scent of the bread was making Aja's tummy grumble. She went to sit on a bench, but it was already occupied by a homeless man. More ragged and dirty than Aja.

"Got any spare change?" the man asked.

Aja reached in her pocket. Thirteen cents. "It's all I have."

"You keep it." The man said, eyeing Aja's sandwich.

Aja hesitated. No, not the sandwich. But the man was so thin. Who knew when his last meal was? She looked longingly at the turkey and cheese falling from the bread and handed the man the sandwich.

"Nah, really?" he asked.

"Yeah, whatever, go ahead." Aja then wished she'd at least torn it in half.

The man took the sandwich. "Thanks," he said as he hurriedly walked away, biting a hunk of bread as he left.

"Well, wasn't that a nice gesture. I didn't think you had it in you."

Aja recoiled at the voice. Dumpster Dempsey.

"Those homeless people are vermin though. You shouldn't feed them or give them money. You'll just encourage them." Dempsey pulled her large purse over her shoulder protectively. "You look like you've been rolling in the mud too."

Aja was pissed. She'd given up her perfect sandwich, was on the run again, and seeing the Dumpster just added fuel to the fire. "That was my dad," Aja shot back. "Since he had to work late, I brought him his dinner."

Dempsey's eyes widened.

"Mom sends her love," Aja yelled at the lingering dust cloud the man had left.

"Aja, you're not homeless. Your mom is the psychic. You live where that hand waves from the front yard," Dempsey said, but seemed just a tad unsure now.

Aja was tempted to ask to use the woman's phone, but she didn't want a barrage of questions or for her to eavesdrop and realize Aja was on the lam again. "There's a lot you don't know about me." She turned and stormed off.

Aja hung around the parking lot, hoping to see someone else she knew. No luck. The only familiar face was the security guard, who by now had spotted Aja trolling around the lot.

She was sick of running. Sick of everything. She hadn't done anything wrong, yet felt guilty. It was dark now so Aja decided to walk home. As she approached her driveway, she saw two police cars parked. The officer she recognized as Doug sprang from a car yelling, "There she is." He crouched behind his car door as if Aja had a gun pointed at him.

She held her arms up mockingly. "Don't' shoot, I'm unarmed." Then she threw in, "And innocent."

The other police car door opened and Freddy Kruger stepped out, slowly, deliberately. That scared Aja more than if he'd come screaming at her guns blazing.

"Get him away from me." Aja screamed and started to back away.

The front door to her house opened and her mom ran out with the female officer from the other night, Officer Smith.

"Aja, are you all right?" her mom asked. "What is going on?"

"I was falsely accused of stealing, and this jerk was going to take me to God knows where." She pointed at Freddy.

"You ran, makes you guilty to me," Doug said, leaning against his car door.

"I ran, toad breath, because this guy scares the bejeezes out of me." She pointed at Freddy.

"Aja, don't talk like that," her mom admonished.

"What? Bejeezes?"

"Let's not make this worse," her mom whispered.

Officer Smith walked to her. "Aja, you need to come to the station. You've been accused of a crime."

"I didn't do it."

"Why did you run?"

"Because the police officer you sent was the guy stalking me. No way am I getting into a car with him."

"Did you file a report?" Officer Smith asked.

"Not yet, we were going to do that soon," her mom said. "Aja's been busy with school and work."

"So I'm to believe a teenager, who has a record, and ran from a police officer when accused of a crime?" Officer Smith raised an eyebrow.

"Yes," Aja huffed. "I did not steal anything." An image of the forty dollars flashed in her brain. "I'm trying to finish school and make a little money so I can get the hell out of this pit town. I don't have time for all this drama."

"You need to come to the station so we can talk."

"Fine. But I'm riding with you."

CHAPTER 19

The police station was dull with green-tinted fluorescent lighting. For more than an hour, Aja had sat alone in a conference room with one-sided mirrors, wondering who was watching from the other side. She thought of the time wasted that she could have been finishing her homework while waiting. She wished her mom could come in and sit with her.

A door opened, and Officer Smith entered with a man dressed in a sport coat and khaki pants.

"Aja," Officer Smith said. "This is Detective Powell; he wants to ask you a few questions." They both took a seat.

"Where's my mom?" Aja asked.

"She's outside waiting," Detective Powell answered. He put a manila file folder on the table in front of him but didn't open it. "So do you want to tell me about Mrs. Poston's jewelry?"

"If I knew something about it, I'd be happy to, but I don't know what that old biddy is talking about." Aja slumped back in her chair.

"Were you in her apartment?"

"Yes, when she ordered me in to help her get something off her shelf."

"How did you know where the key was?" Officer Smith asked.

"The first time she asked me to help her with something she pulled the key out right in front of me."

"So you've been there more than once?" the detective asked.

"Twice. Only when she's demanded that I help her. Otherwise, I try to avoid her at all costs."

"She said you were snooping through her things."

"I was looking at pictures she had out. I asked her about them. That's all."

"Did you want to get to know her better, her habits, her schedule?" The easygoing demeanor of the detective began to harden.

Officer Smith sat and watched the interrogation.

"No. The only reason I'd want to know her schedule would be to avoid her." Aja shot back.

"So you could break into her apartment when she wasn't around." His eyes became cold.

"Read my lips." Aja met his gaze. "I did not steal from that pain-in-the-ass."

Officer Smith tried to defuse the tension. "Aja, please, just answer the questions calmly."

"Do you know what it's like to be falsely accused?" Aja yelled. "That woman has been out to get me since I started working there."

"Seems like a good place to make a dishonest living, preying on old, helpless people," Detective Powell said. "Let's look at your previous crimes." He opened the folder and began reading. "Disorderly conduct, four years ago in Arizona."

"The peace protest? I was at a sit-in with my mom, and we got hauled off by police with shields and sticks. It was stupid." Aja remembered that afternoon. She was already mad at her mom because Aja had actually been invited to a birthday party at a skate rink. The whole eighth grade class was going. Always the new kid, she never got invited to parties and was so excited. Her mom was going to take her right after the protest. Instead, she spent the afternoon in a holding cell. A crushing day.

"Here's another charge. You broke into a chicken pen and tried to steal the poultry?"

Aja wanted to laugh at that, but didn't because when they were caught a group of the farmers leveled shotguns at them. She was fifteen and frightened out of her mind. "We weren't going to steal them, just set them free. They were being treated inhumanely." She sat up. "Those are juvenile records. How did you get them?"

"Just answer my questions." He glared at her. "Another disorderly conduct," he went on, "against a city bus?"

"One of my mom's friends was in a wheelchair and always had

a hassle from the drivers to let her on, so we all stood in front the bus so he couldn't drive away until she boarded. We did that one a few times," she added with a tinge of pride in her voice.

Officer Smith interrupted. "Aja, did your mom take you along to all her causes?"

Aja shrugged. "I believed in her." She thought again of missing the skate party and the giant Peace button ripping her new expensive shirt.

"Your mom's a psychic?" Officer Smith asked.

Aja winced. "Yeah, and an artist. She sells her stuff."

"Well, too bad she couldn't see she was raising a criminal. Here's a charge, after you turned eighteen, of breaking into a car?" Powell held up a document.

"Those charges were supposed to be dropped." Aja said. "Someone left a dog in a hot car, and I tried to break the window out."

"According to this, you succeeded."

"Yeah, but the dog owner got in trouble, too, and she was supposed to drop the charges against me for a lesser fine against her." Aja had tried to use her needle-nose pliers on the window with no luck. She'd found some workers parked in a pickup, and they used a hammer to shatter the glass. They left before the police got there. Aja told them she did it. The owner was more worried about her car than the dog.

"These are charges you were caught doing." Powell made a show of fanning the documents at her. "Do you want to tell me about the ones you didn't get caught with?"

"Why don't you just get a rope, dude. Take me out back and string me up. This is Texas, ya'll." Aja gave a flippant wave of her hand. "Guilty until proven innocent."

Officer Smith held out both arms, like a referee at a boxing match. "Detective, give me a few minutes with Aja."

"You?"

"Please," she said.

"I hope you can get her to tell you where the jewelry is." He looked at Aja as he stood. "If I find out you've taken the stolen stuff to a pawn shop, you'll be serving some time. You're an adult now. No more hiding as a juvie."

Aja met his eyes directly. "I didn't steal her jewelry." She hoped she sounded fiercer than she felt. Remembering the money she'd taken from Mrs. Dempsey, she looked away. Thankfully, no one had mentioned that.

As soon as he left, Officer Smith turned to her. "Aja, we don't want to falsely accuse you of anything, but Bea Poston is insisting you did it. Not only did she see you in the halls after work, but other residents saw you."

Aja sighed. "One of the residents lost his wife a few days ago. I'd helped him with her, and I felt bad and went to check on him."

"That would be Leigh Jensen?"

Aja nodded.

"If you didn't like Bea Poston, then why did you help her? You were off work, right?"

"I don't know," Aja shrugged. "She didn't leave me much choice. She ordered me into her apartment, and I thought it would be easier to help than argue with her." Aja had a strange sensation. She looked at the one-way mirror. "I don't want that creepy officer Richards anywhere near me." She continued to stare at the glass. She knew, without a doubt, he was on the other side. Watching her.

CHAPTER 20

Aja's first and only paycheck was two hundred and fifty-eight dollars. She had to sign it over to the police station to make her three-hundred dollar bail. Her mom made up the rest. She still needed to pay Mrs. Burnett back, but again she had nothing. Three weeks of hard work poofed away for bail.

On the way home, her mom was silent, making Aja more uncomfortable. "I didn't do it, Mom. You know I'm not a thief."

"It's so out of character for you, but I know you've been trying to raise money to move." She glanced at Aja, then back to the road. "You know I'll support you in anything." She paused. "But stealing?"

"You? My own mom? You don't believe me?" Aja asked incredulously. "That cuts hard."

"I'm sorry. I do believe you. You are not a thief. At least not usually, but what about the forty dollars you took from that teacher?"

"That was payback for her saying those things. But it was wrong. I know that." Aja looked at her mom. "It was the first time, and, I promise, the last."

Her mom seemed to calm. "I may have raised you to be a fighter, but I know you better than anyone. Your heart is too big to steal."

"Thanks, I think," Aja said. "I am so tired, and I'm still behind on homework. It seems like the whole world is against me finishing this stupid year." She sat up. "Can you take me by work so I can get my books and purse?" She looked at the clock on the dash. It was almost midnight. "Oh, never mind, they're closed anyway." Summer school was looking certain for her.

"Aja, we're not allowed back there."

She knew her mother's use of "we're" was to soften the blow of Aja not being welcome.

"It's even too late to call Janie to see if she can get my books for me."

"I'll see about getting them for you tomorrow."

"And my car is there."

"I'll take you to school."

"At least that creepizoid officer can't come around. That's a relief," Aja said as she leaned, exhausted, against the car window. Officer Smith helped them file a restraining order against Clay Richards.

"She said she'll have to run it by a superior before she can file it," her mom reminded her. "I guess police officers get special treatment." She stopped to make a left turn. "But I'll wring his little weenie if I see him around." She turned to Aja. "You still have your needle-nose pliers?"

"Yeah, but *he* has a gun."

Her mom smiled. "Don't let the jerks get you down, sweetie. We'll fight this." She turned onto their street.

"I don't know if I feel better or worse, thanks," Aja said. The absurdity of the situation was unreal.

When they pulled into their driveway, Aja noticed her book bag on the porch. She got out and found a note from Janie attached. Aja opened the letter and saw Janie's scrawl: *Sorry. I heard about what happened. Mrs. P is a bitch. I have your purse. Call me tomorrow. XO Janie. P.S. Call Walker too.*

At least Aja could get some homework done tonight.

It took all of Aja's strength to roll out of bed the next morning. She'd stayed up until two o'clock finishing her homework. She knew her mom wouldn't wake her.

In the kitchen, her mom was cooking oatmeal, the real steel-cut stuff, over the stove. "I wasn't sure if I should get you up since you went to bed so late."

"Mom, if I miss any more school I'll be suspended. I have to go."

"Well, at least eat a good breakfast." Her mom set a big bowl of oatmeal in front of her.

Aja didn't sit down, drizzled a puddle of honey on top, and said, "I'll eat on the way."

"I'll write you a note if you're late. Sit and eat."

"No offense, Mom, but your notes don't carry weight anymore. Let's go."

Aja took a big bite of oatmeal, grabbed her book bag, and ran to the door. In the car, she pulled out the old cell phone her mom had given her to use to call Janie. "We didn't have any cool phones to use? This one's practically rotary." She held each button down to make sure it connected.

Her mom didn't say anything as they pulled out of the driveway.

Janie finally picked up, her voice sleepy, and Aja tried to talk around a bite of food. "Janie, it's me. Thanks for bringing my books. I need to come by and get my car."

"I'll be there at three. Stop by, and I'll give you your purse, too. I didn't want to leave that on your porch last night. Mrs. Poston was fighting mad last night. What happened?"

"She said I took some of her jewelry. I swear I didn't, Janie."

"Why would you do something like that? But you're the talk of the residents. They were all hot and bothered last night. This is the most excitement they've ever seen." Janie's giggle was muffled, probably by her comfy pillow.

Aja craved her bed. Wanted life to be normal again. Whatever that was, considering the way she and her mom lived. They were always a little off-track of real life. "This whole thing sucks," Aja said. "I'll call you after school, and I'll have my mom take me to my car." Aja disconnected the call.

"Umm, honey, you can't go pick up your car." Her mom stared ahead. "I'm pretty booked today, but let me see if Clara Wells can help me get it. Where are your keys?"

"In my purse. With Janie." Aja stirred the last of her oatmeal into one ball and ate the whole thing.

"Leave me her number." Her mom looked perplexed. "Aja, according to Officer Smith, you need to stay home in case they want to talk to you. And you're not allowed near the residence center. I'm sorry, sweetie."

"They can kiss my ass," Aja hissed. "I'll do whatever I want. They allow psycho-cop out on the streets, but want to hold me prisoner? Stupid."

Her mom sighed. "For now, let's play by the rules."

"Since when? Are you going soft now when I need you the most? You've never backed down from a fight before," Aja said defiantly.

"I'm still on probation from that chicken-coop coup. I don't have enough money to post bail if I screw up, and I don't want you here alone."

At school, Aja felt like everyone knew what happened. It was as if she had a red scarlet letter painted on her head.

Dumpster called her to her desk when Aja entered the room.

Aja went to the desk, hugging her books close to her. A McDonald's bag was crumpled in the trash next to the teacher's desk. The smell of grease still lingered. "Yeah?" Aja asked.

"I've spoken to Principal Carlisle about you and your homeless father. He thought you needed a court advocate to speak with you."

"What homeless..." Aja remembered the sandwich yesterday. "He wasn't my father."

"You said he was," Dempsey said.

"I was mistaken," Aja answered.

"We have to protect the students here and can't have beggars near the school. If you know that man, he may be back. Does he sell drugs to little kids?"

"Are you freakin' kidding me?" Aja said, too loud. The students that were taking their seats stopped to listen.

"Aja, please go see the principal, now."

"I can't miss any more school."

"You only have yourself to blame." Dumpster's stock line.

"Can you give me my assignment?"

"No. The principal is expecting you."

Aja was dismissed.

In the office, Aja took her usual seat. Mr. Carlisle was in his office, looking at the computer screen. Aja knew he was playing solitaire or online poker. Sometimes her psychic gift was nice.

Mrs. Burnett's office door opened, and she walked a student out. She stopped when she saw Aja.

"What are you doing here?"

"Dempsey sent me."

"For what?"

"Nothing. That's just it. She hates me and can get away with using her power to control me. I'm about ready to skip out of here forever. I'd rather be a drop-out than deal with this."

"Go sit in my office." Mrs. Burnett went into Mr. Carlisle's office and shut the door.

Aja did as she was told. A few minutes later, Mrs. Burnett came out, looking angry and began to write a hall pass. "Aja, go back to Mrs. Dempsey's class. Do your assignments and don't talk back to anyone."

Aja stood and took the pass. "What was that about a court advocate?"

"We got a call about what happened last night. You are already on a tenuous line here. You may be suspended based on the charges. Please come see us here after each class to check in. I'm sorry, Aja."

"I didn't do it."

"I hope not. I've really stuck my neck out in your defense, but things keep happening. I can't believe everybody else is always wrong."

Principal Carlisle strode over. "I'm more than ready to suspend you. You may be a danger to the other students. But the judge said for you to go to your classes and then home. I guess you're also a flight risk."

"Did you search her backpack?" he asked Mrs. Burnett.

She hesitated. "No, I didn't."

He turned to Aja. "Hand it over."

"Why?"

"Aja," Mrs. Burnett said quietly. "Please."

Aja almost dropped the bag from midair, but stopped. The mountain of problems kept growing higher and higher. She handed it to him.

He dumped it out on a chair and carelessly sifted through the books. "So your dad's a homeless guy?"

Aja bit back a smart remark. "No." Aja had always harbored a fantasy that her dad was some rock star like Bon Jovi or Bono. She knew her mom hung out with some bands when she was younger. Her mom sidetracked any questions Aja asked about him and stuck with the sperm donor answer.

Suddenly, Aja became scared. What if whoever did steal the jewelry stashed it her backpack to frame her? It had been left unattended at the center last night. She waited anxiously as Mr. Carlisle went through each pocket.

"Wait, what's this?"

Aja felt beads of sweat on her lip. "What?" she asked, her voice shaky.

He pulled out her pliers. "What are these for?"

Relieved, Aja shrugged. "They come in handy for a lot of stuff."

He handed them to Mrs. Burnett, then dropped Aja's backpack on the pile of books he'd made a mess of. "Done. Go to class. We'll keep the tool."

"But..." Aja stopped. "Fine." She grabbed the pile of books and papers, all out of order now, and stuffed them in her bag.

"Check back here after each class," Mrs. Burnett reminded her. "There will be a court advocate here later, after school. Even though you're eighteen, you're still a student, so, for now, you're being treated as a juvenile. But if anything else happens, Aja, you will be suspended."

CHAPTER 21

Aja's mother was waiting in the administration office after school. She sat next to a stout woman in a gray business suit. Mrs. Burnett stood next to them. They turned when Aja walked in.

Her mom stood and went to Aja. "Honey, this is Ms. Lewis from social services. The court asked her here to talk to you." Aja could tell her mom was on edge. On one hand, she seemed resigned to follow the rules, but Aja could tell it was grinding on her to give in.

"It seems," her mom went on through gritted teeth, "that you will be supervised at all times, but the officer that's stalking you is still out driving around." She looked at the advocate hard.

Mrs. Burnett spoke. "Ms. Harmon, that's another matter. We are here to help Aja."

"Help?" Her mom turned. "My daughter's done nothing wrong, yet she's the one confined?"

Ms. Lewis said, "We can just as easily have her remanded to a juvenile detention center. She can finish school there and would be supervised around the clock."

"A juvenile detention jail? An alternative school?" Aja asked. "They're teaching twenty-year-old eighth-graders second grade math there." Aja looked at Ms. Lewis. "Would I get my diploma?"

"It would be equivalent to a GED."

"A GED may get me into bartending school," Aja shot back. "I want a real diploma."

"Our system is overflowing with juvenile offenders. You accept what is presented to you, even if it's not your dream package. If you'd stayed out of trouble, we'd never be having this conversation."

"But I didn't *do* anything."

"Neither did any of the others, according to them," Ms. Lewis said.

"Aja, you have the potential to get a scholarship into almost any school you want," Mrs. Burnett said. "I hate to see what you're doing to your future." She shook her head.

Her mom stiffened with anger. "Aja's future will be fine. Just because she has a mind of her own, she drives you people crazy. Aja does not have to conform to all the stupid rules." She looked at Aja proudly. "Don't let them break you, sweetie. You're better than all of them."

Principal Carlisle stepped from his office, apparently listening to the conversation. "Maybe you could look into your crystal ball and tell Aja what she's going to be when she grows up."

Aja's mother flared. "At least I have balls. Crystal or not."

Aja winced. When her mom's temper heated up, she'd rail on anybody. "All I want to do is graduate," Aja said. "And, worse, I haven't done anything wrong, but I'm getting blamed for some bad sh...stuff!" She turned to Ms. Lewis. "And I don't want a GED either."

"Aja, I wish I could believe you," Ms. Lewis said, "but the evidence is telling me something else."

Aja looked at Mrs. Burnett. "I'm not a bad person. I shoot my mouth off some, but I'm harmless."

"You are entitled to shoot your mouth off all you want," Aja's mom said. "Free speech." She turned to Mrs. Burnett and Ms. Lewis. "It's her constitutional right."

"Ms. Harmon, you're not helping," Mrs. Burnett said.

"I can see where Aja gets her criminal propensities." Carlisle smirked. "Have you paid back the money you stole?"

"No," Aja whispered, defeated.

"Here's the money." Aja's mom opened her wallet and counted out thirty-one dollars. Then she opened her change purse and took out a handful of coins. "Here, we'll still owe you about five dollars." Aja's mom put the money on the counter.

"Don't worry about it," Mrs. Burnett said. "Let's get Aja help."

"And this is the thanks we get for trying to help," Mr. Carlisle scoffed.

"I feel like a puppet and you are all pulling my strings to the breaking point." Aja tried not to cry. "For the first time ever, I'm ready to move *now*." She shot a glance at her mom, then turned to Mrs. Burnett. "I was wrong to take the money, but I could hear everything you were saying about me that day, that I was total loser. I was mad. I did *not* take the jewelry. I was only trying to help Mr. Jensen that night." She bit back tears. "I felt so sorry for him. This is what I get for being nice. Blamed by the wicked-witch of the old-folks-home for something I didn't do. Life is real fair."

Aja ran out of the office, almost crashing through a group of cheerleaders. Aja wondered what life was like for them. Stability, friends, a real home. Probably none of them had spent time in jail. Her whole life she'd been an outcast. Different, always the odd girl out. And she was sick of it.

CHAPTER 22

Aja stood next to her mom's car in the school parking lot. She'd started to take off and run home, but decided to wait in case that was the straw that got her tossed into the detention facility.

Her mom walked out of the building with Ms. Lewis and Mrs. Burnett. They approached Aja. Ms. Lewis looked pissed.

"Another stunt like that will get you your own bed in custody, young lady," Ms. Lewis seethed.

"Don't talk to my daughter like that." Aja's mom glared at the advocate. "I will take care of her, and I can assure you I'll be riding you and your department's ass. Aja has a voice, too. Probably like most of the teens you've incarcerated. Take time to listen to them and quit running your own mouth. You just might learn something."

"I've learned that most of them lie through their teeth." Ms. Lewis got back in Aja's mom's face.

"And *I've* learned there's good in everybody."

The two women were almost nose to nose when Mrs. Burnett stepped in. "Thanks Ms. Lewis. I promise to supervise Aja while she's at school, and I'll have a talk with Ms. Harmon, too. If there's a problem, I'll call you." She glanced at Aja, who nodded.

"We will be keeping an eye on you," Ms. Lewis snarled, staring at Aja. "If you're not at home when an officer comes to check, I'll personally bring you in."

"Just keep Clay Richards away from me. Anybody else is welcome." Aja hoped that her mom wasn't hosting any more drawing classes soon.

When Aja and her mom pulled in their driveway, she saw her own car parked and Walker sitting on their porch. He stood, looking cute as ever, his dark hair offsetting his almond eyes. Aja turned away and thought how good he and Kendall looked together. Both of them tall, dark and ravishing. It bothered her that he had some pull over her. His ability to get along with everybody fascinated Aja. She was always ready to pull the trigger on distrust.

"Hey, Walker, thanks for bringing Aja's car home," her mom said.

"Anytime." He handed the keys to Aja. "Nice ride."

"You two talked today?" Aja asked, miffed. "Glad you guys are such buds."

"He offered to help," Aja's mom said, raising an eyebrow at her daughter. "Get off your grumpy-horse."

"I called your mom to see if you were okay," Walker said, though he kept a distance from Aja. "She asked if I could drive your car here."

"I'm fine. Never better," Aja shot back, slinging her book bag over her shoulder.

"What's going on, Aja?" Walker whispered. "Mrs. Poston..." he didn't finish.

Aja's mom gave him a quick hug. "Stay for dinner?"

"Mom, probably not a good idea," Aja answered for him.

Walker looked at Aja.

"You're not afraid of those truant officers are you?" Aja's mom asked.

"I'm tired. Falsely accused and apparently second in line to Kendall."

Walker held up a hand. "Let's leave her out of this."

Aja walked around to the side of the car where he stood. Her mom hesitated, then said, "I'll see you inside."

Aja dropped her book bag on the driveway. "You know, you keep saying you're not together, but every time I see you, she's there." She thought of the kitchen disaster where Aja was globbed with food and Kendall was all shiny, clean and bitchy.

"Her family is friends with mine and everybody wants to see us together—except me." He put his hands in his jeans pockets. "My mom is beginning to come around, but she's the only one. I hate to upset my grandparents, so I didn't make a scene. Kendall is what I'm used to. Even though I'm trying to break from my safe life, I'm afraid of hurting anybody."

"Well, I'm in a bit of a pickle anyway, so it's probably best if you keep your distance from me."

"Yeah, I heard." He looked in her eyes as if asking the question.

"I didn't do it." Aja snipped. "I don't know why that old woman hates me so much. She probably misplaced the jewelry and thought I should take the fall. Walker, can you please tell the Jensens I didn't steal anything? Oh, and tell Dr. Landers that I'll get the CD he burned for me. I hope Mr. Jensen's daughters will be able to take care of their dad." She looked at Walker. "I hate that everybody thinks I'm a thief. And tell Janie I'm innocent."

"You promise me you're not a thief?" he asked, doubt in his voice.

Aja stopped, shocked. "I don't have to promise you anything," Aja exploded. She grabbed her bag and stormed into the house. She made sure to slam the door hard to make her point.

Not two seconds later, the doorbell rang. Aja opened the door to see Walker standing on the porch holding her purse.

"You forgot this."

Aja took the purse. "Thanks." She stepped back to close the door but hesitated. "You haven't known me long, Walker, but believe me, I am not a thief. I can be a smartass, but not a criminal."

"It's like you're this really cool outlaw that keeps me intrigued. You're everything I'm not." He took a step back. "What about your jail time?"

She felt like she'd been slapped. "What do you know about that?"

He shrugged.

"Considering it's a 'sealed file,' it sure seems like the whole world is in on my life. Ask Edna Jones or Clay Richards, or go talk to my school principal or counselor. Who knows, it might just make the papers tomorrow."

Aja's mom came to the door, drying her hands on a towel. "Walker, I'm making tofu and veggies for dinner. You sure you don't want to stay?"

"Sounds delicious," he said, as he shook his head. "Maybe another time."

"Mom, maybe you could sit with Walker and tell him about all the times I've been in jail. Let him know what a real criminal I am." Aja turned and stormed into her room.

"Whoa, what's that about?" Aja heard her mom ask.

"I asked her about her being in jail." Walker's voice sounded muffled through Aja's door. "I mean, between that and this jewelry thing."

"You know, Walker, anything she's done has been to help or fight a good cause. She should be proud of all she's accomplished. I know I am."

Aja had to crack her door a little to hear her mom.

"It seems like trouble follows her," Walker said.

"Don't be like the others who've judged her the wrong way." Her mom paused. "Thank you for bringing her car. Let me take you home."

CHAPTER 23

For the next two weeks Aja had Mrs. Burnett check her attendance after each class and she had to meet with Ms. Lewis two evenings a week. The woman was an awful bitch who asked Aja the same questions over and over as if trying to make Aja lie. Aja was weary of her life. At least her grades were excellent, much to Mrs. Dempsey's chagrin.

Aja felt like a prisoner in her home. According to Ms. Lewis and Detective Powell, she had to be home by seven and only attend school during the day. Her mom fought them, saying Aja could do whatever she wanted to since no charges had been filed. But Aja was down to her last month before graduation and figured it was easier to comply.

"Don't let them get to you. They are violating your rights. If you want to stay out until midnight you can." Her mom steamed and huffed a lot, but didn't make Aja go to any of the protests she tried to stage at the police station. Even her mom's friends weren't fighting this fight.

Janie called frequently to keep Aja up on all the gossip at Golden Leaves.

"Oh, man," Janie said. "Mrs. Poston is still going on about you, telling the residents to check for missing valuables. She will not shut up about it."

Aja's stomach broiled. "It really hacks me off that she's running around telling everybody that I'm guilty of something I didn't do. Where does she get off?" Aja groused, and slammed her math book shut. She was not in the mood to finish her homework. "Hey, how's Mr. Jensen?"

"Not good. They put him in the hospital wing here because he was so dehydrated. But he keeps asking about you. He calls you Princess Bride."

"Yeah, I know."

"He really took a shine to you."

"He did?"

"He even told Mrs. Poston that you would never steal anything. But he's really hurting without his wife. It's hard to watch."

"I'd like to see him. Can I visit him in the hospital?"

"No, probably not. It's not the big hospital, just the extra care ward here at the home."

"So, I guess Mrs. Wicked Witch never found her jewelry?"

"No." Janie snorted. "And if she did, do you think she'd own up to it?"

"Of course not. Man, I'd like to put that old biddy in her place."

"Should I tell her you said so?"

"No!" Aja toyed with the pages of her books. "Have you seen Walker?"

"Yeah, he has dinner here a few nights a week. But, hey, Kendall is nowhere to be seen. They had a huge blowout in the parking lot about a week ago. I think it was because she was talking about moving here. Hopefully, she's back home."

After school, Aja saw a car in front of her house. Instead of going in the back, she opened the front door and saw her mom sitting on the couch with a woman holding a notepad.

"Here she is," her mom said. "Aja, this is a reporter from *The Truth*." Aja recognized the title of the local underground newspaper. "I called her because we just got the letter saying that we can't get a restraining order against Clay Richards."

"Why?"

"It's your word against his, and he has to patrol this area. I'm shocked." She nodded to the woman. "That's why I called the news. We need to let the community know how dangerous he is."

The reporter looked at Aja and asked, "So, you think he broke in to your home?"

Aja nodded.

"And, according to the report you filed, he said he wanted to take nude photos of you?"

Again, Aja nodded. She could feel the woman's doubts seep in like fog.

"In his report, he responded, saying he walked in on a nude modeling session at this house. That's what he was referring to, not that he wanted you to do anything wrong."

This time, Aja shook her head but stayed silent.

"And someone named," the woman looked at the report, "Bea Poston said you were coming on to him at the nursing home."

"Not true," Aja whispered.

"This sounded like a good story, but you'll need to provide proof. Right now, it's a little tenuous."

"It doesn't matter anyway," Aja said. "Who'd believe me over him?" Her teachers, principals, former employers would all be against her. She was crushed.

"No, don't back down." Her mom stood. "He's wrong, and we can't let him get away with it. Not only am I worried about you"—she looked at Aja—"but it's our responsibility to get this jerk off the streets."

"It's our word against his," Aja cried. "You're a psychic, artist, singer, and I'm a juvenile delinquent. We've moved to a different place almost every year. Who's going to believe our word over his?"

Her mom turned to the reporter. "You believe us, don't you?"

The woman raised an eyebrow. "Your daughter has a point."

"Why would we make this up?" Her mom was indignant.

The reporter shrugged and stood to leave. "I'll need proof. The story would be good if you can validate some points. I can't report on it with so many holes in it."

"And this guy gets away with it?" her mom asked. "Am I going to have to be a vigilante and take him out myself?"

"Mom, stop." Aja had a flash image of her mom going at Richards with her needle-nose pliers.

The reporter looked cautiously at Aja's mom. "I need proof against him." The sideways glance she gave Aja's mom said *she* was the unstable one.

"He is guilty," Aja said, defending her mom. "It's too bad he can hide behind his badge and reports. We may not look credible, but we're the victims." Aja puffed out and stood next to her mom. "Dig deeper on him; I'll bet you find something."

"I'll see what I can come up with." The woman nodded and left.

As soon as the door closed Aja turned and glared at her mother. "Why can't you be a normal mom? Have cookies and milk ready for me when I come home. Not another stupid cause!"

"Aja, this is who we are."

"Who, *you* are. Not me." Aja whirled to go to her room.

"What's normal?" her mom called to her.

Aja stopped and turned. "Maybe a world where you act like a real mom, you know, ground me for talking back to grown ups, not celebrate it. Sometimes I think you like your causes and protests more than me. *I'm* the teenager, *I'm* the one who's supposed to be in trouble all the time, not you."

"Do you want to grow up to be just like everybody? I'm trying to teach you to be independent and embrace your own self—to be individual."

"As long as we stir up trouble doing it, right? You can't do anything without making it a cause!"

"Find your voice, Aja." Her mom pleaded. "I do it for you. For you to find your own way." She turned and said softly, "I'm sorry."

Aja's phone rang and she stomped to her room before her mother could say anything else. She glanced at caller ID. It was Janie. "Hey, Janie."

"Aja, hi, this isn't Janie. It's Lauren, Steve Jensen's daughter. Janie let me use her phone to call."

"Oh, hi, how's your dad?" Aja sat on her bed and tried to calm down after yelling at her mom. "Janie said he was in the hospital."

"We can't get him to eat anything." Something like a small sob escaped. "We're not ready to lose him, not now after Mom."

"Yeah, I'm sorry. I know your dad really loved her. It was sweet seeing how much he cared." Aja remembered his trembling hand holding his ailing wife's feather-like hand. "I'd hoped to go to the funeral."

"He keeps asking for you. He said you helped take care of Mom."

"I asked Janie if I could visit him, but I'm not, you know, welcome there."

"Would you come if I asked if it would be okay? I'll do anything to make him happy."

"Sure." Aja hesitated. "Lauren, I didn't steal anything."

"I don't have the energy or time to worry about that," Lauren said. "If you can visit dad and make him smile, it would mean the world to us."

"Is he strong enough to meet somewhere like a restaurant?" Aja asked.

"No, he can barely walk, and he's getting IV nutrition." Lauren sighed. "It's so hard now without Mom." She began crying. "They were two peas in a pod. I should be a good daughter and let him go with her. It's what he wants. But I can't bear to lose both of them."

"Call Edna Jones and ask if I can come by," Aja said. "If she says no, maybe I can sneak in somehow." She swallowed hard, thinking she was already walking on a thin line.

"Thanks, Aja."

Aja clicked off the old phone and went to recharge it, since the battery died almost every phone call. As she plugged in the phone, she looked out her window. A police cruiser passed slowly by, and she chilled when she saw who was driving.

CHAPTER 24

Aja considered dialing 911 on her old phone but the cord had come out and the battery had been knocked loose when Aja plugged it in. She dropped the phone on her dresser and ran to the front door.

"Where's the fire?" Her mom stepped out of the kitchen.

"That jerk just drove by our house."

"Clay Richards?"

"Yeah. Should we call 911?"

Aja's mom didn't answer but picked up a long wooden dowel that she used to stretch her canvases. "Which way did he go?"

"Mom, really?" Aja watched her go to the door. "I'm not sure you're going to take him out with that."

Her mom smacked the doorframe with the stick. Clay Richards was nowhere to be seen. "Okay, let's call the police. People like him are the reason I fight causes, and," she added, "to protect you." She reached in her pocket and pulled her phone out.

"Wait," Aja said. "Who do you think they'll send? The closest officer on duty, which is him."

"This is insane. The guy is stalking us."

Aja felt the now familiar tingle of terror down her spine. She still hadn't told her mother about him following her home and to the hospital. "Call the female police officer, what was her name? Smith? See if she's on duty."

"No, this is war." Her mom dialed 911 and reported a stalker who had just driven by their house.

"Mom, don't, it's only going to make it worse."

But it was too late. As Aja predicted, Clay Richards roared into their driveway thirty seconds later. Aja slammed the front door. "Go lock the back. Why did you call him here?"

Aja's mom dialed 911 again and reported the stalker in their drive and to hurry. She bolted the back door and kept the wooden dowel in her hand.

"I know there's a police officer here, but the stalker has a gun," her mom yelled in the phone. "Hurry, he's at the door!" Aja's mom hung up and slid the phone in her pocket, a sly smile on her face.

Aja was mortified, but there was no way she'd leave the house with him so close.

Before long, there were three police cars, lights flashing, parked haphazardly in front of Aja's house.

Richards had been banging on their door. "Police, open up."

Aja's mom went to the front door and yelled, "You are not allowed on this property."

"You called us."

Aja could sense his sneer through the thin door.

"I called the police because of you. What were you doing, driving by our house?"

Aja heard scuffling on the porch and voices. She looked out the window and saw Officer Smith. She tried to get her attention by knocking on the window, but Clay Richards face suddenly appeared in the glass. Aja jumped back. Her mom was there with the wooden dowel locked and loaded, ready to swing.

Aja grabbed her mom's arm. "Put that away," she whispered fiercely. "The last thing we need is to get tossed in jail because you hit a police officer."

"He's on our property."

"*We* called 911. Let's talk to Officer Smith." Sometimes, Aja felt like the mature one. She hated all the drama, most of which her mom created.

"Mom, stop! Why can't we do something normal for once? Aja threw her shoulders back and went to the door. She looked at her mom and said, "Put the stick down." She unlocked and opened the door.

Clay Richards was right there. Aja gulped and said, "You, off our property. Officer Smith, can we talk?"

Officer Smith stepped on the porch and said, "I got this, Clay."

"Don't think so, this is my beat." His beady eyes bore into Aja. "Didn't you call the police?"

Aja could feel her mom right behind her. "We called because I saw you drive by. You're not supposed to come around me."

"I thought you got the memo that wasn't approved." He rested his hand on the handle of his gun. "I patrol here."

"You've been harassing us, and my daughter saw you when you broke into our house." Aja's mom growled at him like a pit bull. "You take one step in here and I'll ram this up your ass." She held the wooden stick up.

"Are you threatening me?" He seemed to enjoy this.

Officer Smith came to the door and said to Richards, "I just got off the phone with the supervisor. I'll take this call. You can finish your patrol."

The look he gave Smith made Aja back away in fear that he was going to pull his weapon and shoot her point blank.

"Don't play power games with me," he spit out at Smith. "You'll lose."

Aja let Officer Smith in the house and closed the door on Richards.

Smith looked at the two of them and asked, exasperated, "Is the stalker you're reporting Officer Richards?"

"Yes," Aja's mom answered. "I don't want him near Aja."

"May we sit?" Smith asked.

Aja's mom and Officer Smith took a seat on the couch. Aja went to close the curtains and noticed Clay Richards next to the cars talking to another officer. Richards pointed his finger ominously to the house. A few neighbors lingered on their front lawns. Embarrassed and angry, Aja shut the drapes.

"You can't call 911 for something like this," Officer Smith was saying to Aja's mom.

"I'm going to call out the troops every time I see that jerk." Aja's mom slapped the wooden stick on the coffee table. "Who does he think he is, driving by here?"

"If you keep it up, you'll be charged with making false calls. Not only will you be fined, but you could spend time in jail."

"Me? Why? We're innocent!" Her mom was outraged. "I'm worried for my daughter's safety."

Aja sat in a chair across from them. "I'm sorry we called, but he really scares me. Nobody believed me when I said it was him who broke in. It seems like every time I look behind me, he's there."

"He was found innocent by the review board."

"Yeah, we're the troublemakers." Aja sighed. "Maybe I'll go buy myself a police badge so I won't be the bad guy anymore."

"Look, I don't want to take sides, but you're not helping your case by making a scene."

The doorbell rang. Aja tensed, fearing Clay Richards was still on the porch, waiting for her. Aja stood and looked out the peephole. But it was Ms. Lewis, the court advocate, looking peeved.

CHAPTER 25

"So is the circus in town?" Ms. Lewis asked when Aja opened the door. Aja noticed that the police cars were still in the front.

"We called the police…" Aja started, but Ms. Lewis cut her off.

"I know, I just spoke to Officer Clay Richards, and he told me you and your mother are making trouble again." She stepped over the threshold without asking for an invitation.

"Come in," Aja snipped.

"Don't get smart with me." Ms. Lewis turned to Aja. "I told you we were going to check on you." She shook her head. "And this is what I find, a crime scene?" She walked to Officer Smith and held her hand out. "Hi, I'm Hilary Lewis, the court advocate assigned to Aja. Sorry they bothered you."

Officer Smith stared at Ms. Lewis. "It's no bother. It's my job. But it looks as if you're bothered by something."

Aja snickered, and Ms. Lewis gave her a hateful look.

Officer Smith stood to leave. "Here's my card if you need anything." She handed one to both Aja and her mom. She looked around the room glancing at the paintings, some hanging in the living room, some half-finished canvases leaning against the wall. "Did you paint these?" she asked.

"Yes," Aja's mom answered, standing. "I make a little money selling paintings."

"They're beautiful," Officer Smith said, flipping through the paintings. Most were landscapes and flowers, some life figures. "You're very talented." Aja saw her pause at one of Walker, nude, his muscles painted with erotic accuracy.

Aja could feel the disproval emanating from Ms. Lewis, her

eyes fixated on a life-size plaster bust. While pregnant with her, Aja's mom cast her swollen nine-month belly and breasts and painted it rainbow colors. She'd fixed the mold to a light pole, and the beaded lampshade seemed to be the head.

"I'll let you get back to things here," Smith said. Then to Aja's mom said, "I'll talk to my supervisor and see what I can do, but Clay has been here for years. He may be a little hot-headed, but he's been a good officer."

When they finally let Ms. Lewis out, Aja's mom closed the door hard and bolted the lock. "That woman works my nerves. Come on, let's do some yoga to calm down. Then I'll reheat our dinner."

Aja fell on the couch. "I don't want to do yoga. I'm not even hungry anymore. She's going to report that we called the police. What if I get sent to the detention center?"

Her mom was already on the floor, stretching. "Breathe, honey. Let the tension fall from your shoulders. Find your chakra." Her mom took a deep cleansing breath. Aja gulped back a sob.

Her mom contorted like a pretzel. "This will help us think about how to handle these people." She breathed again.

"Mom, I know I sound like a broken record, but I need to graduate from school. I'm already eighteen and don't want to start my life with a GED."

"You know you can do anything you dream," her mom said, letting a noisy breath out.

"This dream is turning into a nightmare. How did things get so screwed up?"

"Come on, Peanut. Join me. I already feel better."

Aja got off the couch and lay on her back on the floor. She closed her eyes and wished herself on a beach far away from this hellhole.

"Do this pose." Her mom put one leg over the other and stretched her torso. "It will relax you and help with digestion"

"I thought the tofu would help with that." Aja giggled.

"Here." Her mom pulled her phone from her pocket. "It's Walker." Then the phone rang.

"That's so weird, mom." Aja stayed on the floor and answered.

"Hey, Aja. I wanted to call. I've been thinking about you," he said. "Sorry things ended badly the last time we talked." He paused. "Your mom told me why you've been in jail. So along with everything else, you're also a political peace terrorist." He laughed.

"It's a long story." Aja closed her eyes and tried to forget about the whole police force visit. And she really wished she wasn't so happy to hear Walker's voice.

"So, I'll probably get a call from Homeland Security for talking to you."

"If you're lucky, the president will call." Aja stayed on the floor, but looked up. Her mom was still twisted next to her. "You know, Walker, my life is more complicated than it should be. I've never been normal and probably never will be."

"I know. I think that's why I'm so confused about you. You're like the forbidden fruit, everything I'm not." He sighed. "I can't even break up with my ex-girlfriend, and you're out saving the world."

"You did pose nude. That's off the normal chart."

"And you walked in."

"And saw everything."

Aja's mom blew out a deep breath and smiled.

"Go reheat our tofu, Mom." Then Aja asked Walker, "Why did you call my mom's phone and not mine?"

"Your phone went right to voice mail."

Aja remembered trying to charge it. "My battery dies every five minutes." She sat up. "Walker, for now my first priority is to get out of jail and school. Then I'm leaving Texas. My life is a roller coaster; I never know what's going to happen next. And you need to resolve your issues with your girlfriend."

"That's another reason I called."

"Kendall?"

"Aja, she told my grandparents that she saw you putting the key back the night Mrs. Poston's jewelry was stolen."

Aja was stunned. "She's lying."

"This is why I'm so confused about everything. I want to believe you, but why would she make up a story about that?"

"You tell me. I am not a thief." Again, Aja remembered the forty dollars. Maybe her mom was right. Karma *was* dictating the way this was playing out. "I didn't steal that woman's jewelry. Period."

"Aja, I don't know what to think anymore."

Right now, Aja wished she were a better mentalist, like Kreskin, where she'd have to power to bend spoons, then take it another step further and fling them at someone's head. "Believe what you want, Walker. I know the truth."

CHAPTER 26

Aja stood in the school office, waiting for Mrs. Burnett to sign her attendance slip. It was such a hassle to run here in between each class. Plus, she was still steaming mad about Kendall's accusation.

"Aja," Mrs. Burnett stepped from her office. "Do you have a second?"

"I've got to get to my next class."

"I'll give you a pass." Mrs. Burnett went to her desk. Aja followed her in and sat in a chair.

"Aja, I just got your SAT scores in."

Most kids took the test their junior year, but Aja never lighted long enough in one school district to follow through. She'd just taken the test six weeks ago. "How'd I do?" Aja asked. She thought the test was pretty easy, but sometimes she saw life differently than others. She either aced it or totally flunked it.

"You're in the top five per cent of students. You almost got a perfect score." Mrs. Burnett slid the results to Aja. "Do you realize that this alone would have gotten you some amazing scholarship offers?"

"Would have?"

"Most of the scholarships are spoken for by now." Mrs. Burnett clicked her computer and stared at the screen. "That said, I'm not giving up." She navigated on her computer.

"I want to go to Stanford."

Mrs. Burnett smiled. "Who doesn't?" Mrs. Burnett pulled a thick file from her drawer. "Aja, these are your school transcripts, records, grades from your other schools. There is no continuity.

Your grades, for the classes you finished, are good, but it's like putting a puzzle together. Then you're almost through with your senior year. You haven't applied to any schools yet. Most students have already been accepted to schools."

Aja shook her head. The application fees were always too expensive. She had to choose either applying to colleges or getting her car fixed so she could drive to work to pay for the application fees. The circle of life. And then she probably shouldn't have bought any of the cute clothes from Abercrombie. Her small way of trying to fit in. "I can't afford to apply."

"With your grades and your...um, ambitious personality, you'd have many opportunities." She continued to click on her computer. "This program shows you what your chances are for college admissions at every college in the U.S. Aja, don't let the application fees stop you. I'll help you."

"No, I could barely pay you back the forty dollars."

Mrs. Burnett sighed and stopped typing on the computer. "And there lies the other problem. Your background. You're a little bit of a firecracker. Ms. Lewis would have to release you so your record doesn't hold you down."

"Keepin' the poor man down."

"Don't get on a bandwagon, Aja. There are opportunities for students. Come back after school today, and we'll work on getting your applications started."

Aja squirmed in her chair. This afternoon, she was going to try and sneak into the hospital wing at the assisted living center to visit Mr. Jensen, since Edna told Lauren that under no circumstance could Aja visit. Aja had talked to Janie, who was going to pick her up on the way to work. Then Aja was going to have to haul butt to get home by seven.

"I can't today. I promised to, uh, do something for somebody."

Mrs. Burnett raised an eyebrow. "I'm here to help, but you're already too late for most of the scholarship money."

"Can we do it tomorrow?" Aja asked.

"Here, get these papers filled out tonight and bring them to me first thing tomorrow. Now, let me write you a pass to get back to class."

At four fifteen, Aja sat in her car in the mall parking lot waiting for Janie. They'd agreed to meet here, since it was pretty close to the assisted living center. Aja put her long hair up in a bun and wore a ball cap and big sunglasses just in case someone recognized her. Aja wondered if Walker was going to be there with his grandparents and whether or not he and Kendall were really over.

She had one of her "feelings," an underlying sense that someone was watching. She'd kept looking over her shoulder. Probably just nerves because she was doing something wrong—again.

A horn sounded, causing Aja to jump. She looked and saw Janie waving and rolling her window down.

"Come on, hurry, I'm late as usual," Janie said.

Aja got out of her car and slid in beside Janie. "Thanks for doing this." Janie's aura was warm and friendly. Aja had missed her.

"Anything for Mr. Jensen, even if it makes me an accomplice to a life of crime," Janie said, laughing.

"I know, right? We've got criminals out raping and pillaging, but you and I have to worry about our butts because we want to visit the elderly."

"You're such a bad influence." Janie sped out of the lot. "Do you have a ride back to your car in case Gabe or I can't get you back here on time?"

"I think so. My mom is seeing someone at five-thirty, but should be able to meet me at six forty-five. That should get me home by seven."

"Is she driving to the hospital?" Janie asked, with the implication that even Aja's mom wasn't allowed on the property.

Aja pulled her baseball cap lower. "I'm going to make a mad dash to the road, she'll meet me there."

"I'll see if I can find you a tablecloth to cover you up. The residents will think you're a ghost."

"Then maybe they'll quit harping on the theft and get some new juicy gossip to talk about." Aja sunk low in the seat when they drove into the lot. "I just need to be home by seven in case that awful court advocate shows up again."

"What about Lauren Jensen? I thought she said she'd take you home."

"Not tonight, one of her kids has a soccer game. She was going to send her husband, but I said no worries, I'll find my way home. Besides, I'm not planning on being here long. I could even walk to the mall to get my car."

Janie laughed. "I admire you. I don't think I'd work this hard to get out of high school. But then, you'd wind up like me. Thirty-one-years old, a waitress, with no future and not sure what I want to do with my life."

"But you're good here. Everybody loves you." Aja knew Janie was comfortable with her life. She sensed that Janie was satisfied working with the residents, a contented happiness.

"And I like them," Janie said. "Even if it is sad when it's their time."

"Yeah, I don't know why I'm so worried about Mr. Jensen, since I hardly know him. It was just strange seeing the pictures of them when they were younger. So different from what they became. It's like, poof, a whole lifetime of memories are saved in photo albums. All that's left are pictures and dentures."

"And memories," Janie said. "And seeing their children grow."

"And love, I guess," Aja sighed. "He really loved his wife."

They pulled into the circular drive of the resident's hospital. Aja opened the door. "I didn't even bring a gift or anything."

"That's okay. He'll be happy to see you." Janie leaned back to look at Aja. "No one should recognize you in here, but just in case, keep your head down. He's in the second room on the left. Call me if you have any trouble."

"Thanks, Janie," Aja said, and lowered her cap visor and threw her purse over her shoulder. Again, she felt the ominous threat of someone watching. She looked back and didn't see anybody.

Aja's heart pounded as she opened the door. The one-desk nursing station was empty, so Aja quickly walked to Mr. Jensen's room. His door was ajar, and she could hear voices. She hoped there were no visitors from the home who would be happy to report her.

Tentatively she tapped on the door and pushed it open. "Hello, Mr. Jensen?"

He was lying on a bed hooked to IVs, apparently asleep. Aja

saw Lauren and her sister, Katie, sitting next to him. The room was warm. Near the bed were a small couch and two chairs.

"Aja, I'm so glad you came." Lauren held her hands out to welcome her.

"Hi," Aja said, and let Lauren lead her inside. She pushed the door closed with her foot, in case someone walked by and saw her here. "How is he?"

"He sleeps so much now," Lauren said, as she dabbed her eyes. "Dad, look who's here."

Mr. Jensen's eyes fluttered open, and he took a moment to focus on Aja. He grinned. "It's Princess Bride." He struggled to sit higher. "You helped with Buttercup." He held a liver-spotted hand out to Aja. She sat in one of the chairs next to the bed. His face became sad. "I've lost her. My Buttercup." He closed his eyes as if to hold in tears.

"I'm sorry, Mr. Jensen. She knew you loved her." Aja wasn't sure what to say. She took his hand and scooted the chair closer. "Tell me about her."

His eyes opened again and he smiled.

CHAPTER 27

Aja lost track of time sitting in the hospital room with Mr. Jensen. Lauren and her sister left soon after Aja arrived. But when Mr. Jensen started talking about his wife, he became animated and happy. His girls had brought a few photo albums, and he told Aja about each picture. From their wedding to family vacations. She laughed to see a much younger version of him and Mrs. Jensen wearing Mickey Mouse ears at Disneyland. He held her in a dance dip while Lauren and Katie, much younger, laughed next to them.

Aja asked him some questions about physics, a class she needed to finish. He explained the answers with such clarity and eagerness that Aja wished she'd had him as a teacher.

A nurse had brought a tray of food, set it on the portable tray and left. Aja smiled, wondering if Janie had added the piece of chocolate cake for him. "Here, Mr. Jensen, have some dinner." Aja pulled the tray closer to him.

He waved the food away. "I'm not hungry."

Aja's phone rang and she looked at the clock. Six forty-five. Damn, she was supposed to be at the road for her mom to pick her up. Then they still had to get Aja's car from the mall.

She answered the phone. "Mom, give me a few minutes. I'll be out as soon as I can."

"I need to get home. I have a seven o'clock appointment. Let me drive in and pick you up."

"No, I'll come out. Just wait."

Aja hung up and took a forkful of food. "Mr. Jensen, please take a few bites for me. That was my mom. I have to go soon."

He nodded and let Aja spoon some meat into his mouth. Then he pointed to the mashed potatoes. Aja scooped some for him. Before she knew it, the plate was empty. Her phone had rung a few more times, and it was already after seven.

"I have to run, Mr. Jensen. I'll come back again."

He smiled. "And bring your physics book. I'll go over those formulas with you." He patted his tummy and closed his eyes.

Aja moved the tray away, grabbed her purse and ran out. She flanked the back of the building and tried to hide in the shadows of the trees. She called her mom, who didn't answer. Probably already at her appointment. She always made a point to let Aja be independent and take care of her own life, but still it pissed Aja off that she couldn't wait a few extra minutes for her. She dialed Janie on the off chance that the dinner rush was over. Seven o'clock, and these people were already heading for bed. Janie didn't pick up.

She hoped Ms. Lewis wasn't planning on checking on her tonight, since it was already after curfew. She'd been riding Aja's ass hard since the night they'd called the police.

Aja ran toward the road. The sun was still hot and had just started to go down, but there was still more than an hour of daylight left. The way the shadows hit the trees made the ground seem to move. Aja considered calling Walker. Maybe he was finishing dinner with his grandparents (and probably Kendall), but Aja was desperate. He could think what he wanted about her, but now she needed to be home, and he was the only person left to call. She slowed down and pulled her phone out. The battery fell off the back. Stupid phone. She missed her old phone that Freddy Krueger crunched. It wasn't a cool phone, but at least it held a charge and the battery.

She bent to pick up the battery when she heard a voice. The voice.

"Well, well, are you running from another heist? And past your curfew?"

Aja's gut clenched. She whirled around and saw Clay Richards walking toward her. He was too close for her to make a run for it, but she was tempted to try anyway.

"As I recall, you're not supposed to be on this property," he said, sneering at her.

"And you have to stay away from me," Aja's voice was wispy with fear.

"No, I don't. Remember? You're the criminal, not me."

"You broke into my house."

"Says who?" He walked closer.

Aja backed away. With sudden clarity, she knew he'd been at the mall parking lot watching her when Janie picked her up.

"Stay there. Don't make me tase you." He reached for a funky looking device on his belt. "I want you to be aware. I don't want to have to wipe drool off your pretty face while you're convulsing from the shock of the Taser."

Aja knew she had a pretty good chance of out-running him. Even if he shot the Taser, he'd probably miss a moving target. But the thought of him landing a direct hit scared her just enough to stand down. She'd be at his mercy if he shot her.

"My mother's picking me up," Aja sputtered.

"Then why are you hiding in the trees?" He held the Taser out, then replaced it on his belt.

"You know I'm not supposed to be here. She's picking me up at the road." She took a step back. "I'm already late, so I need to go."

"Did you steal some valuables from some poor old person again?" He matched her steps.

"I came to visit a friend."

"A friend." He gave a sinister smile. "You sure could use a friend." His pace quickened, and he was almost on Aja. She turned and ran, but he caught her collar and violently pulled her to him.

Aja had been confronted by police officers, harassed by men, teased by students. But Clay Richards was a whole different kind of evil. All the others she'd been able to flip off. This guy scared her to the deepest depths of her soul. Her knees went weak, and she almost fell, but an instinct kicked in and she struck back and slapped his face. This just pissed him off more, and he pushed her to the ground facedown and landed on top of her. He held her hands behind her while his knee ground into her back. She couldn't breathe. He took twisty ties and cuffed her wrists.

"So you're a fighter, huh." He pulled the ties excruciatingly tight. "I don't want you all bruised when I take those nude pictures of you." He leaned close to her ear, laying his weight heavier on her back. "You're so pretty." His breath smelled like onions and evil.

A car passed near by. Aja tried to look up but couldn't raise her head. She was afraid the driver couldn't see them through the trees, and the setting sun would be in their eyes.

"Help," Aja croaked. She had no voice or enough air to scream.

The car drove on.

"Don't make me stuff something in your mouth." Clay pushed harder on her back, blowing all the air out of her lungs.

Aja closed her eyes and tried to breathe. Through the nose, out the mouth. She silently thanked her mom for making her do yoga all these years. With his weight on her, she couldn't catch a deep breath but gulped enough air to be able to think again. She did not want to pass out.

"Police station," Aja gasped. "Take me there."

"All in good time," Clay said, running his hands down her arms. He started to reach under her shirt when Aja heard the car pass by again. It had a familiar clunk to it, one she hadn't noticed when it came by the first time. Her mom's truck made funny noises; it had to be her.

Aja tried to squirm away and get his hand out of her shirt. The truck stopped and Aja heard the familiar door creak. "Aja?"

Oh, blessed relief, she'd never been so happy to hear that voice.

"Mom!" Aja barely got the word out before she felt Clay dig into her back again. She thought of all the action movies she'd seen where the good guy was able to twirl out from under the bad guy and twist the bad guy's neck with their legs or flip over and subdue the evildoer with some fancy moves. But Aja was paralyzed with his weight on her. Helpless. She prayed that her mom could see them.

"Oh, my God!" Aja's mom screamed.

Aja turned her head enough to see her mom sprinting toward them. She wanted to cry with relief.

"You bastard! Get off her." Her mom barreled fast at them. Clay Richards shifted his weight some, but stayed on Aja. She could tell he was fumbling with something on his belt.

"No!" Aja tried to scream. "Stop, Mom," she cried hoarsely. But she was too late. Clay Richards shot her mom, point blank, with the Taser.

CHAPTER 28

Aja sat in the now-familiar police room, alone. Her back and ribs ached where Clay had held her down. Worse, where his hand had touched her she felt filthy, almost scalded. After not being able to breathe, Aja now cherished each painful breath she took in. She'd never been so afraid in her life as when Clay was on top of her, reaching under her shirt. Aja also worried about her mom. She'd been told that her mom was fine and was being questioned in another room. She furiously rubbed her angel medal.

She hoped her mom was okay. It hurt Aja to see her flop like a fish from the electric shock of the Taser, the wires of the gun strung off of her like tentacles. She was helpless, but aware of what had happened. Aja closed her eyes to the memory, but the image only became more vivid.

The door opened, and the detective who'd questioned her before stormed in with Ms. Lewis at his heels.

"Looks like you'll be spending your nights at the detention center," Ms. Lewis said.

"How's my mom?" Aja asked.

"She's being taken care of," Detective Powell said. "You both may be spending time in jail."

"My mother did nothing." Aja cried. "She was trying to help me. That bastard Clay Richards had me face down and tethered, with his knee in my back and his hand up my shirt."

"That's Officer Richards to you, young lady," Ms. Lewis retorted.

"That's sexual predator, old lady."

"Remember, Aja, I'm the one holding the cards to your future,"

Ms. Lewis said, crossing her arms. "You'll be lucky to get a GED."

"Do you want to see the bruises he left?" Aja stood, ready to pull her shirt up.

"He told us you ran from him and he had to restrain you," Officer Powell said. "Now, sit down."

"And you believed him?" Aja's eyes filled with tears of fear and frustration. "You give a guy like that power and a gun without even considering what he's capable of? The guy is a pervert in a uniform." Aja fell into her chair. "It's a no-way-out situation."

"He said you were on your way to the nursing home, probably to steal from the residents there."

"I was *leaving* the hospital there after visiting with a patient." Aja waved her hand.

"You're not allowed to be on the property," Ms. Lewis said, taking a seat.

"I know."

"Then why did you go?"

"Mr. Jensen's daughter called. She was worried about him. I thought I could help." Aja wiped her face with her hands. Her wrists were bruised by the plastic cuffs. "I want to see my mom. I don't trust you. After what Clay Richards did to me, I can see how twisted your thinking is here."

"Both you and your mom are the ones with a past history of being troublemakers," Detective Powell said, tapping the table with his fingers.

"There's a big difference between being taken in for a sit-in protest and being a victim of sexual assault. I think your priorities are screwed," Aja spit out.

"As are your views," Detective Powell said, still drumming a beat with his fingers. "Didn't you steal money from a teacher at school?"

"I paid it back." She squirmed a little. Mrs. Burnett had really paid it to Dempsey before her mom gave her the money.

"So you're a thief, too."

Aja stared at him. "That was a crime of passion." She had a feeling, small, but she knew that this detective was dirty, too. Not evil like Clay Richards, but he'd taken money from something. Then the feeling was gone. Of course she couldn't say anything because she had no proof, and she was the one being interrogated.

They wouldn't even believe that Clay Richards had done what she said, even though she could feel the throb of the bruises on her back and ribs.

Officer Smith knocked on the door and opened it. "Aja, I just want to let you know I've just visited with your mom. She's doing okay."

"Thanks. Can I see her?" Aja asked.

"We're in the middle of an investigation. Don't interrupt us." Detective Powell turned on her. "I'll talk to you later."

"You like to throw your weight around, don't you?" Aja frowned at Powell when Smith backed out the door.

"We're not finished talking to you." He smacked the table with the palm of his hand.

"Aja," Ms. Lewis said, "you need to control your smart mouth."

Aja had the feeling again of Clay Richards watching her. It made her feel dirty and scared. She turned to the two-way mirror and shot her middle finger at it. "Get him out of here," Aja cried.

"Did you just shoot me the finger?" Powell yelled, standing so fast his chair fell back.

Aja never took her eyes off the mirror. "I want a lawyer."

CHAPTER 29

After the interrogation, Ms. Lewis escorted Aja home so she could pack a bag for her stay in the detention center. The appointed lawyer said she'd talk to them tomorrow and to go ahead and stay one night at the juvenile lock-up.

"Will I get to school tomorrow?" Aja asked, slumped in the car seat.

"No," Ms. Lewis answered perfunctorily.

"Why not?"

"Because you were told not to go to the retirement home. You can't be trusted."

"You realize I was helping someone."

"No, I think you were there stirring up trouble."

"Do you hate everyone?" Aja barked back.

"Just liars." Lewis stared ahead.

"That's rude." Aja sniffed. "Call the Jensens, they asked me to come."

Ms. Lewis said nothing as they turned on Aja's street.

Inside the house Aja's mom was there with Clara Wells. She ran to Aja and gave her a big hug. "Honey, are you okay? I keep picturing that asshole on top of you."

"And I keep seeing you getting tased. How are you?" Aja pulled away to look at her mom.

"I still can't believe it happened." She rubbed her chest where the prongs had gone in. "This is crazy. I'm pressing charges, then we're getting out of this town as soon as possible." She took Aja in a hug again, her bruises taking a direct hit. "I'm so glad you're home."

Ms. Lewis stood in the doorway. "Not for long. She's spending the night at the detention center."

"No, she is not!" Her mom stood in front of Aja protectively. "Haven't you done enough to her?"

"And I understand you're being charged with obstruction of an arrest. So I'd suggest you don't start trouble. Especially considering you're still on parole." Lewis turned to Aja. "You have five minutes to get your things. Toothbrush, change of clothes, no phone, computer or music pods."

"Whatever," Aja said, pulling away from her mom.

"I don't understand you all." Clara Wells got up from the couch. "These two wouldn't hurt a fly and are good-hearted people." She shook her head. "Really, can't you find any real criminals to harass?"

Ms. Lewis crossed her arms and didn't acknowledge Clara.

Aja's mom started to follow Aja to her room.

"Oh, no you don't," Lewis said. "Aja can go alone."

"Oh get a life!" Clara Wells spat. "Her mother was tased by a corrupt police officer, and Aja was physically assaulted by him. I think they can pick out some clean underwear together without more abuse from you."

"Do you want to come with us?" Aja's mom asked Ms. Lewis.

"Five minutes." Lewis held up five fingers.

"Then what, you'll come in shooting?" Aja spat.

Lewis wiggled her five-minute fingers at her and said nothing.

Aja's mom grabbed her by the arm and they went into her bedroom.

"Mom, are you really okay? I was worried. I thought..." Aja's mom cut her off.

"I'd take a lightning strike for you. I don't want to tell you how it felt to see that jerk on top of you." She put a hand to her eyes. "How can this be happening? Why are the bad guys getting away with this? I would have killed him if he hadn't shot me first." She rubbed her chest again. "Aja, let's run." Her mom went to the window and looked out. "Now, with nothing." Aja saw the familiar flash in her mom's eyes. "It will be our greatest adventure." Her mom spoke excitedly. She reached in her pocket and fished a small wad of bills, mostly singles.

Aja was sorely tempted to jump out the window, too. She

fought down the overpowering urge. "Mom, think. If we run, then we *will* be criminals."

"Since when did you become so, I don't know, compliant?" She spat the last word out like it was vermin.

"We shouldn't have to run. We've done nothing wrong."

"Exactly. We've done nothing but are the ones being punished. It's bad karma, honey. All this started when you took that money."

"Karma? I know it was stupid, but none of this is because of that."

"Something is working against us."

"Mom, really? This is because no one believes us. It has nothing to do with..."

"The fact your mom's the town psychic and all around nutcase?" Aja's mom continued to stare out the window.

"I told that detective that I wanted a lawyer. Maybe whoever they find for me will be able to help. Someone's got to believe us."

"What about your school counselor, what's her name— Burnett?"

Aja sighed as she rifled through her drawers. "I don't think she believes me anymore."

"The family you visited in the nursing home; they'll vouch for you."

"Yeah, I could probably get them to verify that they asked me to go, but that's only part of the problem."

"They invited you there."

"I know. Let me just go stay at that awful place tonight. You call Janie; she'll be able to contact the Jensens, and I guess I'll have to plan on summer school to get my diploma." Aja almost cried into her underwear drawer.

Ms. Lewis suddenly stood in Aja's doorway. "I said five minutes; I meant five minutes."

"Coming," Aja sighed. As she walked past her mother, they fell into a hug. "I'm sorry, Mom. This sucks."

"You don't have to go tonight." Her mom wouldn't let go.

"Yes, she does. I was nice enough to drive her, but I'll be happy to call for a police escort." Ms. Lewis moved to allow Aja to go first.

As Aja walked by Lewis, she could feel into the woman's soul. Despair, distrust, a black hole of sadness. Maybe this woman had seen so much bad that it was hard for her to find good in people.

But there was something else. Aja stopped and turned to Ms. Lewis. "Who's Julia?"

Ms. Lewis looked as if she'd been slapped. "What?" she asked, shocked. "How did you..." Then she became angry. "Get in the car before I call for someone else to take you in handcuffs."

CHAPTER 30

Aja couldn't sleep. Not just because of the constant noise of the stark detention center. Every sound echoed off the green cinderblock walls. Her roommate snored softly, seemed comfortable on the thin mattress. They'd not had time to talk before lights-out. Aja just knew her name was Tish and she'd been caught shoplifting. Aja could also see scores of marks scarring her thin arm, probably from cutting herself. Tish had made it clear that this was her space and she didn't want "no new bitch takin' her things."

The door to the room was left open to a common room, so they weren't locked in like a cell. Aja knew the doors to the outside were locked and monitored by a security guard. She could hear voices from the other rooms, whispers mostly. Throughout the night, she'd hear the plumbing, girls getting up to go to the bathroom. No one patrolled to check on them.

Aja must have fallen asleep. She was awakened by voices in her room. She turned over and saw Tish and two other girls going through her things.

"Hey, what are you doing?" Aja sat up, groggy, her back painfully stiff from the bruises. "That's my stuff."

"And whatcha gonna do about it?" Tish asked. "Maybe I want some of it."

Aja stood slowly and walked to the girls. Nobody backed away. She grabbed her bag, with Tish's skinny arm up to her elbow in it, and pulled. Tish pulled it back.

"I wanna see whatcha got. Give it." Tish wouldn't let go.

"If you ask nice, maybe I'll show you," Aja fumed. She couldn't believe she was getting in a girl-fight over the few items she was

125

allowed to bring. She felt the impression of her guardian angel pin. She was relived they hadn't taken it.

Tish let go and took a step back. "I'm the head bitch here. If I want something, then I get it." The other two girls flanked her. "You sure got some pretty long blonde hair, how 'bout we shave it off when you're sleeping?"

"How about not, head bitch." Aja pulled the strap tight on her bag.

"Three on one, Tish," one of the girls said.

"Wait, she just called me a bitch." Tish took a few steps toward Aja.

Aja was ready. All her life, she'd rallied for peace, been arrested while being part of non-violent movements, sit-ins, all-for-one, never hurt another, always do the right thing. She'd been physically carried away by officers and never fought back. Today, after all that had happened, she wanted to slug somebody. "Bring it," she growled.

"Oh, you're on." Tish acted like she was rolling up her sleeves on her scrawny arms. "I ain't scared of you, blondie. I'll beat your ass to a pulp."

Aja stood ready. She'd never fought before. Hoped that instinct would kick in. Other than a few yoga moves, she had nothing except anger, extreme over-the-top anger.

"You know what, blondie." Tish took a step back but still poised for battle, "I ain't gonna fight your skinny ass on an empty stomach. I'm gonna eat my slop, then I'll kick your ass."

"Whatever floats your boat," Aja said, relieved, but a little pissed too, because she really wanted to punch something.

"Come on, ladies, let's eat." Tish turned to her friends and they started out the door.

Aja turned, took her bag, let out a guttural noise and slammed the bag hard on the bed. She felt like the Incredible Hulk. She wanted to put her fist through the wall or scream at the top of her lungs.

Tish hung in the doorway watching. "You kinda scare me, bitch."

Then Aja started laughing wildly. "Good. I am to be feared," she yelled dramatically. She laughed until tears came.

"They shoulda put you in the mental ward, bitch, your nut's

cracked all the way." Tish moved out the door. "You sure you ain't murdered somebody?"

Aja wiped her tears. "I'm here because I helped an old person and I didn't do my homework." She started to cry.

"Damn, you in a hard-ass school." Tish leaned against the door and watched Aja; her friends had gone. "Look, I'm gonna let you off the hook. I'm not gonna beat your ass today."

Aja nodded, still crying. "Good." She wiped her face with her hands. "Let me know when you're ready."

"Better come eat." Tish turned and walked out.

Slop was right. Aja wasn't sure if she was eating oatmeal or plaster. The small scoop of eggs was cold and mushy, and the overly processed white bread toast would have had her mother in a tizzy. Aja only ate whole-sprouted grain bread.

Tish waved Aja over to her table. "Sit here."

Aja hesitated but sat next to her and her two friends. She couldn't lean back on the hard plastic because of the pain in her back. The cafeteria was boring, typical of a school's eating area. Tish wore a white tank top and a gray jersey sweatshirt with Abercrombie emblazoned across the front. That job seemed like a lifetime ago, Aja thought.

"So you tellin' me you're here because you didn't do no homework?" Tish slathered her toast with margarine and grape jelly. She looked at the others with an almost predatory gaze, as if protecting her turf.

"It's a long story," Aja said. "What about you all?" Aja asked the girls, but looked at Tish. She was struck by how pretty the girl was. She had delicate Asian features, shoulder-length black hair with streaks of fuchsia in it, and she talked like a truck driver. Aja thought she might be sixteen, maybe seventeen, and was surprised at how dumb the poor girl sounded. Aja couldn't see the cuts on her arm, with the shirtsleeves covering them, but Tish was so tiny she looked like she'd bleed out with a paper cut.

"This is our bitch-Ritz hotel," Tish said, taking a messy bite of her toast. She wiped grape jelly off her mouth with her hand. "We here all the time, 'cept Sissy." She waved her toast at one of her friends sitting across from her. "She gets to go home every day, but comes back for school and *detention*." They laughed and high-fived.

"What about your parents? Don't they want you home?" Aja tasted the cold egg mixture and pushed them away.

"My momma said she give up on me. I'm old enough to take care of myself anyway, get a job. I don't need no stupid school and that's why I have to stay, to get my GED. I'm glad I don't have a baby to take care of like Sissy here."

Aja thought her life was screwed up, that she was a total outcast, but she, at least, wanted to go to college, do something with her life. Tish's bar was a limbo low. She couldn't get lower.

"Aja, what kind of name is that? Is that like a place in China or Japan?"

"No, it's from an old music album that my mom liked."

"Weird."

"A-ja Harmon," a woman who worked at the center called out. She said Aja with a hard j. She stood in the doorway to the office.

Aja turned.

"There's someone to see you." The woman nodded for Aja to follow her.

"Probably your proby officer to give you the rules," Tish said.

Aja followed the woman into an unsecured lobby and saw Mrs. Burnett holding books and papers.

"Mrs. Burnett, I can explain."

"Aja, I don't know why I'm even here," Mrs. Burnett admonished. "Every time I turn around, you're in more trouble. I'm afraid I can't do anything about this last semester of school. I'm sure you'll have to go to summer school, but I don't want you to get farther behind in your studies."

Aja cringed. "I swear, Mrs. Burnett, that creepy guy Clay Richards is turning things around. I did nothing wrong. He's stalking me."

"No excuses, Aja."

"I saw Mr. Jensen last night because Lauren called and said he'd been asking for me. I was trying to help."

"Aja, I spoke to Lauren this morning." Mrs. Burnett sat on an old couch and placed the armload of books on a chipped coffee table. She hesitated before she asked, "Did you eat Mr. Jensen's dinner last night?"

"What? No!" Aja sat on a couch across from her. "He ate it all."

"He hasn't eaten since Mrs. Jensen died."

"That's why I was late getting out of there. He kept asking for more."

"He ate it all?" Mrs. Burnett asked doubtfully.

"Do an X-ray on his stomach. I wouldn't touch that mush in a million years."

"I don't know what to believe anymore," Mrs. Burnett said. "Aja, at least work on these college applications. I called Stanford; they were impressed with your scores, but not your record. I have a friend at Santa Clara."

"That's in San Jose," Aja said, happily. "I'd love to go there."

"It's an expensive school, and the scholarships for next year are spoken for. My friend said she'd look at your application, but, Aja, I have to say that your moving from school to school, your juvenile record, and now this." Mrs. Burnett waved a hand around the center. "I'm not holding high hopes."

Aja sat back. She and her mom had always struggled financially. They'd lived from job to job, and the little extra money Aja made working she'd blown on clothes or car repairs. There was no way they could afford such an expensive school.

Mrs. Burnett slid the books toward Aja, "Here. At least do your schoolwork and start on these college essays. If what you say is true then..." Mrs. Burnett didn't finish her sentence.

Aja looked to the cafeteria, where she saw small clusters of kids like Tish, and thought of her own future. She decided that, somehow, she'd raise her own bar, bring Clay Richards to his knees, and get into a good school.

CHAPTER 31

Later that afternoon, after "class," which consisted of elementary-level math and English and an art-music session, no learning, just goofing off for an hour, Aja met with her mother and the court-appointed attorney, Maggie Snow. Maggie was a petite woman with a short sensible haircut and looked so young she'd probably just gotten out of law school.

"So you're telling me this cop sexually assaulted you?" Maggie asked, making notes on a yellow legal pad.

"Yeah, want to see the bruises?" Aja asked.

"From sex?"

"No, from holding me down with his knees. He had his hand up my shirt, then he tased my mom."

"I think we may be able to pursue a case against him being too aggressive. Did he actually rape you?"

"No," Aja said.

"First, we need to talk about you being admitted here. I understand there are some theft and trespassing charges pending against you?"

"I didn't steal anything. I did go to the hospital to see a friend."

She held a hand up. "It's my job to prove your innocence."

"Clay Richards broke into my house, too. I know he would have hurt me. The guy scares me."

"He said he was responding to a call and never went inside."

"He was there before I made the call. He's the reason I called."

"I don't understand how he keeps getting away with everything," Aja's mom said. "He needs his nuts nailed to a wall."

The attorney looked at Aja's mom. "It's his word against Aja's."

"Can I get out of here today?" Aja asked.

"Don't think so. I need to file some motions with the court."

"I want her home today," Aja's mom said. "She's done nothing wrong. The system is screwing her."

"The system is what we have to work with." The attorney put her legal pad in her briefcase. "I need to get to the courthouse now to file a motion to have your case heard ASAP. I'll come back later to photograph those bruises. That'll be worked up as another case."

Aja hugged herself. She could still feel his cold fingers under her shirt, and the thought of it made her sick.

"No matter about your past record, if this guy really did assault you, I will do my best to bring charges against him." Maggie packed her papers in her briefcase. "I'll get an investigator to begin checking Richards's background."

"Thank you," Aja's mom said. "But, please, try to get Aja home. She shouldn't be here."

"I'll see what I can do," Maggie said as she squeezed Aja's arm. "There are a few layers here to peel back. The trespassing and resisting-arrest charges against you are what I've been appointed for. I'll look into the assault. For now, sit tight and stay out of trouble." Maggie looked pointedly at Aja's mom. "That goes for you, too."

"She's innocent. I want her home," her mom said defensively.

"Mom, it's cool. I'll be okay until tomorrow," Aja said, then looked at Maggie. "You can get me out of here by then?"

"Let me get to the courthouse now." Maggie snapped her briefcase shut. "I'll be in touch." She nodded and left.

Aja's mom turned to her. "This whole thing is a nightmare. Clara Wells and I are getting a group to help fight this."

"Mom, he deserves to be nailed, but come on. Why don't we let this attorney see what she can do? What if you get tossed in jail?"

Just then the woman working at the center came in and said, "A-ja, you have to come in now. Visiting is over; we're locking up."

"Come with me now," Aja's mom whispered. "We'll bust out of here and run." She had tears in her eyes.

"Soon, Mom." Aja stood and tried not to cry. "Can you check on Mr. Jensen? Call Janie and see how he is."

Her mom nodded, crying softly.

Aja watched her go. Her mom was still beautiful, lean and muscular, and had always held herself proud and strong. She looked much younger than her forty-one years, but today she looked withered, her laugh lines turned to wrinkles. It was like she'd crumple at the mere whiff of a breeze.

After the doors closed and locked with a buzz that went through Aja like an electric shock, she gathered her books and went to the center's common room. There were groups of teens at a few tables talking. Most sat in front a TV. Aja found an unoccupied table and started her schoolwork.

She finished her homework and opened the college application forms. She read the topics for the college essays and thought about what she could write. Topic A: Describe an event that has shaped your life. Topic B: What are your future dreams? Looking back what would you change? Topic C: Tell about an unforgettable experience and how it shaped you.

Aja smiled. At least with her checkered and diverse past, she'd have no problem coming up with ideas.

CHAPTER 32

Aja was still mulling over the essays when Tish and Sissy flopped down at her table.

"Whatcha doing? We already done school today." Tish pushed Aja's stack of books away. "Physics? You're kiddin,' right?"

Aja shook her head. "No, I want to graduate at the end of this semester, but because I'm here, I'll probably still have to go to summer school."

"Why do you care so much about school? It's stupid."

Aja shrugged.

Tish looked at the college applications. "What's that for?"

"College."

"Man, if I was graduating, I'd stop. Who wants to go for more school? You're one crazy bitch."

Aja laughed. "I guess I am."

"'Specially if you had to come here for not doing your homework. Never heard of that."

Aja changed the subject. "Do you know that social worker, Ms. Lewis?"

"Lou-Lou Lewis? Yeah, she your T.O.?"

"T.O.?" Aja asked.

"Truant officer, bitch. For someone so smart, you're dumb."

Aja could read Tish easily; she went ahead and let the vision in. She got a flash of Tish's home life. A mother who competed with her, told Tish not to do something, yet the mom did it. There was a man who tried to hurt Tish, and her mom blamed her. Aja got an eerie feeling in her stomach warning her to stop the vision.

"Don't ignore me, bitch. I asked you a question." Tish broke Aja's image.

Aja jerked back to reality. "Sorry, what?"

"You zoning on drugs? I asked why you want to know about Lou-Lou."

"Who's Julia?" Aja asked, remembering the vision she had when she passed Ms. Lewis.

Sissy spoke for the first time. "Oh man, don't say that name around her. Julia was one of Lou-Lou's truant kids. Old Lou-Lou felt sorry for her, thought she could save her ass."

Tish laughed. "Yeah, that 'ol bitch Lou-Lou took Julia to live with her, then the little bitch cleaned her out. Left town with Lou-Lou's money and jewelry. *Hil*-arous."

The black cloud that was Ms. Lewis's aura made sense to Aja now. Trust turned to dust. No wonder the woman was such a hard ass. Aja noticed both Tish and Sissy pass a look between them that said there was more to the story.

"Good luck with her being your T.O.," Sissy said. "I got a kid, and she still makes me come here every day 'cause I'm not eighteen yet. Soon as I turn old enough, I ain't never crossing that dike's path again."

Tish laughed. "You shoulda named your baby after her."

"Don't make me hurt you," Sissy said.

"You get to go home at night?" Aja asked Sissy.

"Yeah, lots of us just go to school here."

"Come on, it's slop time," Tish said, standing. "Quit that." She pointed at Aja's books. "I got a headache just looking at those books."

As they stood, Aja said, "Haven't you ever enjoyed any classes?" She glanced at her physics book. "Have you ever mixed baking soda and vinegar? Every science fair always has a kid making a volcano."

"Science fair? No way." Tish took the lead to the cafeteria.

"What about the Mentos trick, ever done that?" Aja asked.

"What, try to fit all of 'em in your mouth?"

"No, get a liter of Diet Coke and put a roll of Mentos in. It explodes."

"Cool. Hey, Sis, bring a Coke and Mentos tomorrow," Tish said. "I want to blow up this joint."

"It's not going to leave a hole in the building." Aja laughed. "It just makes a big mess."

They walked to the cafeteria, where only a few students were lined up to eat. "Where is everybody?" Aja asked.

"They all gone home." Tish grabbed a tray. "Only us hardass criminals get to spend the night."

Sissy broke away to leave for the evening. "My ride's here, see ya'll."

Aja got a sick feeling in her stomach, first when she saw the brown glop they were serving for dinner and second, for being one of the hardened criminals who was locked in.

CHAPTER 33

The next afternoon the attorney, Maggie, and Aja's mom came to the detention center to take her home. She was going to be able to go to school and home, like before, but this time Ms. Lewis said she'd be stopping by every night.

"Before we go, I want to get those photographs of your bruises," Maggie said, pulling a camera with a funky ring-flash around the lens. "Let's find a private room."

They were allowed to use an office next to the lobby. Aja raised her shirt enough to show the painful bruises. "I couldn't sleep last night because they hurt so bad." She didn't mention that a veil of fear also kept her awake, fearing she'd be locked in this place forever.

Aja's mom became livid when she saw the bruises. "I'll kill the bastard myself."

"Mom, remember, peaceful resolutions for all." Another of her mom's favorite mantras.

"Sometimes revenge just feels better," her mom sighed.

They finished with the photos and left the building. Aja sucked in a big breath of air, not because she couldn't go outside in the locked detention yard, but because the feeling of freedom was sweet. The deep breath hurt her bruised ribs.

"Your counselor, Mrs. Burnett, wants us to stop by school on the way home so she can give you your assignments." Her mom started her truck, which spit and huffed with the effort. "She said she gave you some college essay topics, too?" Her mom looked at her. "She said you aced your SATs."

"Yeah, she's really trying to help me go to college." Aja pulled the folder of finished homework out to give to Mrs. Burnett.

"Janie called," Aja's mom said as she pulled into traffic. "She said to tell you that Mr. Jensen's not eating again. He keeps asking for you."

"Is he okay?"

"She said he's still getting IVs, but they want him to eat real food."

"I wish I could see him." Aja smiled, thinking of the trouble she, Tish and Sissy got into by blowing up the tube of Mentos in Diet Coke earlier that day. It was worth having to clean up the sticky mess. Mr. Jensen would have been happy. Aja left instructions on how to make a volcano. As she was leaving, she saw Tish in the rec room building a small hollowed-out mountain with Play-Doh.

They drove for a few minutes in silence, then Aja asked, "Has anybody called?"

Aja's mom glanced at her. "No, he hasn't."

"I didn't say Walker." Aja sighed and thought of Kendall and her meanness and lies. Maybe that was the way to be in life. Screw the rest of the world and just take care of yourself.

"Don't be like Kendall, honey."

"Mom, stop!"

"Sorry, I just saw it. You know I usually can't read you." She sighed. "Even though many times I wish I could."

Aja slumped in her seat and tried to keep her head clear.

They pulled into the school parking lot, empty since school was out for the afternoon. Mrs. Burnett was waiting for them in her office.

"Aja, Mrs. Harmon, thanks for coming." She looked at Aja. "Did you get your assignments done?"

"Yeah." Aja handed the folder of homework over.

"Here's today's homework." Mrs. Burnett gave Aja a new stack of papers.

"Thanks for doing this," Aja said, taking the assignments. She wondered if Mrs. Burnett thought of Aja as her "project," like Ms. Lewis and Julia.

"You have a test in English tomorrow, and Mrs. Dempsey is aware you'll be in class."

"Okay."

"And Aja?"

"Yes."

"No science experiments please, like with Mentos," Mrs. Burnett said sternly, but with a slight smile. "Ms. Lewis got a call from the detention center, and she called me."

"Noted." Aja smiled back.

"Did you look over the essays?"

"Yeah, I'll work on them more tonight."

Aja's mom had been quiet during the meeting. As they stood to leave, she turned to Mrs. Burnett and said, "You don't have to feel sorry for Aja."

"What? I don't."

"Yes, you do."

Aja cringed.

"I'm not a bad mother, just different."

"I see." Mrs. Burnett stood behind her desk, looking as if she'd been stripped of her clothes. "I can tell you you've raised a very bright young lady."

Stalemate.

"I know," Aja's mom said, looking with pride at her daughter. "She's very special, thank you."

"Aja," Mrs. Burnett turned to her. "Lauren Jensen called. She's asking the assisted living hospital for permission for you to visit Mr. Jensen. You seem to have made an impression on him. I'll let you know more about that tomorrow."

"Thanks, Mrs. Burnett." Aja followed her mom out, but turned back and said, "Thanks, really, for everything."

CHAPTER 34

After school the next day, Aja and her mom pulled into the residence home's parking lot. Aja had butterflies in her stomach and hated herself for wondering if Walker would be there, as well as being nervous because everybody here thought she was a thief, including him. They were to meet the director, Edna, and Lauren Jensen in the lobby and walk to the hospital to see Mr. Jensen. The one person Aja didn't want to see was Mrs. Poston.

When they walked into the lobby, Edna stood near the front desk with Lauren. She turned and greeted Aja curtly. "Aja, I'm only allowing this because of Mr. Jensen. Otherwise..." she let the sentence hang in the air like a deflated balloon.

Lauren approached her. "Dad said he was going to help you with homework. His eyes really light up when he talks about you, and he still calls you Princess Bride."

Aja smiled. "He was helping me with physics. I need to tell him about some new...um, friends I just made. I showed them some science experiments, and they thought it was fun."

Aja's mom rolled her eyes. "Yeah, Aja made quite an impression."

Aja failed to mention that she almost wasn't released because of the commotion she'd caused.

"Come on, let's go," Edna said in a clipped tone.

"What is that little crook doing here?"

Mrs. Poston's voice snapped through Aja like the crack of a bullwhip.

"She is being supervised," Edna said to her.

"She needs to be handcuffed. I heard you broke the law again when you tried to steal from Steven Jensen in his hospital room. You slunk back here looking for more trouble."

Aja tried to keep her mouth shut but said curtly, "I came to visit him. And I did not steal your jewelry."

Mrs. Poston waved her hand, sputtering incoherently about Kendall seeing Aja in the hallway that night. Edna took Aja's arm and led her out, followed by Lauren and her mom.

"That's exactly the scene I was trying to avoid," Edna huffed. "I should have had you meet me at the hospital. What was I thinking?" she said, more to herself.

Aja craned her neck in the parking lot, looking for Walker's car. It was still early for dinner if he was coming. She chastised herself for looking—even he thought she stole the jewelry—but she wanted him to believe her innocence. For some reason, it was important to her. He seemed to see the good in everybody else why not her?

Entering the hospital, Lauren took the lead. She knocked at her father's door and opened it. "Dad? Hey, look who's here."

Mr. Jensen looked like he'd lost more weight. Aja recalled his wife the first night she'd met them. He turned his head slowly and raised an arm, taped and badly bruised by the IV line.

"I'm tired, just want to rest." He set his arm on the bed.

"Hi, Mr. Jensen." Aja stepped from behind Lauren.

It took a moment for him to focus on Aja, but when he did, he smiled. "Princess Bride," he croaked. "You helped me with my sweet Buttercup." His face became sad again and he said, "You know we lost her."

"I know, Mr. Jensen, and I'm sorry." Aja took a seat next to the bed. The others stood near the doorway. She saw that his lunch tray sat cold and uneaten. "You need to eat something." Aja turned to Edna, "Is Janie in yet? Can you call her to see if she'll bring a tray for him?" She looked back at Mr. Jensen. "You love Janie's cooking."

He tried to sit a little higher but couldn't. "Maybe a bite or two," he whispered.

Edna left the room, hopefully to call Janie.

"Can we help you sit up?" Aja asked, beckoning her mom and Lauren to help pull him higher in the bed.

All three hooked their arms under his and scooted him up.

Then Aja adjusted the motorized bed to a sitting position.

This seemed to energize him a little, and he stared at Aja. "You look so much like my Buttercup." He adjusted the sheets and settled in.

Aja sat down again. "Guess what, I helped some girls with physics." She went on to tell him about the Mentos and volcano demonstrations.

Now he was alert. "Vinegar and baking soda is just simple physics of acetic acid and sodium bicarbonate making carbonic acid. Now, the Mentos experiment is fun, that's nucleation." He laughed. "That was always a favorite of the students."

"Yeah, I'm sure it was." Aja smiled at Lauren and her mom while they all listened to him talk animatedly about science.

"You're smarter than that," he went on. "Those experiments are done in first grade."

"I was helping some girls with their homework," Aja said, wondering if Tish ever got her Play-Doh volcano built and if it sparked an interest with her in something other than her dead-end life. As many times as she called Aja "bitch," Aja wished she'd gone over some vocabulary too.

Janie and Edna came into the room, Janie exuberant. "Hey, stranger, great to see you!" She put a hot covered plate on the bed table and hugged Aja. She turned to Mr. Jensen and said, "I made your favorite, roast beef and mashed potatoes with extra gravy."

He didn't say anything but looked genuinely happy with having so many people fawn all over him.

Aja pulled the tray closer and lifted the lid. "This smells great, Janie, thanks."

"Janie, you need to get back now," Edna said, but with a little more warmth than when she'd spoken to Aja earlier.

"Okay, bummer, I wish I could visit. Can you stop by after?"

"No!" Edna said. "Lauren, you will stay and supervise Aja and her mom, right?"

"Sure," Lauren said, a big smile on her face as she watched Aja spoon dinner to her father. He ate each bite with vigor.

Edna glanced at her watch. "It's four ten, I'll come by to escort you out at five." She waited for everyone to acknowledge her then she left with Janie.

"Call me," Janie said to Aja as she left.

Mr. Jensen finished his plate. Aja's mom always called them "happy plates" when she was young. They talked about school, and he asked where Aja was going to college. She deflected the question for now.

"You know my Buttercup needs me," Mr. Jensen said to Aja.

"I know she does." Aja looked over his shoulder and felt the love in the room.

Mr. Jensen took a few big bites of dessert before he patted his belly and fell asleep.

A few minutes later, Edna was at the door, purse over her arm. "It's time to leave."

They all stood. Lauren said to Edna, "Look, he ate everything." Then to Aja, "You really have magic around you." She gave her a big hug.

Aja arranged the covers over Mr. Jensen and refastened some tape that had pulled up around his IV. If only Lauren knew the magic, Aja thought. Mrs. Jensen was there, too, by her husband. Aja sensed the feeling of love, knew it came from his wife.

As they closed the door behind them, Aja's mom held her a few steps back and whispered, "You felt her, too?"

Aja turned away.

"Aja, you have the gift."

"The curse. I don't want it."

Her mom put an arm around her shoulders. "Take it at your own speed."

"Ladies," Edna snapped, standing impatiently by the lobby door. "We're leaving—*now.*"

They walked through the steaming hot parking lot, Edna keeping a close eye on Aja and her mom. Aja tried to clear her head. She wasn't ready to talk to her mom about her abilities. Wasn't sure she was ready for them.

A car pulled in front of them and Aja heard her name. She looked up and saw Walker, window rolled down, and Kendall next to him with her arms crossed defensively.

CHAPTER 35

Edna sighed heavily when Aja stopped by Walker's car.

"We heard you were in jail," Kendall said, arrogance lacing her voice.

"Bitch camp, mostly. You've been, right?" Aja said, glaring at Kendall. "They teach you all about lying."

"Young lady, we don't use that language here," Edna said. "I'll see you to your car."

As Aja and her mom started to follow Edna, Aja quickly turned back and asked Walker, "How are your grandparents?" She wanted to scream at Kendall for spreading lies but held her tongue. And she wanted to ask Walker why they were still together.

"Fine, same. I know Janie misses having you in the kitchen." The pitch of his voice rose a little, like maybe he wanted to tell Aja he missed her too. "Kendall came to Texas for a surprise visit," he said, clenching his teeth a little as he glanced at her.

Kendall said something Aja couldn't hear, but sounded like she said "skank," as Aja and her mom walked with Edna to their car. After they got in, Aja watched Walker meet up with Edna and go inside as she and her mom drove away. She glanced back and saw Kendall drive away in the Buick, surprised she'd actually be seen in such an uncool car.

"Do you want to talk about sensing Mrs. Jensen?"

"No."

"Why? I suspected you had the gift. Don't be scared of it."

"Quit calling it a 'gift,' it's weird." It scared Aja more than she wanted to admit. When she allowed a vision or feeling, it seemed to take a small piece of her and leave her vulnerable.

"Do you want to talk about Walker?"

"No! Can we just not talk about anything?"

Aja's mom patted her leg. "I've just missed you these past few days."

"What are you going to do when I go away to college?"

"I don't know." Aja's mom sighed. "I've wondered that too. Part of me is excited for you to spread your wings. Another part dreads you going away." She glanced at Aja as she drove. "I want to get out of this town anyway. It's time to move on. Maybe I'll go with you."

"Don't you want a normal life? A real home? We're like gypsies, casting black magic, then moving on. That's why I don't want the 'curse.' I just want to be a normal person. You know, have someplace to come home to, not live like we're migrating every season."

Her mom was silent for a minute. "Aja, there is no normal. I'm sorry we've jumped around so much. We've had some fun, haven't we?"

"I guess," Aja whispered. She and her mom were closer than most. Maybe it was because, for every new city they moved to, her mom was the only constant part of her life. Aja had never been away from her mother, and since Aja rarely cultivated friendships she and her mom were friends. Sure, her mom encouraged Aja to be independent and try new things. She pretty much was cool with anything Aja wanted to do.

"We need to stop at the store and pick up stuff for dinner, and then I'm going to call the attorney Maggie when we get home," Aja's mom said, changing the subject. "She was going to show the pictures she took of your bruises to a judge or somebody so we can file charges against Clay Richards."

"Did they allow the restraining order?" Aja asked. The healing bruises didn't hurt as much as the memory of the malevolent feel of his hand on her skin.

"I don't know," Aja's mom said. "I hope so."

At the grocery store, Aja checked the time. She wanted to make sure to get home before Ms. Lewis showed up. They'd been at the store thirty minutes by the time they checked out, still plenty of time.

They pulled into the driveway next to Aja's old Toyota and

were shocked to see her car marked with white shoe polish, words saying, "Ima bitch; psycho; crazy; lying whore." And the word that was written boldly on the back window was "Skank."

Aja jumped out of her mother's car and slammed the door. "What the..."

"Why would someone be so hateful?" her mom asked.

It galled Aja that someone had come to her home. She'd already felt violated by Clay Richards, but now kids from her school? Always the odd ball, Aja had been able to dodge direct hate. Usually, she was only avoided by other classmates. This was the first time she'd been attacked at her home.

They were only words, but they bit hard. It steeled Aja's resolve to leave this crummy city. She was almost willing to chuck this school year and transfer to another high school and finish her senior year next year. But she was so close to graduation.

"I'll get the hose," her mom said, holding the bags of groceries as she walked around Aja's car. "This is pathetic." She put the bags on the porch and unwound the hose.

Aja took the hose and started spraying her old car.

"We need some soap." Aja's mom picked up the bags and went into the house.

Aja sprayed water and rubbed the lettering. It came off, but not easily. She felt like someone was watching her, the hairs on her neck prickled. She looked up the street and saw a police cruiser, lights on even in daylight, the menacing silhouette of Clay Richard's pinhead behind the reflective windshield.

CHAPTER 36

This has gone too far, Aja thought. Richards's boldness and arrogance angered her so much she had that urge to punch something again, specifically his nasty face.

Her mom came outside, holding a bucket and sponge. "What's the matter? You look like you've seen a ghost." She followed Aja's gaze to the cruiser.

"That's not him is it?" Aja's mom began walking toward the car.

"Mom, ignore him." Aja kept her eyes on his car.

"No, I'm calling 911 again."

"Don't." Aja felt defeated, beaten down. The system was winning.

"Our rights are being violated. He's been warned to stay away."

"Come on, Mom, let's just clean this up and pretend he's not there. He knows we've seen him. I don't want to give him the satisfaction of him seeing us run." With a burst of angry energy, Aja took the bucket and soaped her car. She vigorously scrubbed all the lettering off as her mom sprayed the hose on the suds. A few minutes later, Clay drove by slowly but didn't stop. Aja and her mom stopped and stared as he went by.

"Bastard," Aja's mom said. "You still have your pliers?"

"No," Aja answered, working on the back window. "They were confiscated at school."

"Too bad I hate guns," her mom scoffed. "I'll give you my pliers," her mom said spraying water on the car and, unintentionally, on Aja.

"Hey, stop!" Aja ducked but laughed.

Then Aja's mom sprayed straight in the air, creating a rain shower over both of them. "Rain, rain, go away," her mom sang as she and Aja danced under the water.

Suddenly, she stopped and became serious, a look of fear crossing her face. She looked toward the house. "He was there," her mom whispered. "Just now." She dropped the hose and ran inside.

"Don't go in there if he's there," Aja screamed and ran in behind her mom.

Inside, Aja could sense that he'd been there. Like the stench of death, his aura lingered.

Aja's mom ran to each room, dripping water as she ran. "He's gone. But he was here."

They went to the kitchen to check the back door. It was closed, but unlocked. That frightened Aja. Did he have a key?

"What's this?" Aja's mom picked up some photographs from the counter near the door.

"I don't know."

"What the..." Aja's mom's hand went to her mouth. She held the pictures up so Aja could see them. Worry creased her mom's face.

Aja almost choked when she saw the first photograph. It was of Aja sitting at her desk in her room, studying. It had been taken from outside through Aja's window. There were a few of those, but the one that seared her insides was the photo of Aja's police mug shot pasted on a naked body taken from a centerfold.

"Now we call the police," her mom cried. "This is too much to take."

Aja was numb. "No, don't call. He'll come back." She could barely talk. "Call that lady, Smith."

Aja's mom nodded, her hand still over her face. They both stood there shocked, unable to move, still dripping water from their impromptu rain shower.

"Don't touch them." Aja's brain started to work. "Put them back where they were. Maybe his fingerprints are on them. All the more reason not to call 911. If he comes back, he'll have an excuse to have touched them."

Her mom dropped them on the counter like they were burning her fingers. Then her mom grabbed Aja in a big hug. "Oh, my God.

What the hell is going on?" They stood that way for a few minutes. "I'm going to call Clara Wells and see if we can stay with her. I don't feel safe here." She released Aja from the hug. "Then we'll call Officer Smith. Go pack a bag."

"Okay." Aja went to her room. She needed to change out of her wet clothes and took dry shorts and a top into the bathroom. After a peeping Tom incident in Arizona, she and her mom were extra careful about changing in front of windows anymore.

Aja changed and put some toiletries in a tote bag. She heard her mother on the phone, hopefully talking to Officer Smith. Aja packed her schoolwork and went to the kitchen, where her mom sat at the table on the phone. She was still wet and drippy.

"Okay, we'll wait here, but hurry. We're both frightened, and he was just watching us outside." Her mom paused. "Yes, it was him. Positive."

When her mom hung up Aja asked, "Is she coming?"

"Yeah, but she's not on duty today so she's calling someone who is. Hopefully they'll come without raising red flags at the station."

"Call Maggie."

"Good idea. Let me change out of these wet clothes first."

"You change, I'll call." Aja took the phone and Maggie's business card.

By the time her mom came back in the kitchen, Aja had left a message at Maggie's office. "They said she was unavailable but they'd get a message to her right away."

Aja stood and went to the kitchen window. She knew he was still out there, waiting. She was tired of being scared by him. Her fear was slowly turning into something else: survival. Kill or be killed. This time justice would be served, and somehow she'd be the one to hand it to him on a platter.

CHAPTER 37

Within the hour, their house was filled with people. Officer Smith was there wearing casual clothes. Another uniformed officer Aja had never seen was bagging the photographs. Maggie was there supervising and asking questions.

Clay Richards had driven by but didn't stop, even when he saw the police car in the drive. Fiona, from across the street, came by to see what all the ruckus was about—again.

"You guys are really testing our crime watch group," Fiona said. "How can two women get into so much trouble?"

"It's a long story," Aja said. They were in the living room, having been shooed out of the kitchen since the officer was there. Aja glanced at the clock: it was almost seven. She wondered if Lewis would show up, too.

"I thought you all were going to be great neighbors," Fiona shook her head. "You guys making drugs here or something? Is the psychic stuff a front?"

"Fiona, you know us better than that," Aja's mom said, coming in from her bedroom with a small suitcase.

"I thought I did," Fiona said.

Aja's mom put her suitcase by the front door. "Fiona, did you happen to see anybody writing on Aja's car today?"

"Come to think of it, I did. Pretty little thing, tall, wearing those expensive sweat pants with PINK written all over her butt. I never understood paying so much for sweats. You can get them at Walmart for five bucks."

"And you didn't call anybody, or ask her to stop?" Aja's mom asked.

"Nah, you know kids. They're always writing all over cars, especially before graduation. I really didn't pay any attention. She seemed like a cheerleader or something, so I figured she was a friend from school." Fiona laughed, a raspy smoker's wheeze. "It happened to my kids all the time. Supposed to mean you're cool or something, but that stuff is hard to get off."

"Did she have dark hair?" Aja asked, remembering Kendall taking Walker's car.

Fiona shrugged. "Like I said, I wasn't really paying any attention. She had a ball cap on, too. She may have been a brunette. I couldn't really tell you."

Aja looked at her mom. "It was probably Kendall." She struggled to remember what she was wearing as she sat in the car, but she could only picture Walker's face.

"Walker's friend?"

Aja nodded. "I don't know how she knew where I lived."

Fiona left, and Maggie came into the living room from the kitchen. "I need to talk to you both when they get finished here. I found out some things that will help our case."

"What kinds of things?" Aja asked.

Maggie looked at the police officer in the kitchen and whispered, "Later. Too many ears here now."

Officer Smith overheard her. "We'll be out of here soon. Or should I say, he'll be out, since I'm technically not working."

"Thanks for coming," Aja's mom said. "If there's anything I can do for you, please let me know."

"Thanks."

Twenty minutes later, everybody had left. Maggie, Aja, and her mom sat in the living room munching on a quickly made salad since the kitchen was a mess with the fingerprint powder. "I talked to a few of the girls in the detention center. Turns out Clay Richards has done some bad things to a few of them."

"Bad things?" Aja gulped.

"Yeah, like sexually assaulting at least one of them."

"Who?" Aja asked.

Maggie pulled a file from her case and opened it. "Patish Nguyen. According to her, Clay Richards 'felt her t's and a' quote, unquote. She said he was her mother's sugar daddy who kept her supplied on 'shit.'" Maggie paused. "I'm not sure what kind of drugs yet, but according to Patish, her mom got mad when she thought her daughter was trying to take him away from her." Maggie shook her head. "I don't understand people."

"Why didn't she press charges?" Aja asked.

"Girls like her don't often report abuse. For some, it's a way of life," Maggie said.

"Do you know her?" Aja's mom asked, turning to her daughter.

Aja shook her head. "Patish? I don't remember anyone by that name."

Maggie glanced at Aja, "She said she knew you. She also talked about a girl named Julia. Apparently, the truant officer Hilary Lewis was trying to help this girl, but Richards was harassing her too. Scared her so much she ran away."

"Wait, Pa*tish*...Tish?" Aja said.

Maggie looked at the file again. "Yeah, I think. Thin girl with pink-streaked hair?"

"Yeah, that's Tish." Aja sat up. "Richards abused her too? How does this guy get away with it?"

"Again, why didn't that girl Julia report him?" Aja's mom asked. "Two girls being harassed warrants some investigation."

Maggie shrugged. "He may have scared her so much she was afraid to say anything."

Aja remembered Tish's bullying. It was no doubt a front for a scared little girl. A defense mechanism. "Tish probably never had a chance in life," Aja said quietly. "And I thought I was screwed up."

Aja's mom gave her a puzzled look. "Since when did you think you were screwed up?"

"Well, you know, our constant moving and instability. Getting tossed in the slammer and *celebrating* it."

"Aja, you know better than that, those were for good causes." Her mom seemed hurt.

Maggie stepped in. "After working with so many types of people I've found there is no normal. We all just keep moving forward and try not to step in the dog crap." She smiled, tempering the argument. "Now let's go over your case. I'm appointed as your legal counsel for the trespassing charge. But, I'd also like to build a case against Clay Richards. Are you up for that?" she asked Aja.

"Oh, yeah," Aja said. "I want to totally nail this guy."

"Okay, then let's get started."

Maggie stayed for almost an hour, going over what to expect and said that she'd follow up with the investigation of the photos left in the kitchen. She also showed them the pictures she'd taken of Aja's bruised back. Aja was afraid her mom was going to run screaming to find Richards right then and see that he'd never be able to have children.

"I'll make him walk with a limp for the rest of his life," her mom cried.

Maggie put the photos away. "It's probably best if we try to take him down legally."

Aja laughed. "I guess your peaceful resolution for all doesn't apply here?"

Her mom backed down and smiled. "You're right. But I've never been this mad or threatened before."

"We should take a self-defense course that will teach us to be one with our needle-nosed pliers."

Her mom giggled.

Maggie gave them a puzzled look.

"Long story," Aja laughed.

The phone rang, and Aja's mom got up to answer it.

"Did you show the judge those pictures?" Aja asked Maggie.

"He's reviewing the case now. That's where I was earlier." She looked at her watch. "It's getting late. We'll be in touch tomorrow." She stood to leave.

Aja's mom came back. "That was Hilary Lewis. I told her what happened and that we were not staying here tonight. She wasn't happy about it, but didn't argue."

"I'll try to contact her tomorrow," Maggie said.

She left Aja and her mom alone. It was almost dark, and although Aja wished she could just curl up in her own bed, she thought of the pictures Clay Richards had taken of her at her desk. "Make sure all the doors and window are locked," Aja said. "I'll follow you to Mrs. Wells's house so I can go right to school tomorrow."

Aja went to her room to grab a few more things. She stopped in the doorway and looked out the window. She didn't see anybody outside but turned out the light anyway. It was dusk, and her room was deeply shadowed. She went to her stack of books and included a few old vocabulary workbooks in her stack. Maybe she'd go by the detention center tomorrow after school and talk to Tish.

CHAPTER 38

Aja was still required to check in with Mrs. Burnett between each class. But instead of it being a chore, Aja looked forward to talking to her. Mrs. Burnett had helped her apply to a few colleges and edited the essays she'd written.

"I love the one about the future and growing old," Mrs. Burnett said as she handed Aja an edited copy of one of her essays. "You really brought out beautifully how fragile life is and how quickly it passes. Quite a bit of insight for someone so young."

Aja shrugged. "After seeing the people at the retirement center I wondered what their lives were like when they were my age. Especially the Jensens."

"Lauren was thrilled to see her father so happy."

"Maybe they'll let me go back."

"I'm sure they will. Now go on, you'll be late."

Aja hustled to her next class.

All her teachers were allowing her to turn her homework in without hassle. Dempsey was the only one still giving her attitude, but she accepted Aja's homework. No mention of summer school had come up.

Her phone had been vibrating all during math, but Aja wouldn't look at it because she was already walking on a tightrope and she didn't want to fall. She did not want to have her phone taken away and sent to the office. But she worried that there was some kind of emergency, and she was itching to see who it was.

When math ended, Aja stayed seated and pulled out her phone. Walker and Janie both had texted and called her numerous times. She didn't have time to check the messages, meet with Mrs.

Burnett and get to her next class, so she decided to wait and check with them after school.

Trying to concentrate during her next class, Aja couldn't help but think about Tish. How could she have allowed Clay Richards to hurt her? Aja felt sick thinking about Tish's mom pushing the girl away. No wonder she had so many cut scars on her arms. She remembered the little girl that had been slapped by her mom at Abercrombie. Even though the woman abused the child, it was her mom that the little girl went to for protection. For Clay Richards to have watched and photographed Aja made her shiver to her bones. Fearing for herself and her mom because they only had each other.

After an eternity, the last bell rang. As Aja headed to the office to check in with Mrs. Burnett, she flipped her phone open and read the texts. Both Walker and Janie said that they now knew Aja hadn't taken Mrs. Poston's jewelry but gave no details. Janie's message was all caps, *"CALL ME ASAP!"* Aja wished she could call that second, but she had to go the office first. Aja was a little pissed because she'd told them she hadn't taken the loot. I guess they didn't really believe me, she thought sourly.

Luckily, Mrs. Burnett had an appointment so she couldn't visit with Aja long.

"Here's a website that offers scholarships. Your homework tonight is to apply to at least five of them." Mrs. Burnett put her purse over her shoulder and took a stack of folders from her desk. "Most require an essay, so they'll take some time to complete."

"Okay," Aja said, taking the sheet of paper with the lists on them. "Thanks."

"All your teachers are reporting positive things about you. I'm glad to hear that. You're down to the last two weeks." Mrs. Burnett's tone had a warning flag attached. She glanced at Mr. Carlisle's office. "Best to stay clear of certain people and keep your head above water, if you know what I mean."

Aja followed her gaze to Mr. Carlisle, who was happily tapping away at his computer. "Understood, thanks."

Mrs. Burnett nodded. She and Aja walked out together.

"Mrs. Burnett, I'm going to swing by the detention center and give some of the girls my old workbooks."

Mrs. Burnett hesitated but kept walking. "Aja, you should

probably stay away from there, too. Most of those girls would love to get you into trouble. Something you don't need."

"I don't think those girls were given enough opportunity to learn. You know, someone who believed in them."

"Trust me, they've all had their chances." Mrs. Burnett stopped and turned to Aja. "I'm sorry. You're right. I appreciate that you see something in them. But, Aja, proceed with caution. Don't get taken down. There's a fine line between being good and bad."

"I know that, but if I can help I'd feel better."

Mrs. Burnett smiled. "I see why Mr. Jensen speaks so highly of you. You have a good heart..." She paused, looked away, and didn't finish her sentence. "I'll see you tomorrow, Aja."

Aja knew the implication, the words Mrs. Burnett didn't say were that she was hanging by that fine line between good and bad. She hoped the wire didn't break.

As soon as Aja got in her car, she called Janie.

"I'm so glad you called. Guess what?" Janie paused, excitement came through the phone. "Guess who took Mrs. Poston's jewelry?"

"Who?"

"Kendall!"

Kendall?" Aja asked. "Why would she take anybody's jewelry? I thought she had a bunch of money. How do you know it was her?"

"This is where it gets good. You totally missed the fireworks at dinner last night."

"What happened?"

"Kendall didn't join Walker and his grandparents for dinner last night."

Yeah, Aja thought, she was skanking up my car.

"Walker's grandmother had one of Mrs. Poston's brooches on. Big old gold thing that was hard to miss. Mrs. Poston went ballistic on her! She thought you gave it to her. But when she told Mrs. Poston that it was Kendall's and that she'd only borrowed it, Mrs. Poston called her a liar. It was a total girl fight with senior citizens. Priceless!" Janie was so excited she could hardly talk. "Then Walker's grandmother took it off and threw it at Mrs. Poston. Edna and Gabe practically had to pull them apart."

"That's crazy. What about the rest of the jewelry?"

"I heard Walker found it at his grandmother's in a bag. I saw him and Kendall in the lobby later. I heard him tell Kendall to apologize to you."

"I won't hold my breath for that. What did Mrs. Poston say about Kendall taking it?"

"I'm not sure she realized Kendall took it. I think the catfight wore her out. She left yelling at pretty much anybody that got in her path."

"Did her helmet hair get messed up?" Aja laughed.

"Didn't budge," Janie said. "I'm on my way to work now, so I'll let you know any new developments. I felt bad for Walker's grandfather, though. It was rough seeing him so helpless not knowing what was going on. Didn't Walker call you? He said he was going to."

"Yeah, but I was in class. I'll call him later."

"He said he felt bad that you're getting drug through the muck."

"Not as bad as I felt because he didn't believe me. Call me later tonight," Aja said and hung up. She decided not to call Walker. Let him come to her.

She called her mom on the way to the detention center to tell her she'd be a few minutes late and what had happened with Kendall.

"See, Aja, sometimes having it all amounts to nothing. You thought she had a perfect, normal life, and look what she's done."

"I know," Aja said.

"I have a client at four thirty, so come in the back. Don't be too late. Maggie's coming by at six. I told Clara we'd come by after. I still don't want to sleep here."

"All right, see you then." Aja flipped the old phone closed.

As she pulled into the detention center parking lot, she saw Clay Richards's police cruiser. She wondered if he was hassling Tish and the others. The usual fear crept along her spine, but she fought it back down. This time she'd look him in his beady, scary eyes and stand up against him. He was not going to bring her down, break her fight.

CHAPTER 39

Aja grabbed the old workbooks and got out of her car. She saw Clay sitting in his cruiser watching her. At least he wasn't inside the detention center. Aja held her head up, took a deep breath, and walked in front of his car. The engine running, exhaust clogged the heavy air. She braced herself in case he honked the horn at her. She could feel his eyes following her, taking in her every move. She felt vulnerable, her knees weak, but she kept going, hugging the books close to her chest.

He rolled his window down and called her over. Aja ignored him and went inside. She had to take a few minutes to calm her nerves; her hands were shaking.

There was an attendant at a desk in the lobby. "Can I help you?"

"I'm here to see Tish," Aja said, fighting an urge to turn around to see if Richards was still there.

"You're A-ja," the woman asked. "Why are you back? I thought you got released."

"I did, but I wanted to bring Tish some books."

"Books? Really?" The woman eyed Aja suspiciously. "You're not going to do any more science experiments are you?"

"No." Aja smiled and bit back a joke about hiding a nail file for the prisoner. "Just vocabulary and I wanted to ask Tish something." Aja could look through a window into the front room in the center. She saw Tish pacing back and forth watching her. Aja couldn't tell if she looked mad or scared.

"Most kids get out and don't want to come back," the attendant said as she stood to let Aja through the locked door.

"I won't be long, thanks," Aja said, walking into the room. The sound of the door locking behind her made her almost turn and run back out.

"What're you doing here, bitch?" Tish asked, looking over Aja's shoulder outside.

"I need to ask you something." Aja turned and followed her gaze to Clay's car.

"I don't know what that asshole's doing here," Tish said nervously. "What you want from me?"

"Can we sit down?" Aja asked, looking around the room. There were only a few girls there, all clustered around the TV. "I have to get home soon."

They sat at one of the small chipped dining tables. Aja set the books down.

"I'm getting out in a few days, and he's been coming by and parking," Tish said nodding her head toward the front. She was scratching her arms under her sweatshirt. Aja wondered if she was reopening old wounds.

"That's who I want to talk about. He's hurt you, too. I'm hoping you'll help us get him tossed in jail."

"Him? He's police. He ain't getting busted. They protect each other."

"Just like we need to do," Aja said.

"Is this about that lady lawyer who talked to me yesterday?"

Aja nodded. "Yeah, we're planning on pressing charges against him, but we need evidence. He jumped me last week and keeps hassling me. If you'll testify and we can find that girl Julia, we might have enough to really have him punished."

"Nah, he keeps telling me he'll hurt me if I say anything." Tish scratched at her other arm so hard it made Aja wince.

"But what he's doing is wrong!" Aja cried. "You have the power over him. If you report him, we can get him to stop."

"If I talk, he'll shoot, bitch."

Aja chilled with fear. In a way Tish was right. He'd already made good on his promise to fight back, having Aja arrested and making it look like it was her fault. He knew who to pick on. Young girls who had problem pasts—easy targets. "He needs to be stopped," Aja whispered.

"Good luck with that. It's your life, and not a long one if you take him on."

"I'm afraid of him, too, but somebody has to stop him." Aja leaned back and stared at Tish. "He picks on girls that he thinks won't fight back. It's our responsibility and our right to report him." Aja thought she sounded very much like her mother.

"Who said I'm afraid, bitch?" Tish had both hands up her sleeves, scratching her arms.

"Who wouldn't be? The guy scares the crap out of me." Aja moved forward and put a hand on Tish's arms. "We don't deserve to be treated like this. We're better than him."

"But he's police." Tish shrugged Aja's hand away.

"He's a jerk."

"Got that right."

"I've got to go." Aja stood. "Think about it, okay?" Aja glanced out the window. It was too small to see all of the parking lot, so she couldn't see if Clay was still there. "Here, I brought you some books." The vocabulary workbooks were from eighth or ninth grade; Aja couldn't remember.

"Why?" Tish looked at them like they were stinky vermin. "I almost got more time added on thanks to that Mentos 'speriment." Tish smiled a little.

"Look, just learn about three words a day. You might find it fun."

"I'm smart enough. School ain't fun."

"Remember, knowledge is power."

"No, punching a bitch out is power."

Aja laughed. "I gotta run. Talk to the attorney when she comes back."

Tish shrugged. "I'll think about it."

Aja left Tish, who didn't even pick up the books. She was buzzed out the door and she blessed sweet freedom. In the parking lot, Clay had moved his car right next to Aja's. She hesitated, turned to the attendant and asked, "Do you have a security guard that can escort me out?"

The attendant looked at Aja for a second, then laughed. "You're kidding, right? We have security to protect us from girls like you."

"Funny, real funny." Aja sighed as she steeled herself to go to her car. She saw movement behind the glass inside the center. Tish was standing, watching her go. She was holding the books.

Aja got her keys ready and, for good measure, took her

mother's needle-nosed pliers from her purse and slipped them into her pocket. She knew she couldn't fight him; he'd win. She hoped that he wasn't stupid enough to try anything, especially with witnesses around.

Aja stood outside the detention center watching Clay watch her. She took her phone out to call her mom, but remembered her mother saying she had a client. She dialed Maggie's number, but her phone's battery died before the call went through. She wished she could call Walker to pick her up, but that was a stupid idea. She was still miffed that he thought she'd stolen the jewelry.

She heard the door to the detention center lock. She turned and saw the attendant through the wire-mesh glass closing up for the day. Damn, one less witness. Aja had no choice. She turned and walked toward her car.

Clay got out of his car and leaned against it, waiting for Aja. He'd backed into his spot so his door was next to her driver's side. She couldn't get into the passenger side because the lock was broken. She'd have to be inside the car to unlock it. Aja walked around her car, checking the passenger door anyway.

"Who'd you pay to inspect this heap?" Clay asked, leering at her. "I'm sure I could find a million violations against you for driving such a trap."

Her car was so old it didn't have an automatic lock, she had to put the key in the door to unlock it, and her hand shook so badly she wasn't sure she could do it. "Excuse me," she whispered, trying to get by him, not sure where her voice had gone.

Now he put his hand on her door. "You're not excused." He leaned in close to her. "So you think you're better than them because they let you out of this place?" He grinned. "You'll be back. I'll see to it."

"Leave me alone and get away from my car." Aja steeled, but was afraid to reach for her pliers. "Why are you even here?'

"To keep up with my arrests." He cocked an eyebrow. "I'm proud to say I know most of the girls in there."

"Afraid to pick on somebody your own size?" Aja huffed, then regretted saying anything smart to him.

"You girls are like rats." He sneered. "People know you exist but don't want anything to do with you. I'm just making sure there's no more trouble."

"If you'd stay away, there wouldn't be any trouble."

"Why don't we take a ride down to the station? I think you still have some charges against you."

"No, I don't," Aja gasped.

He opened the back door to the cruiser and grabbed Aja's arm.

"Stop!" she yelled.

"Are you resisting arrest?" He fumbled for his handcuffs.

Aja screamed, a bloodcurdling, gut-wrenching scream.

He'd almost pushed her into the backseat of the police car when Aja heard a woman's voice.

"What's going on?" It was the night security guard from the center.

"Help me!" Aja cried. "Call the real police."

Clay pushed her onto the seat, and he turned to the guard. "I'm working. Do not obstruct my arrest, or I'll slap some cuffs on you, too."

Aja squirmed out of the car and ran to the entrance of the center, which was now unlocked. Through the window, Aja saw Tish's head bobbing as she jumped up and down.

The security guard walked to the door and let Aja in, then locked the door behind her as she talked on a walkie-talkie. "Yeah, I got her inside. She was scared out of her mind."

"What was she doing there?" the voice from the other end asked.

"I don't know. I just came on." The guard turned to Aja and asked, "Why are you here, anyway?"

Aja was trying to gulp in air. "I wanted to bring some books to Tish; then I'm going home. That guy keeps following me."

"She came to see Tish." The guard said into the speaker as she walked to the window and looked out. "I think he's gone now."

"Visiting hours are over. Send her home. I don't want any trouble from the police," the disembodied voice said.

"All right." The guard clicked off and turned to Aja. "You've got to go." But she hesitated. "How long has he been bothering you?"

"A few weeks now. Scary stuff. He attacked me."

The guard looked at Tish, who was now pounding on the interior door. "I know he's trouble." She went to the door and opened it for Tish.

"I saw what he did." Tish talked excitedly. "You okay? I can't believe you ran, now you really gonna make him mad."

"He needs to be stopped," Aja said.

"That's why I'm almost too scared to leave this place," Tish said, then her voice dropped. "I make him mad a lot."

"He's probably waiting to pull me over when I leave here."

"And they' ain't nuthin you can do about it." Tish wrapped her arms around her own tiny body. "He's like a mad dog."

"You got folks you can call to come get you?" the guard asked, seeming to sympathize with Aja.

"Can I use your phone?" Aja hoped that Maggie was on her way to her house and wouldn't mind stopping here first.

CHAPTER 40

Aja made it home just after six o'clock. She sat on the couch with her mom and Maggie.

"Okay, now calm down and tell me what happened," Aja's mom said, placing a cup of chamomile tea in front of Aja.

"He tried to attack me again, and I managed to run inside, and Tish was there and saw it." Aja's words spilled out faster than she could organize them. "And then Maggie got him good."

"Whoa, Nellie," Maggie said, smiling. "Slow down. We'll get you to the station for a formal statement, but first take a breath and sip of tea."

Aja picked up her cup and blew on her tea.

"You said you got charges against him?" Aja's mom asked.

Maggie nodded. "Here's the deal. The judge approved the restraining order this afternoon." She turned to Aja. "Clay Richards may or may not have known that when he saw you at the detention center."

"What was he even doing there?" Aja took a hot sip of tea.

"We'll get to that," Maggie said. "The judge agreed to look at the abuse case against Richards, but he has hesitations because of the report stating you were resisting arrest and running from him that day at the residence home. He would've been within the scope of police work by taking you down."

"What about tasing me?" Aja's mom said, rubbing her chest where the prongs had gone in.

"But I wasn't doing anything to be arrested for," Aja said.

"We'll have to prove that," Maggie said. "You were trespassing."

"Tell mom how you saved me today," Aja said excitedly. "Maggie made him back off. It was great."

"Aja called me while I was on the way here." She touched Aja's knee. "I'm glad you did. I met her at the detention center and drove out behind her."

"He was waiting to pull me over as soon as I got on the road," Aja said. "He didn't know who Maggie was."

"I pulled into a parking lot and got out of the car with the restraining order in hand and told him he'd have to call another officer to take over."

"He was so pissed!" Aja smiled.

"It took some convincing, but he finally backed down."

"I thought he was going to shoot us both," Aja said, sipping her tea.

Maggie opened her briefcase. "I had my investigator do some checking on Richards." She hesitated before taking a file out. "It's pretty rough stuff. The station should have never hired him, considering his record, but he is a decorated veteran and he grew up here. I think they made some allowances."

"How rough?" Aja's mom asked cautiously.

"While in the service, he had charges brought against him for sexual harassment against some female recruits. All three recruits were transferred out of his division and, unfortunately, I won't be able to get the military records without a huge fight.

"But what we might have here are some statements of a few girls at the detention center that he arrested. Pretty much all the girls he took in complained of abuse." Maggie looked down. "But none of the girls were believed because of their past."

"Just like me," Aja said softly. "What about the pictures we found? Were his fingerprints on them?"

Maggie shook her head. "No, they were clean."

"Do you think we can stay here now that the restraining order is done?" Aja's mom asked.

"It might be a good idea to spend tonight out. He was pretty mad. Give him some time to cool off."

Aja's mom nodded, then got a faraway look. "Hilary Lewis is coming tonight."

"Did she call?" Maggie asked.

"No," Aja's mom said. "I just know."

"We can ask her about Julia," Aja said, not acknowledging the weird look Maggie had given her mother.

"Maggie, please stay for dinner. I'm making a lentil loaf."

Aja scrunched her face. "Again? Can we call out for pizza or something?"

"What time are you expecting Hilary?" Maggie asked, a tiny note of sarcasm laced her voice.

"Oh, I don't know that."

"Trust me, Mom's hardly ever wrong," Aja said, a little protectively.

"With the psychic stuff?"

"Yes," Aja's mom said. "When I'm clearer, I'll do a reading for you free. I so appreciate all you've done for Aja."

"So you can't see how all this is going to turn out?" Maggie half-joked and sat back on the couch.

Aja looked at her mom and said, "It doesn't work like that. Usually you get a feeling from a spirit or sometimes you see things, like in a dream. They may or may not come true."

Aja's mom smiled and puffed with pride.

Aja went on. "Like the tsunami in Japan. I had a dream months before it happened. I saw a big wave going over a shoreline. In the dream, I didn't know where it was. It was just a dream. But then, after it happened, I saw the exact same image on the news. It scared me, really."

"Forgive me if I'm skeptical," Maggie said. "I've never been a big believer in that."

"Yeah, I understand," Aja said and glanced at her mom. "Most of the time I try to ignore it."

They heard a car pull up and a car door shut.

Aja's mom looked at the clock. "That would be Hilary."

CHAPTER 41

Early the next morning Aja rolled off Mrs. Wells's couch before anyone else woke up. She managed to get a little sleep, despite Clara's painting of a huge eye that was positioned over the couch. It seemed to watch Aja all night.

Aja wanted to get to school extra early to use the library's computers, because she'd never gotten the chance to check out the scholarship website.

Navigating Mrs. Wells's bathroom was a riot. There were old-fashioned perfume bottles all over the counter. Aja did not want to accidentally knock one into the sink. Clara had photos of old movie stars and cross-dressers all over the walls. Aja brushed her teeth and tried to figure out which ones were really men. All of Aja's mom's friends were on a scale of strange to bizarre. This was a woman who told everyone that when she died, she wanted to become a carbon diamond. Just like her personality. Fake, gaudy, and flashy, but on the other hand you loved having her around. Aja wondered if her mom had a siren song that attracted all the weirdos whenever they got to a new town.

Before classes Aja only managed to complete three of the scholarship forms by the time school started. She'd gone to all her classes, ignored all of Walker's calls and texts, and headed straight home after school to finish the rest of the applications. She was looking forward to spending an evening at home. Clay Richards wasn't allowed near her, and she had nothing else to do but study.

She came in the front door and saw that her mom had the door to her "temple" closed. Probably with a client. Aja put her ear to the door and heard her mom's voice. She felt relieved, safe. It felt good. Even a full plate of lentil loaf sounded good.

Her phone rang, and Aja quickly punched the silence button. She didn't want to make her mom mad during the reading. Aja glanced at caller ID. It was Lauren Jensen.

"Hello," Aja whispered as she ran into her room.

"Aja, it's Lauren. Can you come by and see Dad tonight?"

"I don't know. What did Edna Jones say?"

"I haven't asked. I'll call her now. Can you come by?"

"Is your dad okay?"

"He keeps saying that Mom needs him. I think he's becoming delusional. It's like he's talking to her." Lauren quietly sobbed. "His mind has always been so sharp that it's really hard to watch him decline."

Aja didn't want to tell her that her father was right. Mrs. Jensen was near her husband, wanted to cross over but was afraid to go alone. They'd always done everything together. Aja had an idea. She hoped her mom didn't have another client tonight. "Lauren, can you come by my house tonight?"

"I don't know. I hate to leave Dad."

"He'll understand. Go ahead and call Edna. I need to check on something here, so call me in about thirty minutes, okay?"

"All right, but what do you have in mind?"

"You'll see," Aja said. She unloaded her homework and sat at her desk, making sure the curtains were closed. Although Clay Richards wasn't allowed near her, she still got creeped out thinking about him watching her.

Finally, after twenty minutes, the door to her mom's office opened and Aja jumped up to ask her mom about Lauren Jensen. She was surprised to see Officer Smith turn and give her mom a hug. The officer dabbed at tears.

"Wow, I didn't believe before. Thank you. I feel better knowing she's at peace," Officer Smith said, then seemed surprised and uncomfortable to see Aja. "Your mom has a gift," was all she said.

"I know," Aja answered. She sensed the presence of a spirit dissipating like a wisp of smoke.

"Mom, do you have anyone scheduled tonight?" Aja asked.

"No, I was going to make dinner."

"Good, I need a favor," Aja said, then turned to Officer Smith.

"Is there any way you could use your police skills to find a person?"

"Depends," Officer Smith said, warily.

"Do you remember the girl Julia that ran away from Ms. Lewis?"

"Yeah, why?"

"Aja," her mom warned. "We've just had a session. I'm sure Officer Smith wants some time to think." Her mom handed Smith an audio CD of their session. "That's so you can listen later, too."

"Thanks," she said, and held it next to her. She turned to Aja. "I can't go looking for someone unless I have a reason. I'm sorry."

"I understand, but..."

Her mom cut her off firmly, "Aja, later, okay?"

Aja backed down while her mom showed Officer Smith out.

Her mom came in looking exhausted. Aja knew most sessions wrung her out and took a piece of her soul, like what Aja often felt when she allowed the spiritual feelings of others in.

"Let me clear my head, then can we do a nice yoga session before dinner?"

"Who'd she see?"

"Her mom."

Aja knew not to ask details. Most of the time, her mom didn't remember specifics about sessions since the spirits, memories or visions came to her as she read. Much of it forgotten after the meeting. She was only the vessel of communication.

"Mom?" Aja said. She didn't want to ask her this favor, especially seeing how fragile her mom looked now. Her phone rang. It was Lauren. "Can you do one more reading tonight? Please?"

CHAPTER 42

Lauren Jensen came by as Aja and her mom were downward dogging in yoga. Her mom agreed to visit with Lauren only if Aja did a full hour of yoga with her.

Her mom turned on her back, eyes closed, and sighed. "You still owe me thirty minutes."

"Deal," Aja said, getting off the floor. "And I'll make dinner."

"Fair enough." Aja's mom held her hand out for Aja to pull her up. "I hope I can find the energy to do her reading."

"I appreciate it," Aja said. "Besides, all those rallies you've taken me to all these years, come on, you so owe me."

"They were character building." Her mom stood and filled her lungs with a deep breath that went to her toes.

Aja let Lauren in. "Lauren, I want you to talk to my mom. She may be able to help with..." Aja paused. "I think she'll help you get some closure."

Aja's mom welcomed her. "I do want to warn you that sometimes, if the passing is recent, the loved one may not come. Often, they're still finding their way."

Lauren looked skeptical. "This is why you wanted to see me? I don't know; I really don't believe in this."

Aja's mom went on. "And she doesn't want to leave your father now."

"Just try, Lauren," Aja said

Lauren stiffened. "This goes against everything I believe in. I mean, really? You summon...ghosts?" She whispered the last word. "They don't exist." She wilted on the couch crying. "But then I do believe in God and heaven." With tears in her eyes, she said, "I don't know what to think anymore."

Aja's mom directed Lauren to her "temple" and closed the door behind them.

Aja's phone buzzed soon after they'd gone into the room. Walker again. She ignored it and began to pull out veggies to cut for dinner. Slicing through an onion that made her tear up, Aja thought she heard a noise in the front of the house. Was it a knock at the door? She froze. No, Clay Richards wouldn't be that stupid. The familiar fear crept through her body. Knife in hand, she went to the front door and peeked out the side window.

There was a familiar vehicle parked in front, and Aja relaxed. Walker's sky-blue Buick was behind Lauren's car on the street. Aja wasn't ready to talk to him, but if he knocked again he'd no doubt bother her mom and Lauren.

She quietly opened the door and stepped onto the porch, knife in hand.

Walker looked at her then the knife. "Whoa, I knew you were upset, but not *that* mad." He smiled.

His smile melted Aja's resolve a little. What was it about him that could get through Aja's protective shield? "I'm making dinner, and mom's with someone. And yes, I am still mad at you." Aja stepped outside and closed the door behind her.

"Didn't you get my messages? Kendall took the jewelry." He put his hands in his pocket and looked down. "I'm sorry I doubted you."

"Yeah, I talked to Janie." She tapped the knife against her leg. "I am so sick of being the easiest to blame when something goes wrong. I've always tried to do the right thing." She thought of the forty dollars she stole. "What's going on with Kendall? Is Mrs. Poston pressing charges against her, like she did me?"

Walker shrugged. "No, I don't think so. I'm not sure she even knows for sure Kendall did it. No one's seen Mrs. Poston since all this happened."

"Hasn't anyone checked on her?"

"Honestly, I haven't thought about it."

Aja looked over Walker's shoulder. "Where's Kendall now? Hiding in the bushes, waiting to write obscenities all over my car again?"

Walker gave her a puzzled look, and Aja told him why she suspected her.

"I'm sorry, Aja." He rolled back on his heels like a kid caught in the act. "Kendall is back in Chicago. For good." He held a hand up. "This time it's really over; she crossed a line that I can't forgive. I've tried to break it off with her nicely, but she wouldn't leave me alone. This time I put my foot down. We're done."

"I don't know, Walker, my name is mud at the residence center. What about my reputation? She runs off to Chicago, and I have people wondering if I have the mark of guilt on me."

He looked away. "I know you didn't do anything."

"Am I allowed back there? No. Do I have a job? No." Aja waved the knife as if to make a point, realized she probably looked like she was going to stab Walker. She didn't need the neighbors to have another tidbit of gossip on her. "Come in, but be quiet so we don't disturb Mom."

They worked together in the kitchen slicing and dicing. Aja drizzled olive oil over a bowl of sweet potatoes, white potatoes and onions, mixed it with garlic and rosemary, then poured it on a cookie sheet. She put it in the oven.

"What else are you eating?" Walker asked.

"Chicken and salad," Aja answered, pulling a tub of organic greens from the refrigerator. "Have you eaten?"

Walker shook his head. "Is it real chicken or a tofurkey blend?"

"It's real. Free of hormones and antibiotics." Aja handed him the tub and grabbed tomatoes, mushrooms and carrots to slice. "You're welcome to join us."

"I don't want to impose. I just wanted to check on you and apologize."

Aja really wanted to stay mad at him, to stay focused on school and leaving Texas. But he was so damned mouth-watering. "You didn't eat Janie's special at the residence home tonight?"

"No." Walker rinsed the vegetables and began slicing the tomatoes. "I just came from school and thought I'd check on you before I went to see my grandparents."

"It'll be past their bedtimes before too long," Aja said. She wasn't sure how Lauren would feel if she saw Walker here. Especially since she was already reluctant about doing the reading at all. "Let's just stay in the kitchen, out of my mom's way."

Aja took a cast iron skillet and put it on a hot burner. She poured olive oil and scooped diced garlic into it. She took three chicken breasts and added them to the sizzling mix. The smell of garlic filled the small kitchen.

"There's nothing like garlic cooking," Walker said, inhaling. "I'd love to stay, thank you."

They worked quietly for a few minutes slicing, dicing, and mixing the salad. Finally Aja asked, "Does Edna know that I'm innocent?"

"I don't know." Walker chopped the carrots harder. "Kendall was so freaked out, she begged me not to say anything."

"What about Mrs. Poston? She knows I didn't do it, right?" Aja held the spatula up that she was using on the chicken.

"I don't know," Walker sputtered. "Like I said, I haven't seen her."

"So you'd rather protect a thief then go to bat for me." Aja flipped a breast too hard, spattering oil on the stove. "Didn't your grandmother say anything to her?"

Walker set the knife on the cutting board and faced Aja. "My grandmother hates scandals, and after the scene in the dining room, she's embarrassed. She left the jewelry in Edna's office to give it back. I think she'd rather sweep it all away. Forget about it."

"And just blame the hired help. Keep it simple." Aja scooped another breast and tossed it over making a bigger mess. "You know the charges against me haven't been officially dropped yet." At least her curfew had been dropped thanks to Maggie.

Walker sighed. "I was planning on visiting my grandparents later. I'll talk to them and Mrs. Poston on your behalf."

"And Edna Jones?" Aja pointed the greasy spatula at him.

"Yes, and Edna."

"Good." Aja heard voices in the living room. Lauren's reading was finished. "Can you keep an eye on the chicken? I'll be right back." Aja hoped Walker got the hint that she wanted him to stay in the kitchen.

Lauren was at the door, clutching the CD Aja's mom had given her. Aja could feel Mrs. Jensen's presence still in the room, and it stopped her in her tracks. The strength of it surprised Aja. She immediately sensed that Mrs. Jensen was conflicted, hadn't been ready to die, and still needed her husband near her. But she didn't want him to leave his children and grandchildren either.

"I can't lose both of them," Lauren cried. "Maybe this wasn't a good idea coming here." She glanced at Aja but didn't acknowledge her. Instead she turned and ran out the door.

Aja's mom leaned heavily against the doorframe. "I need to lie down."

"Are you okay?" Aja asked.

"Four readings in one day is too much," Aja's mom said. "Mrs. Jensen wants her husband with her." She shook her head. "She was strong, having just passed. She's still too connected here." Her mom looked past Aja. "Walker, I didn't know you were here."

Aja could tell her mom was spent. Being a psychic, her mom usually knew when someone was here or on the way. "Dinner will be ready soon," Aja said, going to her. "Why don't you lie down or meditate for ten or fifteen minutes? I'll come get you when we're ready."

Aja's mom nodded and allowed Aja to lead her into her room. "Aja, Mrs. Jensen wants you to talk to her husband. Tell him she misses him, but she'll wait. She kept saying 'As you wish.' I couldn't figure that out."

Aja smiled, remembering Mr. Jensen doting on his princess bride and the famous line from the movie: *As you wish.*

CHAPTER 43

Aja and Walker washed the dishes when they finished dinner. Aja's mom was quiet and subdued during the meal. She didn't even push Aja for the extra yoga time owed to her, just excused herself and went to bed.

"I guess I should be going," Walker said, drying his hands. "I promised my grandmother I'd stop by tonight."

"Maybe I'll go with you and talk to Mrs. Poston."

Walker hesitated. "Let me talk to everybody first."

Righteous anger flared in Aja. "Since I'm innocent, I don't see why I can't." She felt a tickle of apprehension in her gut when she said that, but the fight to prove herself won out. "I want to make sure you really talk to your grandparents." Aja considered stopping by Mr. Jensen's room to talk to him, too. "Give me a sec to tell mom I'm going out."

Walker was waiting by the door when Aja came from her mom's room. "I'll take my car so you don't have to drop me off later."

"I don't mind."

"No, just in case I want to drop by and visit Mr. Jensen."

"Visiting hours will be over," Walker said.

Aja knew he was reluctant to have her there. "I'll take my chances."

She followed Walker in his car and watched him park in front of the residence home. She kept driving and parked closer to the hospital. It was almost seven. She could meet with Walker's grandparents, Mrs. Poston, and hopefully stop by to see Mr. Jensen before eight. She still had a pile of homework to do tonight, and Mrs. Burnett expected perfect work and attendance for these last few days. No excuses.

Walker waited for Aja under the entrance at the home. "Aja, I've been thinking...I don't want to upset my grandmother. Can we do this another time?"

"I'm already here. It won't take long." Aja stepped ahead of him. "If I get tossed out of here, then we'll do it later." She turned and gave him a hard stare. "You know Walker, I hate scandals, too."

He sighed and dutifully followed her inside.

There was no one at the front desk to stop Aja, so she followed Walker down the hall to his grandparents' apartment. She kept expecting to hear Mrs. Poston screech at her, but all was quiet.

Walker's grandparents lived past Mrs. Poston's apartment. As they passed, Aja tensed, more reflexively than out of fear, but Mrs. Poston's door was closed. Unusual for her, the old bat always had her door opened to see what everybody else was doing. Walker was quiet and seemed pensive during the walk.

"Walker, why don't you go visit your grandparents first. I'll talk to Mrs. Poston. I want to make sure she knows I'm innocent."

He seemed almost relieved but said, "Aja, this place is still reeling from the cafeteria scene. I don't want to rock any more boats."

"I won't tell her it was Kendall. I'll let you do that." Aja had stopped walking. "I'm not into revenge or looking to rub someone's nose in it, but I want to be able to walk the halls here without feeling shame. That's important to me."

"Okay, I understand. Come by my grandparents' apartment when you're done." His eyes softened. "Tell Mrs. Poston I'll vouch for you."

"Thanks," Aja said, heading toward Mrs. Poston's door. The hallway was quiet except for loud TVs inside most apartments. Aja figured everybody was in for the night, ready to watch *Dancing With the Stars* or some other show.

Aja knocked on Mrs. Poston's door and waited. Nothing. Aja knocked again, put her ear to the door, and said, "Mrs. Poston, it's Aja, can you talk?"

Still nothing.

Aja knocked louder, which brought Mrs. Poston's neighbor,

Dr. Landers, out. He was still crisply dressed from dinner, but his shirt was untucked.

"Why, Aja, what a surprise." He gave her a questioning look.

"Hi, Dr. Landers. I wanted to talk to Mrs. Poston. Do you know if she's out?"

"Actually, no one's seen her for the last few days. We talked about it over dinner tonight."

"Maybe she's with her family."

"Yeah, I hope so. But Bea usually announces when she's leaving." Dr. Landers leaned closer to Aja. "This place is like a gossip mill; everybody knows what the others are doing, especially..." He nodded toward Mrs. Poston's door and winked at Aja.

"Has anybody checked on her?" Aja asked.

"I don't know. We all have an electronic button wired to the front desk that we have to turn off by 10:00 a.m., or someone checks on us."

"Maybe she's just not feeling well," Aja said, looking at the door.

"Come to think of it, I remember Bea had hers disconnected. She said she hated to have to check in with anybody like a child." Dr. Landers began to look concerned. "And her family rarely comes by."

Aja had to bite back a smart remark, like she knew why they wouldn't visit. Instead she said, "Should we go in and check on her?" Aja almost reached for the hidden key but stopped. That was what had started all this mess—her knowing where the key was. "I can run to the front desk and see if anybody's spoken to her."

"You are a sweet girl," Dr. Landers said. "I never believed you'd taken anything."

"Thank you."

Dr. Landers reached for the fake geranium pot. "She keeps a key under here."

"Yeah, but I don't want to get in trouble by going in uninvited."

"Understood." Dr. Landers smiled. He knocked on Mrs. Poston's door and tried the doorknob. It was unlocked. He shrugged, then cracked open the door. "Bea, are you here?" He pushed the door open further.

Aja couldn't see all of her, only Mrs. Poston's legs. Aja hated herself for thinking that it reminded her of the wicked witch in *The Wizard Of Oz*. Aja and Dr. Landers stepped inside where they found Mrs. Poston face down in her living room. Lying still. Too still.

CHAPTER 44

An hour after Aja and Dr. Landers found Mrs. Poston, Edna Jones sat on a sofa in the residence home's lobby wringing her hands. "Oh, this is terrible. How long was that poor woman like that?"

The paramedics had taken Mrs. Poston a little while ago. Aja and Dr. Landers had sat with her while they waited. Aja had dabbed a wet cloth over Mrs. Poston's face and, per Dr. Landers, let her suck a tiny amount of water out of it. "Even though she's dehydrated, you don't want to give her a lot to drink. She might need surgery." He'd taken her vitals. The poor woman was barely conscious, her pulse thready, and her usual loud voice could only croak the words, "Help me." Aja felt awful for her. Mrs. Poston's helmet hair was flat and stuck to her face. Aja gently moved it away from her eyes as she cleansed her face with the washcloth. It seemed like forever for the emergency crew to arrive.

"And you." Edna glared at Aja. "You always show up when there's trouble. You're not allowed here anyway. Oh, heavens." Edna's pudgy fingers flapped in the air.

"Edna," Dr. Landers said, "If it weren't for Aja, Bea Poston may not have survived the night. You should thank her."

"Why did I allow Bea to shut off the check-in light? I told her something like this could happen." Edna rambled on, trying to justify the action. "It's not our fault. She insisted on turning it off."

Uncomfortable, Aja felt in her pocket for her guardian angel charm but remembered that she'd pressed it into Mrs. Poston's palm as they took her away, telling her that it would bring her good luck.

Walker approached the crowd that had gathered in the hallway just as Edna screeched to Aja, "Were you here to steal from her again?"

"What's going on?" Walker asked. He looked around at the medical trash left by the paramedics lying on the floor. "Who's hurt?"

"Mrs. Poston," Aja answered.

Walker looked at Aja, shock and questions lining his face. "What happened?" he whispered. He looked at her as if she was the one who hurt Mrs. Poston.

"Walker, do you really think I'd do something to her?" Aja glared hard at him.

"Young man," Dr. Landers interrupted, "Aja saved Bea Poston's life. I think you, and most of this group"—he waved a hand at the rubberneckers—"owe this girl an apology. And you, Edna, you especially should apologize to her."

"Everything was fine until you showed up here." Edna focused on Aja. "It seems as if every time there's a crisis, you're in the middle of it."

"Edna, I'll speak to the management about your attitude," Dr. Landers admonished. "Bea Poston would have died tonight if Aja hadn't thought to check on her."

Aja began to back away. "Thanks for sticking up for me, Dr. Landers. Could you let me know if she's all right? I have to go." She turned to leave and saw Walker standing next to his grandparents, both clad in their nightclothes. "Didn't anybody tell Edna I didn't steal the jewelry?" she asked softly.

It seemed that the whole population of the residence home was watching the drama. Aja wished Walker would step forward and come to her defense. She felt naked with all eyes on her. There were too many ghosts in the room—past and present. She'd even lost interest in defending herself.

As she made her way to the door, she heard clucking and whispers as she passed. She wasn't sure if it was from the residents or from the ghosts. She tried to turn off her intuitive brain, but she was so beaten down it was hard to think straight.

The exterior doors swished open, and she walked into the hot humid air to the parking lot. She glanced back to see if Walker was behind her, but he wasn't. She couldn't see him through the throng of people still hovering in the lobby.

Though she'd parked near the hospital in case she had time to visit with Mr. Jensen, she decided, considering how the evening had gone, to just head home. Her car was the only one in the side lot, and she began to get a feeling of foreboding. She stopped walking for a second and looked around. She was alone. No police cruiser, no figures lurking. Keys in hand she jogged the rest of the way, jumped in her car and started the cranky engine. She took a deep breath and tried to shake the awful premonition feeling in her gut. To be safe, she reached over and locked the door as she drove out of the lot.

She figured the scared feeling was because of seeing Mrs. Poston bent, broken, and so near death—and all the residents whispering about her. Even though the woman had given Aja nothing but grief, Aja wished her no ill will. Or did she? She tensed, thinking maybe her powers were stronger than she thought and she *had* caused Mrs. Poston to fall by thinking of bad things for her. No, Aja thought, no, I'd never want to physically hurt the woman. Then why wouldn't this feeling of dread go away?

Driving toward the main street, Aja looked toward the copse of trees where Clay Richards attacked her. That must be it, she sighed. It was dark as a tomb through the trees, and her nerves were spitting fire from the disastrous evening.

A shadow moved from the back seat and, before she could react, she felt something cold against her ribs.

"Keep driving," Clay whispered venomously in her ear.

CHAPTER 45

Aja screamed and looked in the rearview mirror straight into Clay's steel-dead eyes. She forgot to drive and instead thought to run, accidentally pressing the accelerator, propelling her car over the curb and smashing head-on into a tree. Her head smacked into the steering wheel, which hurt, but not as much as knowing Clay was in the car with her. She reached to open the door, but it was locked. Before she could unlock it, Clay grabbed her by the hair and pushed her down. He pressed her head down on the passenger seat, the console cutting into her back as her seatbelt strained to hold her in. Clay moved between the seats hovering over her with a knife.

"You've given me more trouble than the other rats and for that you'll pay," he said through clenched teeth. "Most of you juvenile delinquents know your place." He leaned heavier on her, the seatbelt felt like it was slicing her insides.

Aja couldn't breathe, couldn't move with his dead weight on her. The engine hissed and creaked, and she could smell antifreeze. She prayed Walker or somebody would drive by. She wished she could send a telepathic distress signal to her mom but really didn't know how, since she'd practiced keeping her "gift" off more than on.

Probably afraid someone would drive by, Clay used the knife to cut the seatbelt off Aja, leaned over her, then unlocked and opened the passenger door. "Let's take a walk," he seethed. He crawled over Aja, his knees crushing her abdomen, and jumped out of the car. Grabbing her hair and arm, he pulled her to the ground. On her knees in front of him, Aja's forehead was bleeding from hitting the steering wheel. A puddle of blood formed near her knees and it felt like Clay scalped her when he pulled her by her hair.

"Stand up and walk," he demanded.

Aja had no energy or fight. She couldn't move at all.

"I can kill you right here. I know how to make it look like an accident."

All of a sudden, there was a diffuse, sprinkled light; it made Aja think of a person's aura. The illumination faintly lit the trees, but without reflection, and it reminded Aja of her mom's angel snow globe after a good shake. Oddly, Aja felt her mother's needle-nose pliers pressed into her hand. From where? Then, as if someone else moved her hand like a puppet, she managed to get the pliers around Clay's nose as he bent over her. With strength she didn't possess, she twisted his nose. He yelled and dropped the knife.

Aja kept twisting. He tried to fight her off, but there was some kind of protective force around her. As he fell to the ground, Aja never released pressure. Headlights fanned over them from the street, and Aja saw, in the beam of car lights, clear as day, Mrs. Jensen standing next to the tree Aja's car was twisted into. Aja never saw her lips move but heard her say, "He won't bother you anymore, dear."

Walker ran to her side. "Aja, are you okay?"

Aja let herself cry and nodded. "I will be."

CHAPTER 46

Aja remained in the ER until almost two in the morning. She was whipped, but felt renewed. Clay Richards had been arrested. She finally felt at peace.

"It's over," Aja told her mom as they left the hospital.

"Yeah, I feel it, too." Her mom put an arm around Aja. "The black cloud has lifted."

Aja gingerly touched her forehead, thirteen stitches later and bumps and bruises everywhere else.

"Let this be a lesson never to steal again," her mom said.

"What?"

"All this started when you took that money from the teacher." They got in her mom's truck. "Bad karma."

"That's crazy."

"Aja, we've had some bumps in the road, but those only moved us to another phase in our life. When you took that money, it brought Clay Richards to us. Remember?"

Aja thought about the day she took the money. She rode the edge of trouble her whole life, but had never done anything wrong like that. "I wanted to prove them right."

"Who?"

"The principal and Dumpster Dempsey. They were saying all sorts of bad things about me. I thought I'd give them a reason for talking like that."

"You're better than that," her mom said as they pulled in their driveway. "Now go to bed. We're meeting with Officer Smith tomorrow morning."

"No, I have school."

"Aja, you don't have to go, considering everything that's happened."

"Mom, two more days, then finals. I'm fine."

Aja's mom looked at her for a minute and smiled. "Okay, honey, but I think they'll understand." They both got out of the car. "Maybe I could learn how to be more responsible from you. I am proud of you."

Aja waved her off, but still enjoyed the compliment. She was sore and tired, and she dreaded the alarm going off in a few hours. But still, she felt great.

Mrs. Burnett, having heard about what had happened last night, checked Aja's stitched forehead and bruised face when Aja met with her before classes started.

"How do you manage to get yourself in these messes?" She spoke with affectionate admonishing. "Are you sure you're up to going to your classes? I understand you were assaulted last night on top of you wrecking your car."

Aja nodded. "I hurt inside and out, but I haven't felt this good in a while. The jerk is behind bars, and I feel like I can get on with my life."

"If you start to feel puny, then see me or the school nurse. This is a valid reason to miss school."

"Thanks." Aja stood to leave, thinking that all the other reasons were valid, too. Maybe because this time she had stitches to show for it.

"Oh, Aja?" Mrs. Burnett called.

"Yes?" Aja turned.

Mrs. Burnett smiled. "I got a call from Tish this morning. She wants to finish her GED and look at vocational schools. I think you had a positive influence on her."

"Karma," Aja said. "Good karma."

Officer Smith, Maggie, and Ms. Lewis were waiting when Aja got home from school. Her mom had fixed herbal tea, and they sat sipping and admiring the paintings Aja's mom had done. Ms. Lewis gravitated toward the floral still lifes, only glancing curiously at the nudes.

Aja joined the women and poured a cup of tea for herself. "I'm starving, Mom, do we have anything to eat?"

"I'm expecting Clara Wells in a few minutes. She made you a coffee cake."

"Oh, yeah!" Aja said, happily.

"No lentil loaf?" Maggie asked.

"Aja." Officer Smith took a seat on the couch next to her. "Clay Richards isn't talking, but the girls at the detention center are." She sighed. "I'm sorry we didn't see what was going on."

"There's more good in people than bad," Aja's mom said, looking at Ms. Lewis.

Ms. Lewis didn't respond to Aja's mom, but said to Aja, "I spoke to Tish and Sissy today." She stopped, like something was caught in her throat. "I didn't realize Julia was a victim, too." A tiny tear threatened to fall. She turned to Aja's mom. "You're right. I should have listened to her."

"Find her and tell her." Aja's mom gently touched Ms. Lewis's arm.

"Maggie and I are trying to track her down," Officer Smith said. "Aja, all those girls today opened up like a Christmas gift as soon as they realized we were on their side. Thanks for standing up for them. For making us see them differently."

Maggie spoke up. "Clay Richards's bail hearing is being set soon. The judge is waiting to hear testimony from the girls and you. Officer Smith is going to take your statement today. I'll put the case together and hope the judge sets his bail so high he'll never see the light of day." She sipped her tea. "And all charges against you have been officially dropped."

The front door opened, and Clara Wells came in with her usual flourish. "Aja! I heard you busted some balls last night—or twisted a schnozola. I talked to the doc who worked on him." Clara worked at the hospital. She went into the kitchen with her foil-wrapped cake. "I made this special for you."

"I can't wait, thank you," Aja said. As weird as Aja considered her mom's friends, she was learning to appreciate their individuality. Clara, who wore a tiara and feather boa for her driver's license photo, now sported pink leg warmers over her black tights. Even if her mom's friends had streaks of strange, they were always there for them.

"Why don't we get your statement first," Officer Smith said.

"Oh, heck no. The last time Mrs. Wells made this, I only got one dinky piece that I had to share. I'm not talking until I stuff myself." Aja jumped up and got some plates while Mrs. Wells sliced the cake.

"I get the biggest piece," Aja said. "By the way, how is Clay Richards's nose?"

"Permanently twisted," Clara said. "He'll never smell the same again."

"He didn't smell that great to begin with," Aja joked.

"Ha! Good one." Clara handed Aja a plate with a huge piece of cake, so heavy with butter, cinnamon and sugar Aja could barely hoist it to her mouth as she bit into it straight off the plate.

"Get a fork," Aja's mom admonished, as she took plates to their guests.

Aja sat with the others on the couch and dug into her cake.

"Mrs. Wells, did you happen to hear how Mrs. Poston is doing?"

Clara laughed sharply. "The nurses are threatening to overmedicate her, she's such a pain-in-the-ass patient."

"So she's going to be okay?"

"Twisted her leg, but I was asking my friend about Clay Richards so I didn't find out much about Bea Poston." Clara winked. "She wasn't supposed to tell me anything, you know all those patient confidentiality laws."

"So, Aja, how did you beat up Clay Richards," Officer Smith asked, wiping crumbs from her face. "He's been trained for combat and is a real sharp-shooter. Oh man, this cake is good."

Aja's mom squirmed nervously. "I hate to think of what could have happened." She squeezed Aja's knee. "It scares me more than you know," she whispered.

"I had some help," Aja said to her mom. "A kind of," she smiled, "force field."

Officer Smith talked around a big bite. "In my self-defense class, I'm going to recommend that all girls carry around needle-nose pliers. Who would've thought?"

CHAPTER 47

Finals were a breeze. Aja aced all her classes and had one of the highest GPAs in her school but the worst attendance record. On the last day of school, she sat in Mrs. Burnett's office, glad the school year was over with no summer school tour of duty.

"Well done, Aja," Mrs. Burnett said, sitting at her desk, now cleared of all the files that usually cluttered her office. "What do you think of the scholarships you were offered?"

"I don't know; they're all from Texas schools. I was hoping to get to California." Aja had gotten a few hundred dollars from some scholarships she'd applied for.

Mrs. Burnett shrugged. "I understand, but I'd hate to see you give up some good opportunities here. You could go to community college there, establish residency then transfer into another school."

"That's what I was thinking."

"You should be proud of your grades, and don't wait too long to decide," Mrs. Burnett said. "Most kids are already committed to a school. I'll be around most of the summer. Don't hesitate to call."

"Thanks again for everything," Aja said. "Who knows where I'd be if you hadn't helped me."

"I'm sorry I didn't believe all you said."

"It's cool, I get it. There was a lot of sh...stuff." Aja bit back a bad word.

"Check in with me tomorrow. You will be at graduation Friday night?"

"I don't know." Aja smiled. "I might have to work."

Mrs. Burnett raised an eyebrow.

"I got my job back at the residence home. Fridays are dinner and bingo. Big night at Golden Leaves."

"Lauren said her dad is doing much better."

"Yeah, he's been eating and is even walking a little." Aja didn't tell her that Mrs. Jensen let him know that she'd wait for him. He was still needed here. "He may go home soon."

Ever since the night with Mrs. Poston and Clay Richards, Aja had been hailed a hero and victim and she'd spent time at the residence home. Dr. Landers was her biggest supporter and had convinced Edna Jones to rehire her. Aja had spent her afternoons studying in Mr. Jensen's room. He'd helped her with all her classes, but especially physics.

"They're lucky to have you. But I wish you'd consider going to graduation. You've worked hard for it."

"Thanks," Aja said. "I'll think about it and I'll have a decision made about college before you go on your Alaskan cruise."

Mrs. Burnett looked puzzled. "How did you know I was taking a cruise?"

Aja smiled. "Lucky guess." She'd decided to learn to be more open to her intuitive side.

She left Mrs. Burnett and saw Mr. Carlisle at his computer. He glanced at her, frowned, and looked back at his screen.

"Don't play that poker hand; you'll lose it all," Aja said.

Mr. Carlisle looked like he'd been caught with his pants down. "What are you talking about?" He stood up and closed the door.

As she walked out, she heard him say, "Damn, no!"

Walking out of the school, Aja felt so light she thought she could fly. School was finished. She'd done it. Clay Richards was in jail, and she'd been vindicated for all she'd been blamed for. Life was good again. Or would be, when her physical scars healed.

She scanned the drive-up lot for her mom. Aja's car had been totaled in the accident. It was practically totaled *before* the accident, but at least it got her where she needed to go. Aja wasn't sure where she was going to get enough money to buy a car and move to California. She regretted spending any money on those cool clothes from Abercrombie. Her mom told her to send positive thoughts out to the universe and good things will happen. Aja tried to send a thought out to her mom for making her wait for her in the boiling heat—it wasn't positive.

A familiar sky-blue Buick turned into the school lot. Walker. Aja's heart clutched a bit. She hadn't talked to him since the night they'd found Mrs. Poston and she'd ignored the incessant phone calls from him ever since. It still bothered her that he would think that she could have hurt the woman.

He pulled in front of her and rolled the window down. "Need a lift? We can start over, like the day I gave you a ride to work."

"I'm waiting for my mom," Aja said, crossing her arms.

"I called her, and she said she'd be happy for me to pick you up." He smiled, heating up the hot air more.

"You two sure talk a lot."

"I told her I wanted to apologize to you for ever doubting you." He leaned over the passenger seat to better see her. "I'm sorry, Aja. Can we start over?"

"Walker, you've doubted me since you found out I'd been in jail. You actually thought I took the jewelry, and you keep waffling between me and Kendall. I don't know what to think." She remembered the feeling of goodness he'd projected when she first met him and still admired his ability to see the good in people.

"I've spent my life following the leader, doing what's expected, trying to make everybody happy. You're teaching me to be stronger. I'm sorry Aja. Really sorry."

"You need to teach yourself to be stronger. Quit relying on others."

"You're right." He looked away thoughtful. "I'm learning to think for myself more." He looked at Aja with hope in his eyes. "I admire you for your ability to realize who you are. You don't back down. I need to figure out how to do that." He smiled. Did you really think I'd hurt an old woman?"

"No, although I wouldn't blame you for thinking of it the way she treated you."

Aja crossed her arms deciding whether or not to get in the car. The sun made her stitches practically sizzle.

He looked at her slyly and grinned, "And besides, your mom invited me to have some of the coffee cake Mrs. Wells brought over."

Aja sighed; she couldn't resist him. "Okay, but you only get a small piece."

"You drive a hard bargain."

"Can you take me to work later?" Aja asked. "Are you seeing your grandparents tonight?"

"Yes and yes. And I know they'll be happy to see you, too."

Aja got in and let the air conditioner blast her face. Her stitches itched from the heat and sweat. "What about Kendall?" she asked irritably. "Does everybody know she stole the jewelry?"

"Yes." Walker slumped in his seat and looked out the hot windshield. "She sent a letter to Mrs. Poston, my grandparents, and Edna Jones apologizing for taking the jewelry. She wasn't happy about it, but her parents threatened to cut her off if she didn't do the right thing. I told her and her family that if she didn't I would let everybody know, both here and Chicago." He sighed. "And we are officially over. This time nobody will try to convince me to stay with her. I've made it clear to my family and hers that we're done."

Before Walker put the car in drive, he turned to Aja and took her hand. His eyes followed the line of stitches in her forehead. "Oh man, that looks like it hurts."

"Throbs mostly, but I'm okay." Aja's side hurt more from the seat belt cutting into her, but it wasn't too bad. She decided to drop the Kendall issue. Only time would tell if they were really through.

"Will you be okay to work?" Walker asked.

"Yeah, I'm fine. I've been going there to visit Mr. Jensen, and I told Edna that I'd be ready to start as soon as school was out."

"I'm glad she rehired you. The whole place was rooting for you after they found out the truth." Walker stroked a small strand of hair off Aja's face. "Especially Dr. Landers and Janie."

"Yeah, they've been great." Aja sat back in her seat as Walker began driving. "I'm going to have to work as much as I can this summer, since I have to buy a car and pay for tuition."

"Are you going to start community college here? I can carry your books for you."

"I don't know, Walker. I really want to move to California."

"The gang at Golden Leaves will really miss you. I understand there's a real art to getting the food to the right mush consistency."

Aja laughed and looked out the window. What was she going to do? She glanced at Walker, wishing she could get an intuitive read off him. Maybe she wasn't practiced like her mom, but for some reason the auras of people she was closest to were like static on a TV. Like she wasn't supposed to know about them, and she'd have to find out for herself. The only read she could get off him was a beam of goodness. Like a magnet, it's what had drawn her to him again and again.

CHAPTER 48

Friday night at Golden Leaves was meat loaf or tilapia. Not the best menu to start work again, Aja thought, almost gagging on the smell of over-cooked fish. After Walker dropped her off by the kitchen, she went in to check on Janie and Gabe, hoping to take a few minutes to visit with Mr. Jensen before work.

After a bear hug from Janie and a welcome nod from Gabe, Janie said, "Mr. Jensen got out of the hospital wing this morning. He's back and hopefully can come down for dinner tonight."

"That's great. How's he doing?" Aja asked, tying an apron over her wrinkled, but clean, white shirt. "I'd hoped to see him before you guys put me to work."

"I think he's okay. You can check on him later. Mrs. Poston is back, too, but probably won't be down. She has a full-time helper until she's back in the saddle. I told her we'd bring dinner to her tonight." Janie stacked salad plates on trays. "I'm so glad you're back. How's your head?"

"The stitches will heal. The brain damage won't."

"But that was there before," Janie joked.

"How is Mrs. Poston?" Aja asked, filling the water pitchers with ice.

"Mean as ever."

"Good." Aja laughed. "The world feels right again." She started out toward the dining hall with the water.

"No, wait." Janie called her back. "Let me do that. You start making the coffee and get the soup bowls ready."

"Wow, first day back and I already got a promotion," Aja said.

"Don't let it go to your stitched head yet." Janie took the

pitchers from Aja. "Just hang out in here until everybody gets seated."

"And stay out of trouble?" Aja asked wryly.

Aja heard the dining hall fill with guests. She started out the door with the juice service, but Gabe yelled for her to help him with the mush-loaf plates.

"Yuck," Aja said, slipping plates of the brown glop into a warming oven. "This looks disgusting."

"Tastes good," Gabe said gruffly.

Janie came in. "Aja, would you come here?"

"Should I bring the salad plates?" Aja asked.

"Not yet, just bring yourself."

Aja wiped her hands on a towel and followed Janie out to the dining room.

"Surprise!" All the residents stood next to a big chocolate cake that said: *Congratulations, Aja! Welcome Back* in wispy cursive of yellow frosting. Bunches of balloons floated from each table.

Dr. Landers strode away from the group and took Aja's hands. "We're all glad to have you back."

Aja was speechless, could barely mutter, "Thank you," as she scanned the faces in the crowd. Mrs. Burnett was there, beaming. Aja's mom and Walker stood next to Lauren Jensen, and with them, in a wheelchair, was Mr. Jensen. An IV with milky fluid hung from a pole on the chair and snaked under his buttoned shirt.

"Princess Bride," Mr. Jensen said, smiling.

Dr. Landers let go of Aja's hands, and she went to greet everybody. "This is such a surprise. Thank you."

Mrs. Burnett clapped her hands for attention and said to the crowd, "Aja has one of the highest GPAs in the school. She's worked hard these past few months. Cheers!" No one had a glass but everybody applauded. Mrs. Burnett looked at Aja with affection. "I can't stay too long I've got to run to graduation."

Janie told the crowd, "Let's eat so we can dig into the cake. You can take a piece with you Mrs. Burnett."

Everybody took a seat, Aja and Janie started serving, although Aja spent a lot of time visiting with and thanking everybody.

Aja spent a few minutes at the Jensen's table. Her mom and Mrs. Burnett sat with them. "How are you feeling?" Aja asked Mr. Jensen.

"As good as an old man can." Mr. Jensen winked. "Glad to be here."

Lauren touched his arm. "If you get too tired, I'll take you home. Don't overdo it, Dad, you just got out today."

"I'm fine, sweetie," he said, then he motioned for Aja to come close so he could whisper to her, "Buttercup told me what happened. I'm glad she was there for you."

"Me, too, Mr. Jensen. And I'm glad you're doing better."

"You're a good girl," he said quietly.

After dinner was finished, Aja and Janie served coffee. Aja was still sore, and her stitched head was aching. Gabe carried the big cake to the kitchen so he could cut it. Dr. Landers stood and called for everyone's attention.

"Aja, for your graduation and for what you've done for Bea Poston and Steve Jensen, everyone here wanted to give you a graduation gift." He produced an envelope from under his napkin. "Congratulations."

"You all didn't need to get me anything," Aja said.

Dr. Landers handed her the card. She opened it and was shocked to see a bunch of money. Everything from one-dollar bills to twenties. "Wow, thank you all so much!" Tears filled her eyes.

"We know you've been saving for school," Dr. Landers said. "And I understand you'll need a car, too. I hope that helps."

"It will, sir. Thank you." Aja felt overwhelmed.

Mrs. Burnett walked up and handed Aja a card. "This is from me."

"Thank you." Aja opened the card, which had shooting starts on it and said, *Follow your dreams.*

"I will, Mrs. Burnett," Aja said as two twenty-dollar bills floated to the ground from the card. "Oh, wow."

"You were the best forty dollar investment I've ever made." Mrs. Burnett winked.

A weak, raspy, but unmistakable voice screeched over the others. "So, China girl, you finally got out of school. Wasn't sure you were going to make it."

"Hi, Mrs. Poston."

"Oh, I knew she'd graduate. She think she's the smartest bitch ever."

"Tish?" Aja was shocked to see her juvie cellmate in light

purple scrubs pushing Mrs. Poston's wheelchair. She wore a long-sleeved T-shirt under the top, no doubt to cover her scarred arms.

"Yeah, I got me a new job thanks to Mrs. Burnett."

"One where you'll get your mouth washed out with soap if you don't stop using vulgar language," Mrs. Poston admonished.

"Well, if you weren't such a bossy-pants all the time," Tish gave it back to her.

"Someone has to teach you young women manners. Push me to that table," Mrs. Poston ordered, pointing to the Jensens.

"Push me to that table, *please*," Tish mocked. "It's a two-way street, being polite and all."

"Don't quibble with me," Mrs. Poston said, waving her hand. "Janie, I'd like some soup, please." With the emphasis on 'please.'

"I'll run and git you some water," Tish said, after pushing Mrs. Poston to the table. "And I'll try not to quibble any on the floor."

"Yes, please do. And quibble means to argue, not spill," Mrs. Poston said, shaking her head. "So much to learn."

Tish got Mrs. Poston water and then found Aja.

"I'm going to apply to be a M.A.," Tish said proudly. "A Medical Assistant. They have a program that I can get into when I get my GED."

"That's great, Tish," Aja said. "I know you'll do well. Especially if you can handle Mrs. Poston."

"She don't scare me. Her bark's worse'n her bite."

"Tish, don't be lallygagging and get back to work." Mrs. Poston snapped her spidery fingers. "And, China girl, come visit with me after work."

"Yes, ma'am." Aja couldn't believe how all the planets had aligned. Tish working for Mrs. Poston, Aja back with the old folks who at first she thought were gross and now felt a real affection for, and Walker who seemed to watch her every move as she went from table to table.

CHAPTER 49

Later that night, Aja sat on her bed re-reading what the residents had written on her card. She'd counted the money, which totaled just over two hundred dollars. She was floored. After work, she'd visited Mrs. Poston, who, in her own gruff way, thanked Aja for checking on her.

"I can't believe no one came to my rescue sooner," Mrs. Poston told Aja. "I pay too much money here not to have someone come by to see if I'm okay. What happened to good customer service?"

Aja also noticed her attendant light had been re-activated.

"Here, this is for you." Mrs. Poston handed Aja a small box with a card. "Now go on. I'm too tired to watch you open it here, and my new assistant has to help me get ready for bed. She's too expensive to keep another minute longer."

"Oh, yeah, I'm rolling in the dough." Tish stood behind Mrs. Poston's chair. "Let's get you off to bed so I don't have to hear you order me around anymore."

"Impertinence," Mrs. Poston muttered as Tish wheeled her to her bedroom.

"What you call me?" Tish huffed.

"Look it up in the dictionary."

Before Aja left the apartment, Tish turned to her and said, "Thanks for dealing with the devil. All the bitc—" She stopped and glanced at Mrs. Poston. "—the *girls* from juvie are glad. We gonna nail his ass."

"Young lady, see that bar of soap? That will be your dinner if you don't clean up your mouth," Mrs. Poston griped. She looked at Aja. "Why are you still here?"

"Just leaving. Thanks, Mrs. Poston."

"Oh, China girl, I almost forgot." Mrs. Poston reached into the front pocket of her crisp button-down shirt. "This is yours." She handed Aja the silver guardian angel medallion Aja had given her on the way to the hospital.

"You keep it," Aja said.

Mrs. Poston nodded curtly, then carefully slipped it back in her pocket. "Thank you," she said sincerely.

On her bed, Aja carefully piled the stack of money and cards from the residents and reached for Mrs. Poston's gift. She opened the box and was surprised to find the brooch that Kendall had taken. On a small piece of paper, in spidery, but impeccable penmanship, Mrs. Poston wrote, *Thank you. You deserve this more than the other girl.*" Aja opened the card, where she found a check for two hundred and fifty dollars. Under "memo" Mrs. Poston had written: *college tuition.*

Aja couldn't believe how her luck had changed. Fate had stepped in and righted the wrong. She heard a light knock on the front door. Even though Clay Richards was in jail, she still felt a small stab of fear. Her mom and Clara Wells had gone out for karaoke and wine.

Carefully, Aja walked to the door. The wooden dowel still leaned against the wall. "Who is it?"

"Walker."

Aja looked through the peephole and saw Walker standing on the porch, holding two Starbucks cups.

"I brought lattes."

Aja opened the door. "Hi." Walker smiled, which always made Aja's knees turn to Jell-o.

"Any chance there's leftover coffee cake?" Walker asked, hope lacing his voice.

"There may be some crumbs on the floor, but that's all that's left."

"Then maybe some tofu?" Walker stepped in and handed Aja a cup.

"That we have."

They settled on opening a bag of kettle corn, then sprinkled it with dark chocolate chips as they relaxed on the couch.

"It's so nice not to have any homework or"—Aja rolled her eyes—"drama."

"The evening's still young." Walker tossed a kernel of popcorn in the air and caught it with his mouth. "So what are your plans?"

"Future or immediate?"

"Both." Walker missed a toss, and the kernel landed in his hair. He grabbed it from his head and ate it.

"Gross." Aja laughed.

"So, are you planning on a community college education or will you use your GPA and go to Harvard?" He smiled and cocked his head, which reminded Aja of a cute puppy. She was tempted to pick him up and hold him.

She demurred and said, "I'm going to take some basics this summer at the community college here. Then I hope to go to California."

"Alone?"

Aja shrugged. "I don't know, maybe. I think mom's pretty happy here for now." She sipped her cooling latte and leaned back.

"Maybe I'll join you in California."

"We could take long walks on the beach, and go to the library together." Aja giggled. "You could try to keep me out of trouble."

"Now, that would be a challenge." Walker sat up. "Is this a psychic vision, you and me on the beach?"

Aja shook her head. "No, just a daydream."

CHAPTER 50

Clay Richards's pre-trial hearing lasted two days. He had his own character witnesses, who spoke of his dedicated years on the police force as well as his military service. But there were many more witnesses, young women, who had been victimized by him. Most he'd had committed to juvenile detention and made them feel like it was their fault. The most damning witnesses were Julia and Tish. He'd repeatedly hurt and threatened them for years.

Ms. Lewis took the stand and said how difficult it had been for her to accept blame for allowing so much abuse to happen. "I trusted him and thought the girls were lying." Aja felt uncomfortable seeing this formidable woman sobbing on the witness stand for "being so blind."

Ms. Lewis and Julia were mending their relationship, slowly. Julia was like a puppy that had been beaten too many times. She wanted to be loved but cringed when a palm was raised, not knowing if it was going to hit her or hold her. She reminded Aja of the little girl who'd been slapped around at Abercrombie.

There was still fire in Clay Richards's eyes, but it no longer scared Aja. She knew he was going to a place where he could no longer bother her.

Now in summer school, Aja took her books to work every night and tried to study when she could. It was nice having so many residents who enjoyed helping her with homework. She found more resources in the people who had lived some of the history she studied.

Aja poured water in the dining room and greeted the guests as they sat down.

"China girl," Mrs. Poston called from across from her table. She was still in a wheelchair a month after her accident, but according to Tish, was working extra hard at physical therapy so she could run after Tish with that bar of soap.

"Yes, Mrs. Poston." Aja made her way to the table, ready to pour a cup of decaf.

"My coffee is cold."

"I have a fresh pot here."

"You should have given me a fresh cup the first time," Mrs. Poston griped.

"Yes, ma'am," Aja said, pouring. "Are you staying for bingo tonight?"

"I doubt it." Mrs. Poston nodded toward Tish, who sat near the kitchen studying a workbook. "Tish has a test tomorrow, and she needs to get home early."

Tish looked up when she heard her name.

"You're going to pass that test, right?" Mrs. Poston yelled to Tish across the room.

"I don't know; it's too hard."

"Then keep studying." Then to Aja she said, "She's smarter than she thinks. She can be a bit of a pill, but I'm giving her some slack. Confidence is what she needs." Mrs. Poston poured cream into her coffee. "What's this? I need fresh cream, China girl, you know that."

"I'll get some," Aja said. As she went into the kitchen, she thought about having confidence. How far could any of these girls go if only they believed in themselves?

"Is everybody served?" Janie asked, stacking the dinner plates. "We need to clear everything out for bingo."

"Mrs. Poston needs some cream. Then I'll get the rest of the dishes."

"Are you staying, or are you and Walker going out?"

"We're both staying for a round, but then I need to hit the books." She needed Walker to drive her home since she still didn't have a car.

"Geez, don't you ever get tired of studying?"

"Yes and no. I don't know what else I'd do. I'm not sure what I want to get a degree in."

"Yeah, me either." Janie scraped more plates for Gabe to soak.

"But I'm needed here now. Maybe one day I'll find my way."

Aja thought of Tish, sitting in the dining hall studying anatomy terminology for her medical assistant degree. Tish had complained to her earlier that Mrs. Poston took a dollar out of her pay every time she said a bad word. She said, "I'm losing money working for that old bag." But Aja knew Tish was moving forward, and Aja had to give her credit for sticking with the job and school.

Tish still scratched at her arms when she was stressed, but even that habit seemed to have calmed. She always wore the long-sleeve T-shirt under her scrubs, no matter how hot it was.

Walker stepped into the kitchen, wearing a red-striped vest reminiscent of a carnival hawker. "Come on, Aja, Janie, I'm calling the numbers tonight. I need one of you to be the bingo spinner."

"What about Dr. Landers?" Janie asked.

"He's helping Tish with her homework and gave me the coveted vest for the evening." Walker turned, held out both elbows and said, "Ladies, may I escort you to the playing hall?" They each took an arm and went in, Aja careful not to spill Mrs. Poston's cream.

"Let the games begin!" Walker gave a shout out to the residents as they settled in the dining hall.

"Well, it's about time, China girl," Mrs. Poston complained. "I hope that cream hasn't curdled, it took you so long."

After a few rousing games, where Walker called the numbers and Aja spun the balls, some of the residents started to fall asleep in their chairs. Tish, who'd decided to stay because she needed the money, helped Janie work the room, making sure everybody had the numbers correct and keeping the sleepyheads alert. Aja felt a quiet tranquility. This was where she was supposed to be now at this time in her life. Not forever, but for now. She could make a difference. For her and for them.

As she watched the residents with Tish, Janie and Walker, an idea began to form.

CHAPTER 51

By the end of the summer semester Aja had received acceptance letters from all four of the colleges she'd applied to. She tried to sign up for the Peace Corps but was crushed when she found out you needed a college degree. She was hoping it would set the course for her life and help her decide what to study.

She and her mom sat on the sofa one afternoon before Aja headed off to work. "I guess I should stay in Texas then," Aja sighed.

"You can go wherever you want. We'll find a way." Her mom smiled. "We always do."

"I've been thinking," Aja said. "What if I stayed here for the fall semester and went to community college? I want to start a program that brings the residents from Golden Leaves to the detention center to tutor the kids there."

Her mom nodded. "Aja, that's a wonderful idea."

"Seeing Tish and Mrs. Poston together is a riot—two people I would have never thought could get along now seem to need each other in some weird way. Mr. Jensen is getting stronger and would love to help with physics. Dr. Landers could teach science."

"And it would bridge the age gap. Older people tend to dislike teenagers, and teens can't see past the wrinkles to see what's inside."

"I'll have to talk to Edna Jones about it."

"I'll talk to Hilary Lewis and Maggie if you want me to."

"Sure, let me plant the seed with Edna first."

"You know you won't have to worry about Clay Richards anymore," Aja's mom said.

"Another of your feelings?" Aja asked.

"No, I spoke with Maggie today. It looks like the charges are solid. He'll be tried soon or may cop a plea."

Aja closed her eyes. She knew this, had an intuitive flash about him a few days before. There was no image with the feeling, she just knew deep inside that he would be found guilty of all charges and other indiscretions from his past would be exposed.

The local news had run with the story for a few days, then let it play out. A news magazine show wanted to do an hour program on it after the trial, but Aja was ready to put it behind her, though her mom thought it would be a good way to expose the injustice of the system and encouraged Aja to pursue it.

"What about Walker?" Aja's mom asked.

Aja shrugged. "I don't know, he could stay another year here, but then he'll have to figure out where to go to college, too."

"Is Kendall still in the picture?"

"Luckily, she'll never set foot in Texas again. Walker said Kendall's parents slapped her hand for stealing, then took her shopping because she'd been so traumatized. At least they're not pressuring for a relationship with Walker anymore."

"Karma," her mom said. "It will come back on her."

"What about you, Mom? I see that look in your eyes again. Are the winds of change blowing?"

"I like my friends here. I like the band I'm with, but I feel my roots growing and, you know me, I've never let them grow long enough to bloom." She leaned back on the couch. "Honestly, I was hoping you'd go to school in Austin. I think I could be comfortable in the Hill Country." Aja's mom had been traveling more often to the Austin area for art fairs and music gigs. "But I'm in no hurry. I want to make sure you're taken care of."

"Don't worry about me."

"I'm a mom; it's my job."

Aja considered that. Her mom had never been a typical parent but Aja never doubted she loved and cared for her, no matter how scattered Aja's childhood had been.

Aja checked the time. "I've got to go. If I get there a few minutes early, then I can talk to Edna about our new idea."

"Instead of taking it to her first, talk to the residents and see what they think. You'll probably have a better chance of success if you have a group supporting you."

"Yeah, maybe we'll have a peaceful sit-in at Golden Leaves. Everybody could line their scooters up in the lobby in front of Edna's office."

"Remember, Aja, every one of those elderly people was a teenager once. They still have a voice and lots of wisdom to go with it."

CHAPTER 52

The residents liked Aja's idea to work in the detention center. A few worried about being locked in with a bunch of criminals, but they softened when Dr. Landers told them that Aja and Tish had been victims of the system.

"We may not be able to save them all, but wouldn't it be grand to help the ones who are willing to help themselves?" he told the group at dinner.

"I'm going to show them proper etiquette." Mrs. Poston stood at her table, her wheelchair parked nearby, since she'd refused to use it during her meal. Tish instinctively headed toward her in case Mrs. Poston lost her balance. "I'm trying to teach Tish, but she's stubborn."

"Not as stubborn as you," Tish shot back. "And she keeps calling me pig million."

"*Pygmalion*," Mrs. Poston said, exasperated. "We'll rent *My Fair Lady* and I'll pay you to watch it." She sat, unsteady, with her Velcro knee cast but Tish was there to help. "For now, young lady, you need to watch your manners and your mouth."

"Yeah, you making more money off of me than you paying me on that cuss jar." Tish helped her sit.

Dr. Landers laughed. "Maybe we'll have movie night with these kids. We can show them some classics, and they can show some of the new movies."

"I don't want to see a bunch of naked bodies or hear foul language," Mrs. Poston said.

"We'll teach you to rap," Tish said, pushing the wheelchair closer to her.

Surprisingly, Mrs. Poston laughed. "Ballroom dancing. That's what you should learn."

Aja was amazed at the interaction between them. Aja had never seen Mrs. Poston laugh. Tish took her assaults head-on, and Mrs. Poston seemed to enjoy sparring with her.

"You gonna teach me in this?" Tish asked, shaking the wheelchair.

"Oh, no. I'll be out of that before you know it, and I'll be dancing circles around your young legs."

"You on!"

"No, *you're* on. Proper grammar please."

Aja's mom was right. Edna Jones pooh-poohed the idea when Aja brought it to her directly, citing liability and danger issues. "These are people charged with crimes, Aja."

When Aja told her the residents thought it was a good idea, Edna still waved her off. "I just don't see how it could work."

"We have the van; I'll drive them once or twice a week there."

"Aja, I'm glad you've turned out to be such a responsible help around here. The residents really love you, but sometimes things are better left alone. These people need to rest. Too much excitement will stress them."

"As if this is our last stop before death?" Dr. Landers suddenly appeared in her doorway. "Edna, I believe Aja's idea will benefit not only us, but the kids in the detention center."

"Sometimes, we have to stick our necks out for change," Aja said, sounding very much like her mother. "We can make a difference. Even Mrs. Poston wants to do this."

"Bea Poston?" Edna asked dubiously.

"Yes, even the 'old bat' is okay to shake this place up," Dr. Landers said, winking at Aja.

"I will have to check with the management and the legal team," Edna said. "I just don't know."

"Here," Aja pulled some documents from a folder. "My attorney, Maggie, did some background on the legal issues, and she said there are only a few things that need to be addressed. She said she'd be happy to help out—for free." She handed the documents to Edna. "And Mrs. Burnett from the high school said she'd be glad to help. She'd talk to some teachers and students to offer additional tutoring and counseling. And she said the school district will provide teaching tools, books and stuff."

"Sounds like you've done your homework." Edna took the file but didn't open it. "I still think it's asking too much of our residents. They tire so easily."

"We'll take our chances, Edna," Dr. Landers said.

"Let me make some phone calls," Edna said, reluctantly.

Their first outing was a meet-and-greet at the detention center so everyone could introduce themselves. The way the teens lined up against one wall and the older residents on the other side of the room reminded Aja of a chess match, each sizing up the opponent. No one made the first move.

Finally, Aja called a few of the girls she remembered and introduced them. The way they looked at the old people, as if they were aliens, upset Aja. "Sissy," Aja said to the young mother. "Tish should be here soon, but for now, can you help me introduce everybody?"

One young man with pants around his buttocks sat on one of the Formica tables. "So what're we supposed to do with a bunch of old people? Play some hoops?" He and another young man laughed and high-fived each other.

"Oh, grow up, Lamont."

Aja was relieved to hear Tish's voice behind her.

"Hey, bitch," Sissy called out.

The few staff members who were there said nothing about the language. They stood off by themselves near the door. Edna stood next to them, looking like she was going to stroke out.

"Young lady," Mrs. Poston, still wheelchair-bound, said firmly to Sissy. "We're here to teach you youngsters some manners. Perhaps we should start with you."

"Who are you to tell me..." Sissy started and stood up in a defensive posture.

"Sis, this is my new boss. I got to be nice or she'll fire my ass...assistance," Tish said.

"Good catch," Mrs. Poston mused. She sat stoic in her wheelchair, a big picnic basket on her lap.

Aja walked in between both groups. "Everybody, these people are from Golden Leaves. They've offered to visit with you and help with your schoolwork."

"Why we want to talk to them?" Lamont yelled. "That one's older than my grandma, and she dead." He pointed to Mrs. Poston.

Mr. Jensen had sat quiet in his wheelchair. Aja was afraid that this outing would be too much for him. But he had insisted on coming.

"Lamont?" Mr. Jensen said, his voice barely audible. "Would you please push my chair to a table so we could visit?"

Lamont laughed and shook his head. "Visit? Old man, you crazy." But he got up and sauntered to Mr. Jensen. His pants would have fallen off had he not held them in front.

"Lamont," Mr. Jensen said, "You might need two hands to push the chair."

Lamont made a 'sheese' sound and continued to strut over. He used one hand on the chair handle and kept the other on his pants. He pushed Mr. Jensen to the group of young men sitting together. They all looked at frail Mr. Jensen as if they didn't know what to do with him.

"So tell me," Mr. Jensen said. "I've always wondered about that fashion trend of your pants hanging off like that. Isn't it uncomfortable?"

"More comfortable than having them around your neck like yours." Lamont gave his pants a tug.

Mr. Jensen laughed. "Do you think I could pull off that style? I have enough trouble keeping my pants up on my crooked body as it is."

"All right, peeps," Tish said. "We're supposed to play bingo." She fanned herself with a stack of playing cards.

Aja noticed Tish was uncomfortable, probably not sure which way to fall in the groups.

"Bingo? Are you on meth?" one of the young men said. "That's for old people. We ain't old."

"We have prizes," Mrs. Poston said. She opened the picnic basket and pulled out packages of baked goods. "Homemade by all the old"—she looked at Tish—"peeps."

As soon as the game began and the delicious prizes lined up, it didn't take long for both groups to cautiously bond. Aja was happy to see that whenever one of the residents won, they forfeited their prize to keep the game going. After two hours, Edna said it was time to go. "We need to get our friends home for dinner." Her voice lilting on the word friends.

Lamont stood to push Mr. Jensen to the door, still one-handed. "So you tellin' me you had a black-and-white TV with no remote? That's crazy, man."

"No cell phones either," Mr. Jensen said.

Aja could tell he was tiring quickly. She'd call Janie on the way back and ask her to get a dinner plate ready for him as soon as they arrived. Aja would make sure he ate early so he could rest.

Waiting to board the van, all the residents chattered about how different this generation was.

"Can you imagine if we wore pants showing our bottoms?"

"Can you believe that seventeen-year-old is already a mother? She said she got pregnant riding bareback, but I grew up around horses and don't know how that happened," one of the women who often ate with Mrs. Poston said.

"Means she didn't use no protection," Tish told her as she helped her into the van.

"And if I said 'ain't,' my mouth would have been washed clean," Mrs. Poston said. "They don't even see that it's wrong. Where is this world headed?"

Aja remembered the vision of a girl getting her wrists smacked while she was in Mrs. Poston's apartment. Maybe it had been Mrs. Poston as a young girl.

"Maybe we can help them," Dr. Landers said. "I spoke to a young man who wanted to be a doctor before the school work got too hard and, I suspect, peer pressure. I'm not sure I can help him enough to ace the MCAT, but maybe enough to find a medical career. Most of these kids just need to be guided on how to move forward."

"Look at Tish," Mrs. Poston said, waiting her turn for the wheelchair ramp to lift her into the bus. "She's trying to change. But there's a lot to undo."

"You gonna undo me," Tish said.

In a few weeks, both groups fell into a routine at the visits. Not all the kids were receptive to the elders and some refused to participate. But there was a handful that, although they acted tough, seemed to enjoy the company.

Mr. Jensen became stronger and was able to walk with a cane. Something Lamont thought looked "smack." Lamont even thought the suspenders Mr. Jensen had given him soon after the first meeting were "fly" and wore them most of the time. He said he was going to start his own fashion trend and look for a cool cane to go with his new clothes.

"When you come visit," Mr. Jensen told him, "you can go through my cool duds and take what you like."

"Duds?" Lamont asked.

"Clothes," Mr. Jensen told him.

"Duds, ha, I like that." Lamont laughed. "Makes no sense, but I still like it."

"Yes, sort of like fly," Mr. Jensen agreed.

Aja was happy to see that, even though a few of the teens' detention sentences were finished, most continued to come when the residents were scheduled. According to them, it was for their community service time, but Aja could tell they seemed to enjoy it. It was decided that the groups needed to reciprocate, much to Edna's dismay, and come to Golden Leaves for dinner.

"Have them come early, dressed appropriately, and we will have them set the tables. They need to learn how to properly set a dinner," Mrs. Poston said while eating one evening. "Tish now knows the difference between a salad fork and a dinner fork. I just can't imagine being older than five and not knowing something so basic."

Aja poured fresh coffee for her and said, "I'm not sure how to set a table either. I saw in a movie that you're supposed to start on the outside and work your way in with silverware when you eat."

"Have you ever been to a nice restaurant?" Mrs. Poston asked, critically. "I mean a five-star restaurant."

Aja thought for a minute. Considering all her money always seemed to go toward car repairs or clothes. And her mom's career, or careers, never brought in enough for something like that. "No, I don't think so." She always thought it was extravagant to spend as much on one dinner as they did for a week's worth of groceries.

"Well, then I'm taking you and Tish for a nice meal."

"Better than Golden Leaves food?" Aja asked.

Mrs. Poston waved her off. "I haven't been out in ages. And you and Tish must learn how to conduct yourselves in public."

Dr. Landers, sitting at the next table, overheard the conversation. "You know, Bea, I think you might have a great idea. Why don't we have the young people here to learn social etiquette, then we'll take all of them out. It would be a treat."

"And who would pay for something so extravagant? I certainly don't have that kind of money." Mrs. Poston huffed.

"I'll be happy to pay," Mr. Jensen said. He'd been dining most evenings with Dr. Landers.

"Thank you, Steve, but we could all pitch in," Dr. Landers said, looking pointedly at Mrs. Poston. "I have to admit, since we've been working with these kids, it's given us all something to look forward to. I always enjoy my afternoons with them."

"You are all making a difference," Aja said. "You're showing them a side of life they didn't know was there." She sat next to Mr. Jensen. "What I think is the coolest is how many questions they have about what it was like before cell phones and TV. It's giving them something to think about."

"China girl," Mrs. Poston said sharply. "As long as you're wearing that apron, you should not be sitting with the guests. I'll have more water, please."

"Yes, ma'am." Aja stood and smiled as Dr. Landers winked at her.

CHAPTER 53

The first dinner at Golden Leaves was similar to the first meeting at the detention center. The tough "criminals" looked so out of place, especially in their new ill-fitting clothes, they didn't know what to do. The young men tugged at their ties, and some tried to pull their suit pants down low. Some of the girls had rolled their dresses up short. The few that were required to stay overnight at the detention center were flanked by the center's two security guards.

Only seven of the thirty or so kids had been actively participating through the summer, so they were the only ones allowed to come.

All the tables had been set, but Mrs. Poston stood next to a table draped with only a tablecloth. "First, I'm going to instruct you how to set a proper table and show you what each utensil is for."

"A fork's to eat and a knife's to cut," Lamont said. "We not stupid."

"And what if you're invited to a dinner at the White House?" Mrs. Poston asked. "You don't want to look stupid then."

"Yeah, I'm 'spectin that invite in the mail." Lamont laughed. He wore the suspenders Mr. Jensen had given him and gave them a little snap.

Aja and Janie stood ready to serve. Tish was dressed up but stood with them in case they needed help serving.

"She's gone over and over this shit with me already," Tish whispered to Aja and Janie. "I didn't know demitasse from big ass, but I do now."

"And you're a better person for it?" Janie asked, amused.

"The only restaurants I go to have a drive-thru."

"This is so stupid," Sissy said. "I don't have a dress that covers my ass."

Mrs. Poston's friend asked. "Maybe that's why you're a teen mother."

"Lady, if you makin' fun of me."

"No, child. I just want you to respect yourself. Then others will, too."

Walker came in, looking dashing in a suit and tie. Aja, who never went for the "suit" type, sucked in a breath. He went straight to Aja, in her stained apron, and offered a bouquet of flowers he'd had behind his back. "I was hoping you'd be my date this evening."

"I'm working." Aja blushed and glanced at her messy uniform. "This dinner is for the guests and residents."

"You're one of us," Tish said. "You a juvie, too."

"Then I'll help you here and take you out later," Walker said.

"That's sweet, Walker, but I want to make sure Mr. Jensen is okay this evening. He's been quiet lately. I think he's been especially lonely now."

Mrs. Poston gave the crew a basic lesson on dining etiquette and which spoon to use to either stir or sip with.

"That's a lot of extra dishes to wash," Tish complained.

Everyone took a seat. Tish and Sissy sat with Mrs. Poston and her friends. Lamont and two others sat with Mr. Jensen and Dr. Landers. Aja thought it was funny that, like a high school cafeteria, the boys and girls didn't sit together. They should have made place cards to mix the groups. Walker had put the bingo vest on and was cheerfully pouring water at each table.

As Aja and Janie served, Aja was surprised to find this group had better manners than the teens at a school cafeteria. Everyone was careful to use the correct utensil, even asking if they weren't sure, and the conversation at each table seemed like a mutual question and answer session about each generation. No one acted cooler than the other.

When dinner was finished, Aja served Mr. Jensen his dessert.

"Princess Bride, I think I'll pass this evening. Maybe Lamont or one of his friends would like my cake."

"Really? Sure," Lamont said as he started to reach over Mr. Jensen. He hesitated, then sat back and let Aja serve it to him. "Thank you," he said graciously, almost embarrassed. "Why he call you Princess Bride?"

"Because she looks just like Princess Buttercup from the movie, *Princess Bride*" Mr. Jensen answered. "It's a wonderful movie if you haven't seen it."

"Sounds like a baby movie."

"Maybe we could watch it on movie night," Aja offered.

"That would be nice," Mr. Jensen said quietly.

"Can I take you back to your room?" Aja asked. He seemed so tired.

"Yes, thank you." He pushed away from the table and used his cane to steady himself as he stood. "You know, perhaps Lamont could escort me back this evening. Lamont, you could take a few minutes to go through my duds."

Lamont looked shocked. "You really gonna trust me to take you alone? You not scared?"

"Of course not." Mr. Jensen took a shaky step.

"I don't know if the security detail's gonna let me go."

"Can I get you a wheelchair?" Aja asked.

"No, Buttercup, I'm fine."

Aja was surprised to hear him call her his wife's endearment. In fact, she'd not felt Mrs. Jensen's presence as much around him.

Lamont went to ask if he could take Mr. Jensen to his room and was told no. They were getting ready to leave anyway.

"It's okay. I'll take him," Aja said. "Let me tell Janie. I'll be right back."

Walker joined Aja and Mr. Jensen as they took him to his room.

"Aja, this has been a great program," Walker said. "I think everybody is really enjoying each other."

"We're not so different," Mr. Jensen said. "Princess Buttercup...I mean Bride." He hesitated. "You have a heart filled with love." As they got to his room he turned to Aja and hugged her as hard as his weak arms could. "Thank you for coming into our lives, my Buttercup and I are forever grateful." Walker opened Mr. Jensen's door, and Aja felt his wife's powerful spirit inside seeming to wait for Mr. Jensen.

"I'll get him settled and in bed, and I'll meet you downstairs," Walker said to Aja. "Then we can enjoy a special dinner. I think Gabe pureed some pot roast. We can enjoy it by candlelight." He winked at Aja as he took Mr. Jensen into the apartment and closed the door.

Aja knew that the love the Jensens had for one another would live on forever. She could feel it through her soul.

CHAPTER 54

The next morning, Aja languished in bed thinking of last night. The dinner with the teens and the elders had been a success. They'd planned on coming back in a week to watch *Princess Bride* with the residents. After the dinner, Walker had surprised her by setting a formal table with candlelight, linens and beautiful china, courtesy of Mrs. Poston, on the garden patio at the resident's center. The food was delicious, even the blended roast beef Gabe had made for them.

Aja smiled, recalling how many of the residents poked their heads around the corner to spy on them while they ate.

"Just checking to see if you need anything," Mrs. Poston's friend said when caught.

"Don't break my china, China girl," Mrs. Poston said as she scooted away on her motorized chair, Tish trailing behind, complaining about wanting to go home and get out of her uncomfortable dress.

Dr. Landers had mixed some songs and placed his speakers and iPod outside for Aja and Walker to enjoy. Mostly old love songs of the '40s and '50s. After they'd finished eating, Walker took Aja's hand and asked her to dance. She felt grimy in her work clothes, but also felt like a princess when he took her in his arms and gracefully swirled her around the garden. Then he kissed her for the first time. The kiss was like fire that heated her core. She'd only dated a few guys, but never felt the intensity she experienced now, like hundreds of fireflies all lit up at once. She felt her heart soar to the sky and an anchor pull her down. This was wonderful, but did she want to be tied to someone? Aja barely had time to catch her breath when she heard a smattering of applause, and she looked to see a handful of residents, clad in their pajamas, smiling and waving at them from the lobby.

It was a perfect date. Aja sighed and hugged her pillow close enjoying the memory. She had not seen Mr. Jensen there with the group though. She wished he could have been part of that moment.

Her phone rang. She got out of bed to answer it. It was just past seven thirty; she didn't have class until ten.

"Aja, it's Janie."

"Hey. What a great evening. Thanks for everything."

"Aja." Janie's voice was serious. "Mr. Jensen passed away last night. In his sleep. I'm sorry." She began crying. "He'd been doing so well."

Aja was hit with a fist punch of sadness. "What? No!" She hadn't seen it coming the way she had with Mrs. Jensen when she'd known it would happen. "I didn't think he was ready." Or maybe *she* wasn't ready to let him go.

After they hung up, Aja sat on her bed, shocked and saddened. She closed her eyes and tried to feel the Jensens' spirit. She didn't feel anything. Was she losing her gift? It was the gift she'd hated all her life, but now needed to connect with them. She found a small measure of comfort knowing that Mrs. Jensen had been waiting in his room last night and they were together now.

She wiped away a tear, heard her mother puttering in the kitchen. Still crying, she went into the kitchen. Her mom looked up, smiled, then saw the tears and took Aja in her arms.

"Are you okay?" her mom asked, concerned, then held her tighter.

"Mr. Jensen died."

"I'm sorry, honey."

"Did you know?" Aja asked.

"No, not until I held you. I'm sure he's with his wife."

"I didn't see it. Sometimes I just know." Aja pulled out of the hug. "He was sad, but I didn't have a feeling about it."

"Maybe he didn't want to worry you, didn't want anybody else holding him here." Aja's mom said. "Let me get you some tea."

Aja grabbed a Kleenex and blew her nose. "Why does it hurt so much? I hardly knew them."

"You connected with them." Her mom placed a steaming cup of tea in front of Aja. "You were meant to be in their life now, to help them transition."

Aja thought of Lauren and Katie, how hard it was going to be for them. She decided to skip classes today and go straight to Golden Leaves. "Mom, can you take me there now?" Still without a car, Aja relied on her mom or the bus to get to college and work.

"Sure."

Aja took a few minutes to email her teachers to say she wouldn't be in class, then stuffed her work clothes in a bag.

Her mom dropped her off about ten o'clock. In the main lobby, Edna Jones was setting an easel, on it a poster stating that Steven Jensen had passed away and listing the time for a memorial service in the residents' chapel.

Aja looked at the document, thinking that it looked too standard, like the names and dates were copied and pasted routinely. It made her sadder.

"Aja, you're not scheduled to work until this evening," Edna said, straightening the poster.

"I heard about Mr. Jensen."

"Sad, I know. He was a good man," Edna said with as much sincerity as ordering a latte.

"Is Lauren here?" Aja asked.

"I think she's in his apartment if you'd like to go up. But please, Aja, don't get underfoot."

"I just want to help." Aja started crying again. "Don't you even care about them?"

Edna looked at her sternly, then softened. She took Aja's arm gently. "Come on, let's sit for a minute. Edna guided Aja to a chair that looked over the garden where she and Walker had dinner last night.

As they sat, Edna looked out in the garden. "Aja, I know you may think I'm hard-hearted, but this is life. Maybe I've built up some immunity to this, since death happens a lot here." She sighed. "You've brought a level of excitement here, a spark of life. Even though I like order and routine, and I can't believe I'm saying this, but I appreciate what you've done, bringing the youth from the detention center here. Lord knows my ulcer still acts up whenever the two groups get together." She put a hand on her stomach. "But it certainly has re-energized some of the residents here. I'm glad you connected so well with the Jensens. They had a full, happy life. That's what we need to remember about them."

"I guess he couldn't live without Mrs. Jensen," Aja said, wiping a tear with her shirt.

"Yes, they're in a better place," Edna said, a pat, sensible cliché she'd probably said a million times.

Aja could practically hear Edna's brain ticking off her to-do list for the vacant apartment, but she appreciated that Edna had taken the time to talk to her.

In the apartment, Aja found Lauren and Katie crying as they sat on the couch. Aja glanced at the bedroom; the bedsheets were crumpled and cascaded to the floor. There were medical patches and trash from the paramedics littered around the bed. But worse, there was no spiritual feeling from either Mr. or Mrs. Jensen. They were gone.

Aja hugged Lauren. "I'm sorry."

"Thank you," Lauren cried. "This is too hard to have lost both of them in such a short time."

Katie nodded and wiped her face with a stringy Kleenex. "Tell her about your dream."

Lauren sat down again. "I dreamt last night that Mom and Dad were together. I could see them, but couldn't touch them. If I tried to reach out, it was like I'd touch water, and the image would ripple and blur." She took a shaky sob. "But they looked beautiful, full of light. I don't know; it was weird, but real."

"They were meant to be together," Aja whispered.

Lauren nodded. "Dad's caregiver found him this morning. He called 911, then called us. Dad died in his sleep."

He died in the arms of his Buttercup, Aja thought, remembering the strength of Mrs. Jensen's spirit in the apartment last night.

Aja spent the morning with Lauren and her sister. She cleaned up the mess in Mr. Jensen's room. Later, she called Walker, who was at school, and told him what happened.

"Oh, man, I'm sorry. How are you doing?"

"Better now that I've thought about it. I didn't know him before he lost his wife, but since we've become friends, I could tell there was a part of him that was missing. So maybe this is the way it should be." She looked around the empty apartment. "I only hope I find love like they did." She blushed, remembering their date last night, and Walker's blazing kiss.

"I think, maybe, I have," he said softly.

CHAPTER 55

Two months later, Aja got in her car, a 1997 silver Honda Accord, courtesy of the Jensens. Mr. Jensen had left it to Aja, with Lauren's blessing, along with a thousand dollars in a college savings plan. The car was clean, no-frills, and best of all it didn't make any funny noises.

Mr. Jensen had even remembered Lamont. The night he died, after the dinner, Mr. Jensen had taken the time to go through his clothes and accessories and put them in a box with a note for Lamont to "enjoy his fly duds, and think of him when he wore them." That tough guy, Lamont, was so moved that someone remembered him his eyes filled with tears, although he tried valiantly to hide them.

Aja was still a little teary-eyed after saying good-bye to her mother, even though her mom had promised to join her in Austin as soon as she settled things here. The lure of California still beckoned, but Aja decided to use the scholarship money and stay in Texas. Mrs. Burnett was happy about that and promised to help along the way. The University of Texas was her *alma mater*, too, so she made sure Aja had more burnt orange T-shirts and sweats than she would ever need.

As Aja got on I-35 south to start her new life, she thought about Mr. Jensen's memorial service. Posters with photo-collages had decorated the church lobby. There was laughter as well as tears and, even through the sadness, she sensed that Mr. and Mrs. Jensen had come full circle together in life and now in death. After her shift that night, Aja had seen them in the garden, where she and Walker had their romantic dinner. Mr. and Mrs. Jensen glowed with love. They danced and dipped and smiled at Aja before their image dissipated, leaving a diaphanous glow like an aurora borealis and a feeling of all things good. Just like her mom's angel snow globe.

Golden Leaves held a going away party for Aja's last night at work. Tish tried to keep up with Mrs. Poston, who was finally off the scooter and on her feet. Aja smiled, thinking of the odd friendship that had forged between the two. They were more alike than Aja could have ever imagined. Tish reminded Aja of a flower that could push up through a crack in concrete, a survivor in any environment. Mrs. Poston was more like a rose with sticky thorns; you needed to handle her with caution, but there was beauty within. Aja was proud of Tish, who'd aced all her tests so far, thanks to Dr. Landers and the other residents who'd taken her under their wings. Mrs. Poston used the money from Tish's cuss-jar to help Tish pay for school.

"With all this money, young lady, you should be well on your way through a master's degree," Mrs. Poston told her.

Janie and Gabe bought Aja a blender for her new apartment in Austin. "So you can make good food like me," Gabe joked. Aja figured she'd use it more for fruit smoothies then blended meat.

Edna Jones had given her a glowing letter of recommendation for Aja's job interview at an assisted living community in Austin. The director there was willing to work around Aja's school hours.

Best of all was Clay Richards's prison sentence, ten years minimum in the slammer. Maggie had done a great job, culling through complaints that had been filed against him, previously ignored because the young girls hadn't been believed. It was Julia's testimony that had sealed his fate, that and the photographs he'd taken of some of the girls he'd arrested that were found on his hard drive. The pictures were of Tish and Julia mostly. Aja shivered, remembering the photos he'd taken of her through her window while studying.

He had stalked Julia relentlessly and sexually assaulted her, but she was too afraid to report him because he was a police officer. She and Ms. Lewis had reconnected, with Ms. Lewis vowing to stand beside Julia during her testimony.

Sissy, Tish's friend, was pregnant again. But Lamont, with help from Mrs. Burnett, was working to get his GED.

Aja passed an eighteen-wheeler on the highway and looked in her rearview mirror. Walker followed behind in his car. Aja smiled. He was pretty special to decide to change his plans of going back to Chicago and go to UT instead. His grandparents had encouraged him to go if he promised to visit often. They were happy to have him stay in Texas, even though his parents, and probably Kendall, wanted him to come back to Chicago.

Aja smiled, remembering the first time she'd seen Walker. Naked, standing on a pedestal, her mom and her art class sketching his muscled body. Aja had to laugh. Her life would never be normal and that was okay. Maybe being a screwed-up outcast, who connected with dead people and could see people's auras, wasn't so bad after all.

At least she'd never be bored. Maybe life was a little like her mom's snow globe. Shake it up and dance in the light of the raining gold dust like the angel inside.

Aja reached over to the passenger seat and took a hunk of the coffee cake Clara Wells had made for her trip. She stuffed a messy mouthful in, careful not to spill too many crumbs in her clean new car. She was sure Walker had already reduced his half of the cake to crumbs by now.

Yes, life was good, and it would continue to be good.

How did she know?

She just had a feeling.

ABOUT THE AUTHOR

When not writing **Jeanne Skartsiaris** also works as a Sonographer. Prior to that she was a medical/legal photographer for a plaintiff's law firm.

She attended creative writing courses at Southern Methodist University and is a member of Romance Writer's of America and the local chapter, Dallas Area Romance Authors.

Also the author of *Surviving Life*.

She lives in Dallas, Texas.

Look for Jeanne – on Facebook at Jeanne Skartsiaris, Author, and Twitter, @jskartsiaris. Or visit her website at www.jeanneskartsiaris.com.